IT'S HARD OUT HERE
FOR A DUKE

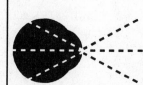

This Large Print Book carries the
Seal of Approval of N.A.V.H.

IT'S HARD OUT HERE FOR A DUKE

MAYA RODALE

THORNDIKE PRESS

A part of Gale, a Cengage Company

Farmington Hills, Mich • San Francisco • New York • Waterville, Maine
Meriden, Conn • Mason, Ohio • Chicago

**LIBRARY OF CONGRESS CIP DATA ON FILE.
CATALOGUING IN PUBLICATION FOR THIS BOOK
IS AVAILABLE FROM THE LIBRARY OF CONGRESS**

ISBN-13: 978-1-4328-4561-2 (hardcover)
ISBN-10: 1-4328-4561-6 (hardcover)

Published in 2018 by arrangement with Avon Books, an imprint of HarperCollins Publishers

Printed in the United States of America
1 2 3 4 5 6 7 22 21 20 19 18

For Gigi, my other mother
For Tessa, my wonderful editor
For Sarah, for Mondays and Wednesdays

ACKNOWLEDGMENTS

This book — this series — would not be what it is if not for a mildly adventurous NYC subway ride with my fellow historical romance author Sophia Nash, in which I, a seasoned New Yorker, led us to the wrong train. This fortunately allowed us time to converse beyond the basic pleasantries, and I learned that she was an expert equestrienne and historian and was thus able to answer my pressing questions about this series idea I was kicking around . . . and which helped me decide to go ahead with it. So thank you to Sophia for sharing her knowledge and for fate for getting us lost!

I am also indebted to my cousin, Sarah, another expert equestrienne, for reading an early draft of this manuscript and sharing her extensive knowledge of all things horse-related with me (and James). This book would not be possible without her, particularly her invaluable assistance on Mondays and Wednesdays.

Many thanks to Gigi for always reading and encouraging my romance writing. She's been there for me from the beginning (or starting three months after) and is still there when I need her more than ever.

And while I am thanking people, I must also extend my everlasting gratitude to Tony, Penelope, my Lady Authors, and the team at Avon. Last, but not least and for always: my momma. For everything.

PROLOGUE

My dear Miss Green,

I write to you with the most shocking news. Though the ton said I was mad to seek Durham's long-lost heir rather than simply hand the estate off to the odious Mr. Collins, it seems I shall soon be vindicated. It is quite the story, one best related in person over a pot of fortifying tea and some of Cook's cakes, so I shall spare the ink and paper here.

The duke is en route and is to be expected — along with his three sisters, all of whom we will need to launch in society. Yes, *we.* I bid you to come to London at once, should your mother's condition allow it. This is my life's work, and I fear I shan't be able to do it without your assistance. Besides myself, you know Durham best.

Yours,
Josephine

P.S. How is your mother's condition? I hope these months with her in Hampshire have done you both some good, though I am eager for the company of my ever-faithful companion.

Southampton, England, 1824
The Queen's Head Tavern

Some men were born to be dukes, and some men were James Cavendish. Despite being an undistinguished American, he found himself in possession of an aristocratic title in a country he had never before visited.

Back home in Maryland he was James Cavendish, the horse breeder and trainer of some renown round those parts. He was known as Henry's son, the one with a talent for horses, an easy and charming way with women, and the one responsible for three sisters who were endless trouble.

But here in England, he was the Duke of Durham.

Whatever that was.

Whatever that meant.

Or he would be, once he and his sisters completed their journey and arrived in London. Oh, he knew the title had passed to him the moment his father took his last breath, shortly after his mother had passed away. Or rather, he learned it sometime

10

later, when the Duchess of Durham's representatives had tracked him down and informed him of that fact.

He had known it while he and his sisters debated traveling to England, and he'd been achingly aware of it for every minute spent crossing the Atlantic. They had docked in Southampton this morning, would remain in this inn tonight, and would continue on to London on the morrow. James had sworn to himself that he would not be Durham until he set foot in London.

In his head and heart he would not *become* the duke until his boots touched London ground. And until he crossed the threshold of Durham House, he would be James. Just James. Just an unremarkable, plain young man of no import or renown, just having a pint in a pub like anyone else.

His sisters — Claire, Bridget, and Amelia, each one more trouble than the last — were settled in a room upstairs, happily having baths and stretching out on full beds after a long journey at sea.

James wasn't ready to sleep. Couldn't, really. More to the point, he wasn't ready to be alone with his thoughts. Worries tangled with regrets. He doubted whether they should have even come so far and feared it was too late to turn back. He wasn't sure he could *do* this ducal business.

Was it better to try and fail than to never try at all?

Not only did James not have the answers, he didn't even want to consider the question. He had a sinking feeling it was too late anyway.

A tavern at night was an excellent place to be when one wanted to avoid deep thinking.

This particular tavern wasn't very different than the ones back home, and he appreciated the familiarity provided by the same scuffed wood floors, rough-hewn tables and chairs, tallow candles. If he concentrated only on the hum and roar of voices, he could tune out the strange accents reminding him that he was on the other side of the ocean. He could pretend he was at Fraunces Tavern back home, that his friend Marcus would stroll through the door any minute, ready to regale him with some of his latest exploits, usually involving whiskey, women, and a deplorable lack of judgment.

But Marcus wasn't here, wasn't going to be here, and James knew no one. There wasn't anyone he particularly wanted to know, either.

Except —

James noticed a woman. She sat primly at a seat near the bar, mostly keeping to herself, though occasionally conversing with the barmaid. She sat with her spine straight, holding her head tall. Her hair shone like unrefined honey in the candlelight.

She seemed too proper for a place like this.

He watched her for a while, wondering. Where was her companion, what was the purpose of her travel, what was she thinking as she traced her fingers along scratches in the wooden tabletop? Where had she come from and where was she going? She must have a story and he wanted to know it.

He caught her eye. She just happened to glance his way, giving him a mere hint of doe eyes and full lips.

She looked away quickly.

Back to the table, back to the teacup she sipped elegantly, back to ignoring him.

She wasn't looking at him. She wasn't looking at him. She wasn't looking at him.

He waited, wanting another glimpse of the soft curve of her cheek, and, hopefully, the slight upturn of her lips.

Finally, after one of those moments that felt like eternity, she glanced his way again. The corners of her lips teased up into a hint of a smile, but those lashes fluttered and her gaze darted away.

Careful, this one startles easily.

James leaned back against the wall, a nearly empty mug of ale dangling from his fingertips. He knew about creatures that startled easily, who would flee at the slightest provocation. He knew to stand still and wait patiently, projecting a sense of calm and security. He knew that waiting was more effective than chasing.

This was fine. James had all night to play this kind of game. Even if they did nothing more than exchange glances across the room until midnight, he'd be happy.

It distracted him from the things he wanted distraction from.

Their gazes connected again.

His heart thudded hard in his chest as he drank her in. Curious eyes. Full lips. Elegant movements.

She looked away.

She dared another glance.

James didn't move from his place against the wall; he was still wanting and waiting for an invitation to speak to her — perhaps a smile, a little nod, or some indication that he was welcome.

Eventually, their eyes connected and she held his gaze. His heart beat hard and steady. He didn't know all the rules of being a duke, the kings and queens of England or a million other things, but he knew an invitation when it came his way. He knew it in her shy smile, the slight tilt of her head beckoning to the empty seat beside her.

Time seemed to slow as he crossed the room and made his way toward her. Once he was standing in front of her, his breath was knocked right out of his lungs. She was pretty, and she was smiling at him, just James. This might be the last time a woman looked at him like that, wanting him just for him, without thinking, *a duke!* This was a moment he was going to revel in and hold on to.

Though Miss Meredith Green lacked birth, and wealth, and many other qualifications one would assume of a gently bred lady, she had been raised to be one. She could curtsy with the best of them, expertly arrange both flowers and seating arrangements for dinner parties, and could recite pages from *De-brett's Book of the Peerage.* These were just a few of her accomplishments.

As such, she should not be here, in the public room of the Queen's Head Tavern and Coaching Inn. Especially not alone and especially not at night, where any old ruffian might think he could take a liberty with her, to put it nicely. Which is why she should *not* have allowed the barmaid to add a generous splash of whiskey to her tea.

Which is probably *why* she was encouraging the ocular advances of a handsome man with whom she was not acquainted.

Meredith had noticed him the moment he walked in, tall and lanky but strong, with unfashionably long brown hair that fell rakishly in his eyes. What color were they? she wondered. She didn't need to know. There was nothing she could do with this information. There was absolutely no point to her knowing.

She badly wanted to know.

So she dared one glance, then another.

Do not look. Do not look. Do not look.

Her better judgment was roundly ignored. Before she knew it, they were somehow flirting from opposite sides of the room without even saying a word.

It was the sort of thing that made a girl's heart beat giddily and her toes start to tap under her skirts. Thanks to years of training, she kept her posture poised and her movements elegant, but under her skirts, her toes were tapping.

This, *this* was what she needed tonight: a distraction. The past few months had been trying, and the next few promised to be challenging as well, albeit in a different way.

She had only tonight to live for herself.

She darted another look in his direction.

He was watching her. This truth elicited a slight smile from her lips. But she shouldn't take pleasure in this.

She ducked her head.

But her heart beat quickly and she wondered: Would he come over?

He shouldn't. He really should not. She absolutely should not encourage him. But life was full of should-nots, and tonight Meredith wanted to say yes.

It had been a bit of a day — on top of quite a week, and one hell of a month. Or two or three. Her visit to her ailing mother in Hampshire revealed a dispiriting truth: the life choices of Miss Meredith Green were few, and less than thrilling. Nevertheless, she had made her choice to return to London and live the restrained and dignified life of a lady's companion.

Emphasis on *restrained.* When one relied on one's spotless reputation for her very existence, one comported herself accordingly. One did *not* give or receive heated glances across crowded rooms.

But Meredith embarked on a little whiskey-infused rationalization: until she stepped foot in London, she could afford to live a little loosely. For one night, she might

indulge in the sort of wicked behavior —
and passion — that she'd have to refuse
forevermore.

That was just the splash of whiskey talking, she told herself. It was just the strain of
recent events wreaking havoc with her common sense. It was her mother's bad influ-
ence. She'd had the great luck to be raised
to be A Lady. She oughtn't forget that.

Do not look. Do not look. Do not look.

She looked. Oh, she looked.

His gaze sparkled. Like he *knew* what inner turmoil and rationalization his glances
inspired. This time, she didn't look away.

Oh, goodness, he was coming over. Her
heart beat faster and faster as his long
strides brought him closer and closer until
he was standing beside her, leaning casually
against the bar.

Gentlemen did not lean.

"What is a beautiful woman like you doing alone in a place like this?"

Lord, what a line! What a ridiculous thing
to say. It took all her ladylike training not to
let her eyes roll. As it was, Meredith's heart
sank, and her smile faltered with disappointment.

But then he gazed at her, eyes sparkling
and lips curved into a smile, like he really
saw her and liked what he saw. Men didn't

often look at her this way, if they looked at all. In Hampshire, there was no one. In London, she was inconsequential.

But this man was looking at her like she was the sun, moon, and stars, too. Meredith decided he could stay, even with a ridiculous line like that.

"You must have a story," he said. "Tell me your story."

"I don't have a story," Meredith replied. But that was a lie. She had the kind of story that one didn't tell. It was tragic — in that it was hopelessly boring. But this man's smile was making her feverish, because it had her considering that tonight, perhaps, her life might become interesting. Just for one night.

"I have a story," he told her. "It's rather unbelievable."

"Do you now?"

"Yes, I do."

Because he was still gazing at her like she was a beauty and because he wasn't so bad himself and because tonight was just tonight, an interlude between the recent dispiriting events and an uninspiring future, she replied with a hint of flirtation, "I suppose you're going to tell me."

"Since you asked . . ." He took a breath, like he was about to embark on a retelling of *The Odyssey* or some other epic tale. That was fine; she had all night and wasn't too keen to think about her own life and problems. Then he changed course. "Forget my story. All you need to know is that I'm a man, passing through, just here for the night and I'll be gone tomorrow. Well, I don't want to think about tomorrow."

"I know."

"You know? How do you know?"

She wanted to sigh with *knowing* — the passing through, the here for one night, the tomorrow she didn't want to think about, either. But she didn't want to have to explain any of that to him. Instead, she said, "I know you're traveling. Your accent gives you away. You can tell a lot about a person by his accent."

"Is that so?"

"People from different regions have different accents. People from different classes speak differently, as well. Of course, one can make many inferences about a person based on those things alone. Their birth, their status, their family, their acquaintances, their education. From that, one might guess at their prospects in life."

If nothing else was right about her, Meredith at least had the right accent: a polished, upper-class accent. Her prospects, on the other hand . . . well, that was one of the things she didn't care to think about tonight.

"So, what can you tell about me?"

"You're American." She'd met one or two travelers from America in London, but never in this part of the country. Then again, she spent most of her time in the capital. But for the past few months she'd been home, trying to care for her aged and ailing mother. "You're American, and sound as if you've had some education. You are plainly dressed, which may be a consequence of your recent arrival from a long journey, but might also suggest that you do not move in refined circles. And, as a young man with apparently limited means, it suggests that you might not be wed."

This conjecture upon his marital status was a stretch, but something she had to know before the conversation continued further. Meredith felt something sparking between them, and it had to be smothered if he were married. And if not . . .

"I suppose you have the right of it," he replied. "I must stick out terribly with these old clothes and foreign accent. There's no wife to make sure I fit in. I don't belong here."

"A man like you will always fit in just fine."

"A man like me?" He lifted one brow.

"You are a man, for one thing; that will open nearly every door in the world. You do have the wrong accent and clothes, you need a shave, and your hair is too long, but that is all fixable with training and a good valet. You are also not completely unfortunate in your appearance and manners. I daresay you'll get along well enough."

That drew a wry smile from him.

"And what about you?"

"I have my place in the world. As long as I stay there, I'll be fine."

"Where is your place in the world?"

"I'm not telling a man I hardly know."

"I'm not a stranger. You know my story."

She laughed. "I don't think I do. In fact, why do I feel that I don't know the half of it?"

"May I order you another cup of tea? We can continue not being forthcoming with each other."

He stood there — leaned there — with those blue eyes sparkling at her, waiting for her answer. Meredith's heart started to pound at the realization that this was one of those moments where the direction of her life hinged on the next word she uttered — the *before* to an *after*.

That is, if she said yes.

Oh, she knew the *correct* answer. Any girl

with an ounce of sense knew to say, "You are too kind, sir. Thank you, but I must decline." Another drink meant more conversation which meant more of a chance for that strangely sizzling something between them to strengthen and draw them closer, sparks flying, until the smolder turned into a flame turned into a fire.

Well, tonight she wanted to burn.

And if she was going to go up in flames, it might as well be with this handsome stranger, who she was unlikely to ever see again. Meredith was innocent in experience but not ignorant in the ways of the world. She knew that this stranger on this night was her one chance to experience passion.

This would be her one night of indiscretion, and it would be a secret she took to her grave. But until that day, she had this one night to feel fully alive. After the events of the past few months of a deathbed vigil, she needed to feel that. With the prospect of lonely nights ahead of her in London, she craved the intimacy this man promised.

And so, listening to her heart instead of her head, she said, "Yes."

Yes to another drink.

Yes to more conversation.

Yes to everything else that would follow.

Just as she had predicted, that one yes led

to another and another and another and to this . . .

Later that night . . .

A kiss. There were sparks when his lips touched hers later, much later, that night, in the privacy of the darkened corridor upstairs.

Meredith felt like she was finally being sparked to life with this kiss, as in the fairy tales she always hated. Life wasn't like that for most girls who lived and breathed in the real world, she knew that well.

But this kiss on this night with this man had her reconsidering heroes and fairy tales and kisses that woke a girl up. There was a spark between them, and she chased it like it was the only light in a world of darkness.

"I don't even know your name," he murmured, hours after they had met. They had chatted for hours and names hadn't seemed necessary.

"Just a girl."

He didn't need to know her name because names were for knowing each other, and this would only be tonight.

Lips parted.

A gasp.

A reach for more of him, of her, of *this* ember smoldering between them and slowly

24

but surely bursting into flame.

Those flames were like hope, like life, like the warmth that had always eluded her.

"I'm James. Just James."

Meredith wrapped her arms around him and murmured, "Just kiss me, Just James."

One kiss led to another, which led to the soft click of a door closing behind them, shutting out the rest of the world. What was before and what would come after ceased to matter. There was only this man, this girl, this moment.

She heard the rustle in the dark as he lit a candle, and then saw the soft glow of a single flame.

"I want to see you," he explained.

It made her eyes feel hot. No one ever wanted to see her, really see her. She was inconvenient, she didn't fit in, she was too much of this or too little of that. But this man wanted to see her; his hunger for her was plain in his eyes. God, it felt good to be seen and hungered for.

It made her feel strong. Bold.

Like the night was just beginning.

There was the soft sound of fabric rustling as she undid the lacings on her dress and let it fall to the floor, revealing herself to him.

There was the sound of his sharp intake

of breath when he saw her in next to nothing, opening herself up to him, laying herself bare.

There was the sound of her pounding heart, roaring in her own ears as she let herself feel, really feel, his touch. Her skin tingled in the wake of his caress.

His touch was gentle as he reached for the curve of her waist, above the flare of her hips and below the swells of her breasts. His touch explored all those curves, slowly, gently, achingly, deliberately.

As if he wanted to know her. Or memorize her for later.

One night. Just this one night.

She stood still, breathing deeply, savoring the trail of heat in her skin, left in the wake of his fingertips. Meredith willed herself to remember this sensation, this man, this night.

One night. Just this one night.

Their mouths met for another kiss. Open lips, tasting each other.

Growing bold, she reached for him. Skimming hands over his chest, feeling the linen of his shirt bunch up beneath her hands. Wordlessly, he lifted it off and cast it aside. For a second, he seemed shy. Or perhaps it was just something in the way his hair fell forward into his eyes.

Now she pressed her bare palms against his warm skin, feeling the ridges and planes of his muscles and the smattering of hair across his chest. She imagined she felt his heart pounding hard beneath her palms.

She imagined it beat for her.

But she wouldn't allow herself to imagine that it meant anything, that this could be anything more than one night of passion.

He pulled her close, and his mouth found hers for another kiss, one that blurred the lines between where he ended and she began. He was hungry for her.

She wanted him, too, with an intensity that did not surprise her. She so often felt shut away, alone, unseen and untouched. Which is why she was here, taking this chance, and giving herself up to this mad passion. And *mad* was not a word she used lightly.

James cupped her breasts, teasing the pad of his thumb across her nipples. A sigh escaped her.

He pressed kisses along her neck. And when his hot mouth closed around the dark centers of her breasts, she moaned with the pleasure of it, especially when his tongue went to work teasing her.

This pleasure he stoked in her made her bold. Meredith reached for the waistband of his breeches, stroking her fingers along the edge where fabric met his skin. Dipping her finger beneath, wanting but unsure.

She felt his lips curve into a smile even as he kissed her.

Then he removed his breeches.

The next thing she knew, they were entwined on the bed, fevered skin against fevered skin. Only for a moment — certainly not forever — it felt like heaven.

Chapter 1

All of London is breathlessly awaiting the arrival of the new American Duke of Durham. He is expected in town any day now, though Her Grace, the Duchess of Durham, has been remarkably tight-lipped about him.

— FASHIONABLE INTELLIGENCE,
THE LONDON WEEKLY

London, 1824
A few days later
As their carriage rolled closer and closer to London, James thought about *her.* Just a girl, she had said, before she kissed him deeply, opened herself up to him, invited him in, wrapped him around her fingers, teased him to unknown heights of pleasure, made him forget, made him feel alive, made him fall half in love with her.

Just a girl. Ha.

He didn't even know her name.

29

He thought of her when Amelia insisted on not only stopping at the ruins of an old castle she'd read about in her guidebook, but also finding a knowledgeable local person to provide a tour, which may or may not have been accurate, but certainly made for a lengthy afternoon activity that delayed their trip.

James didn't mind. He was in no rush to get to London.

He thought of *her* when Bridget and Claire insisted on traveling to one more town over so that they might stay at a nicer inn. Would she be there? Or was she at the one they'd left? Where was she going anyway? So many questions he hadn't asked, because he'd kissed her instead, assuming that she would be there still in the morning.

He thought of her while his sisters alternately chattered amiably and then bickered (over what, he could not discern). Claire provided a lengthy and tedious explanation of Euler's equation, then they all sang songs for hours and hours on end. Lord help a man trapped in a carriage for days and days with three sisters.

And now they were closer, closer, closer with every turn of the wheel.

Closer to London.

Closer to Durham House.

Closer to a future his father had abandoned and a future James wasn't sure he wanted.

James was a simple man, a country boy, accustomed to wide open spaces and expansive blue skies.

The buildings rose up tall, reaching into a sky gray with smoke and smog, and towering over everything.

He enjoyed the solitude and spaciousness of their farm in Maryland, with endless green pastures and cool, quiet forests.

In London, the narrow roads were thick with people, some dressed meanly and some dressed in a finery rarely seen back home. The lot of them combined to make a thick, pulsing mob.

Their carriage was moving at a glacial pace through streets thickly congested with carriages, cattle, and people. His lungs constricted. He couldn't breathe.

And now the carriage was slower, slower, slower.

Stopped.

The Cavendishes had arrived in London.

James looked up at the house. The stately building seemed to soar toward the sky, and the limestone seemed to glow in the afternoon light. This was no mere house; it seemed like a concrete ray of light from

Heaven, ordained by God Himself.

It was a grand residence designed to impress and intimidate. *Success,* James thought wryly. This was his now and it terrified him.

James swallowed hard as a fleet of servants exited the house from the large front doors and decorously lined up on the cobblestones. So elegantly and expertly did they do this that he wondered if they had practiced and if they had been watching and waiting for his arrival.

The women wore dark dresses pinned with starched white aprons and caps. The gentlemen were dressed in blue-and-gray livery, which happened to be of a finer style and quality than the clothes he wore.

He thought of her, again, and her comment on his plain attire. It hadn't bothered him then, but he was keenly, awkwardly aware of it now.

The lot of them just kept coming, lining up and waiting to serve him.

But not yet. *Not yet.*

James had promised himself that none of this became real until he set foot in London, and, as he was currently ensconced in the carriage, he technically had not done so.

Therefore, he could still flee.

His sisters were exiting the carriage, one

after another, spilling forth in a mass of skirts and petticoats and bonnets and curls and girlish chatter. Bridget dropped her diary on to the cobblestones, Claire tripped on the carriage step, and Amelia gaped openly at all of it, her loosely tied bonnet tipping off her head as she looked up and up at the huge house.

He could go.

And God, he wanted to.

His heart was pounding, blood roared in his ears, something was lodged in his throat, and he couldn't breathe. The city was closing in on him, all these people were waiting for him, expecting things from him that he didn't know if he could deliver.

He was a simple man, of simple pleasures. He was happiest on his farm, with dirt on his boots and the company of his horses.

He wasn't . . . this.

James could order the driver to take him away, anywhere. At this moment, he had half a mind to. More than half. They could drive straight to the docks, where he could board a boat for America, back to the land that was green and beautiful and his.

Back to the horses he'd trained from birth. He'd had to say goodbye to them, their big brown eyes somehow knowing that he was leaving them forever, his friends, his *life,* the things that made him *him.* And for what?

Everything in him urged him to flee, to turn and to run. Like a wild horse running from a wolf.

But then he caught sight of a familiar face. One that had made him look twice, then a third time, then he couldn't stop. It was a face of beauty and mystery that had haunted him ever since he woke up expecting her and found she'd vanished.

She was just a girl, she had said.

But she was also *here.*

James stepped out of the carriage.

Oh, hell . . .

An elegant older woman dressed in a blue gown stepped forward to greet him. She was fair and of slight stature but held herself in a manner that suggested an ability to command armies with nothing more than a politely worded order. James recognized her demeanor from his work with horses; dominance needn't be displayed with size or brute force. It was a subtle energy conveyed through a look, a word, and self-possessed confidence.

"Your Grace," she said. He started to turn to see to whom she was speaking but quickly realized she addressed him. "Welcome to

London."

"You must be the Duchess of Durham," James replied to Josephine Marie Cavendish, the Duchess of Durham, daughter to the Earl of Cambria, and God only knew how many other titles or royal connections she possessed.

Was he supposed to bow to her? Shake her hand? He was acutely aware that an entire phalanx of servants watched his ignorant behavior.

"Presently, yes," she said with a pointed smile. *And so it begins.* "I trust your journey went well."

"Yes, very well . . ."

James looked past the duchess to *her,* his Just A Girl who by some twist of fate or the grace of God happened to be here. He couldn't quite wrap his head around it, but he was glad. He couldn't quite wrench his attentions away from her, either — though she steadfastly refused to look at him.

"And these must be your sisters," the duchess said, gesturing to the pack of girls standing behind him.

"What? Yes."

Right. He was the duke now. He had to set an example. Manners, et cetera. Paying attention to the business at hand and not staring like some gawking schoolboy at the

35

girl he thought he'd lost forever. His Just A Girl was *here,* standing with the line of servants, but not quite a part of them. She did not wear a uniform like the others, but she wasn't standing with the duchess, either. He didn't understand how she fit into the household.

Claire elbowed him and muttered something like, *Pay attention.*

James straightened and introduced his sisters, awkwardly aware that there was probably some protocol he didn't know for this situation, and thus he was probably doing it wrong and everyone would laugh about it later, behind his back.

The duchess then performed introductions to the staff.

There was the butler, Pendleton, who appeared to be approximately six hundred years of age. Down the line they went, and James was introduced to the gray-haired housekeeper, a French cook, upstairs maids and downstairs maids, footmen and groomsmen.

Each and every one curtsied or bowed and murmured something about being honored to serve His Grace. He mumbled a reply, hoping it was the right thing to say. Not only had James no training in How To Be A Duke, his father had rarely spoken of upbringing in England and the ducal household. He was at a disadvantage from the start.

But James did his best to focus on the people speaking to him and not the one woman who did her very utmost to avoid meeting his eye. There was no trace of the coy gaze, sweet smile, or laughter from the other night. Today she refused to even look at him.

Why wouldn't she look at him?

Meanwhile, he was waiting for an introduction to *her,* the Just A Girl who had made love to him and left him to wake up alone.

She hovered behind the duchess like a shadow.

They were all about to enter the house when James couldn't let this continue.

"Wait. You missed someone."

He didn't miss the flash in *her* eyes.

"Oh, but of course," the duchess replied. "This is my companion, Miss Meredith Green."

Bloody hell . . .

Their entire house in Maryland could fit in the damned *foyer* of this place — James hesitated to call it a house when castle or gilded fortress might be more appropriate. It was obviously designed to impress and intimidate, what with masses of marble and gold covering every available surface. It worked; this all belonged to James now, but even he felt like a small boy with his mother nearby hissing, *don't you dare touch anything.*

The drawing room was just as bad, or grand. It was a large, airy room with windows overlooking a garden, delicate bits of furniture scattered about, massive paintings hanging on the way, and delicate, fragile breakable things on every available surface. Excess was the theme — everything was patterned, engraved, or gilded, or all of the above.

James had never felt so huge and hulking, like he would inadvertently break one of those chairs or accidentally knock over a precious porcelain vase.

And he was supposed to live here. Ha.

But none of all that could hold his attention for long because *she* was here. It was some miracle to have found her again — and so soon and so close. He would have taken it as a sign if he believed in those sorts of things. Perhaps he would start.

The duchess indicated that they should all sit.

Miss Green sat by the duchess, behind

her slightly. When he last saw her, her honey-hued hair was spread out on the pillow; now it was parted in the middle and pulled back. Her complexion looked just as lovely in the light of day as by candlelight. But her mouth was set in a firm, discouraging line. She now boldly met his gaze with those doe eyes and ever so slightly shook her head *no.*

Then she resolutely looked away.

The message couldn't be clearer.

We never happened.

I don't know you.

We will never happen.

Forget about me.

But that *no* was an acknowledgment that he wasn't imagining things. She had been real. What they had shared had been real. James felt his breath still, his heartbeat slow, his brain getting stuck on one thought: But . . . why?

He knew his reasons for that night, but what of hers? He knew he was a duke now, and probably had vastly more important matters to attend to than the matter of a woman, but tell that to something deep inside that craved her and wanted to know the mystery of her. She hadn't seemed like the sort of woman who dallied with strangers in taverns, and this all but assured it.

"How was your journey?" the duchess inquired.

"It was quite long," Claire said.

"I found it very hard," Amelia added.

"The motion of the ocean had me quite . . . overset at times," Bridget said.

"I'm sorry to hear that," the duchess murmured. "But I am so glad that you have all arrived here safely."

"We are also glad to have arrived safely." Leave it to Claire to be diplomatic. In truth, they all had mixed feelings about leaving home and embarking on this journey. James now had the sense that the crossing wasn't even the half of it. That'd been merely an interlude and now, *now,* the real journey was truly beginning.

"Do we call you Josephine?" Amelia asked.

"We do not."

"Josie?"

"You may address me as Duchess or Your Grace," she said graciously.

"That's awfully formal. And we are family," Bridget pointed out.

"Indeed we are."

Her Grace, the duchess, not to be known as Josie, had long ago married their uncle, the fifth Duke of Durham. When he expired, the title went to his younger brother, Henry — their father, who had long ago bucked all expectations and left England to marry an American woman he'd met and fallen in love with during the war. The four American Cavendish siblings, presently ensconced in a London drawing room, were the result of that union.

But their parents had passed away, in quick succession, before representatives of the duchess had arrived searching for the new Duke of Durham.

They had come in search of Henry; instead they found James, an American man with muck on his boots from the stables, and sweat on his brow from working in the paddock with his horses. And they had *bowed* to him. Marcus had watched the whole scene unfold; he had just laughed and laughed.

Now James was here.

"I have petitioned the king for your sisters to be addressed as Lady," the duchess said, and Bridget straightened. "And of course, Duke, you are to be addressed as Your Grace."

Presently His Grace was sprawled on a spindly-legged chair that felt as if it might collapse under his weight at any second. His legs were outstretched, one boot crossed over the other. He anxiously drummed his fingertips on the arm of the chair.

41

"Just James is fine," he replied, his gaze settled on Miss Green.

She bit her lip.

"It is not," the duchess said flatly. "Among yourselves you may continue to use your Christian names. But in company, you will have to be more formal. Your Grace."

His sisters exchanged smirking glances before bursting into laughter. He certainly didn't chastise them because there was something about hearing that familiar, happy sound in this strange new world. If they could still laugh raucously in these opulent surroundings, perhaps there was hope that not *everything* would change.

The dowager duchess was less amused.

"Do you think this is funny?"

"Is that a rhetorical question?" Amelia asked. Because, obviously, they thought it hysterical that their brother be formally addressed as Your Grace, or duke or anything other than simply his name.

It was hysterical that their little family from a farm in Maryland should find themselves in this monstrous drawing room in their new home in a foreign country halfway around the world. They had been commoners, and now they were aristocracy.

Yes, it was where their father had grown up, but he never spoke of this or prepared them for the day when they'd find them-selves here. James thought of all the hours they'd spent together, father and son, and this — all this — was never mentioned. He could have had a damned clue. But no. And he couldn't even *ask* why his father had kept this from him. He would have to figure it out on his own, the same way he'd had to figure out how to raise three sisters.

"He is Durham now. He is the seventh duke." The dowager duchess pursed her lips and spoke with controlled formality. It had a chilling effect. Laughter died off.

His days of being Just James were over. But he wasn't ready to bury his past self just yet. He took one more glance at her, Miss Meredith Green.

The other night she had been Just A Girl.

The other night she had returned his gaze.

The other night she had been warm and willing in his arms.

The other night he had been Just James.

Now that he was the duke, now that he was Durham, she was cold and distant. He swallowed hard, suspecting that this was only his first taste of all the rules and formalities that would keep everyone at arm's length from him.

"It is his duty to conduct himself in a manner befitting his rank and the Cavendish family. In fact, that is true for all of you."

"Yes, Your Grace," Claire murmured.

"Miss Green, please pour."

Miss Green poured the tea from a gleaming silver tea set, her movements elegant and precise.

"How many cubes of sugar?" Miss Green inquired, her hands hovering over a small bowl of carefully cut white sugar cubes.

"Two, please," Bridget replied.

"Ladies have one," the dowager duchess said.

"Why did you even ask?" Amelia muttered under her breath.

Bridget paused.

"One, please."

And so it began. James wanted her to have all the damned sugar if she wanted it.

"Now that you have arrived, we haven't much time to polish you up before introducing you to the ton. People talk of little else than your arrival and are eager to make your acquaintance."

"The ton of what?" Amelia asked.

The dowager duchess looked perplexed.

"The *haute ton* is a phrase used to refer to all the best families in London society," Bridget answered. James vaguely remembered her obsessively eavesdropping on two obviously wealthy British women on their boat; she must have learned it from them.

"You have done your research," the dowager duchess said with a nod of approval. Bridget beamed.

"I was hoping for some time to explore," Amelia said.

"It is possible to arrange for some excursions to the local sights and museums, so you can familiarize yourself with the city and have something intelligent to discuss with suitors."

James heard Amelia muttering under her breath about wanting to explore for herself, not giving a hang about suitors. His youngest sister was the wild pony of the bunch, the one who was always hardest to train and never fully domesticated. Josie was going to have her hands full with her. With all of them.

"And I would like to visit with the Royal Society. I do hope to meet those who study mathematics," Claire said.

"I can't imagine why," the duchess said dryly, which was the usual response when Claire stated her interest.

James frowned. He didn't like this. They hadn't been here an hour, and already this duchess was trying to mold them into Perfect English Ladies, which would likely

45

necessitate stifling their personalities. His sisters were a constant plague upon his peace and sanity, but he didn't want them to change or give up what they loved, be it math, or exploring, or an excess of sugar in one's tea.

Claire, however, was accustomed to this attitude. "Because I have a brilliant mind for mathematics, and it would be a shame to let it go to waste."

"Ladies do not —"

"Yes, I know," Claire said with a dismissive wave of her hand. She was always impatient with such a limited view of womanhood. "But I do it anyway."

"You would all do well to focus on finding suitable husbands rather than fretting over math problems, excursions, or glancing longingly at the pot of sugar. I am given to understand that you are all, as we say, on the shelf."

They may have traveled halfway around the world, but they still hadn't escaped the Disapproving Marriage-Minded Matron. Their neighbors back home had always despaired of "the poor lot of motherless children without any marital prospects," but any matchmaking attempts had fallen flat. Instead, they had each other and were free to pursue their interests.

Claire wasn't interested in matrimony — or a man who could curtail her intellectual pursuits. Amelia was more wild than civilized. And Bridget was often infatuated with this bloke or that, but wasn't interested in settling for anything less than true love.

None of them were interested in anything less than that.

Their father had thrown a dukedom away for love. Their mother had married "the enemy," according to her American family. Love was the example their children had grown up with. None of them would settle for less.

James hadn't been remotely interested in marriage, not even to get his sisters off his hands. He did mostly enjoy their company. And so the years had passed by without proposals or weddings, and now they were older than the usual age at which people wed and at the mercy of a woman who was clearly determined to see them leg shackled sooner rather than later.

The three sisters turned their heads toward James. The duke.

"I think we would all like some time to settle in before we start marrying my sisters off," he said. "God knows, there is a plague of them, and they'll drive you mad before breakfast. And yet, I find myself fond of them. Most of the time. And would prefer to have them around while we become accustomed to things here. And until we decide *if* we shall stay."

The possibility that they might say to hell with all this was tantalizing. He held it close.

The dowager duchess opened her mouth to protest but thought better of it, because this was the new duke speaking, after all. "Very well," she said. She pursed her lips. "Perhaps you would like to be shown to your rooms and take some time to rest before dressing for dinner."

But it was understood that this was not over yet.

Oh, bloody hell and damnation . . .

The new duke had kept looking at her. Looking at her like he knew her, had seen her undressed, and in a state of rapture, *knew her.* He looked at her like that all afternoon, all through dinner, and all through tea after.

Meredith was terrified that someone (ahem, the duchess) would notice.

She always noticed everything.

She must not notice this.

To be fair, it took every bit of self-control for Meredith to not look at him. Her handsome stranger who had made her smile when she was in low spirits, who had brought her to heights of ecstasy, and whom she'd fled in the night, was *here.*

Not only that, he was the duke. THE DUKE.

As such, he was the one man who would be forever off-limits to the likes of her.

Which was fine. *Fine.* From the moment she'd finally surrendered to her curiosity and smiled at him, she had intended one night only. One night at the Queen's Head Tavern, specifically. One night of passion in an otherwise chaste and respectable life. One night for herself in a lifetime dedicated to others — the duchess, her mother. Her little indiscretion wasn't supposed to be *here.* In London. Living under the same roof. *The duke!*

Because who would have thought that the handsome stranger with an American accent, plainly dressed and alone in a tavern in Southampton, was the new duke?

No one would have thought that.

Dukes were English, not American. They dressed in fine attire — if plain, at least well made. They traveled with servants and took private parlors rather than mix with the riffraff in the common room. Everyone knew this, except the new duke.

She hadn't been expecting him.

Meredith had spent the past six months cut off from the great world in Hampshire, tending to her ailing mother. It had not been an opportune time to leave the duchess, given that she'd lost her husband and the future of the estate was uncertain. Meredith only returned upon receiving word from the duchess that she was urgently needed. The details of the new duke — that he was American, and would be accompanied by three sisters — were only related to her over tea once she returned to London.

Still, she never dreamed that the American man she'd spent the night with was *the new Duke of Durham*.

But now she'd best gather her wits and get a hold of herself. What had happened between her and the duke could not happen again, and no one must know that they had happened, once upon a time.

She would just have to avoid him as much as possible — and she had half a chance, given the vast size of Durham House. All those rooms. All those corridors. There would be plenty of places to hide.

When they were together, she would simply avoid his gaze — even if it took Herculean effort to turn her face from those sparkling blue eyes that looked at her like she was something and someone spectacular.

Her efforts to avoid him were thwarted later that night, on the servants' stairs, of all places. The dimly lit and secluded servants' stairs.

She was venturing up, ready to retire for the evening, and he was descending. The stairway was so narrow there was no avoiding each other.

"Hello. Miss Green. I was just on my way out for some fresh air before retiring. I did not wish to disturb anyone."

He smiled down at her as she slowly climbed the stairs toward him.

"Your Grace."

She nodded her head and made like she intended to keep going. Like she was going to walk right past him. Which was her plan. It was a good plan. A sensible one.

"Wait. Please."

She paused. It was a reluctant pause. Because pausing was not part of her plan. It could lead to intimacy, to trouble, to Things She Should Not Do. But he was the duke now, and she was little more than a servant. It wasn't that she had to obey, it was that it was inadvisable to flout him. She could not encourage any intimacy with him, yet she also needed to maintain his favor, lest he insist she depart. Meredith didn't think the duchess would ever stand for that, but it wasn't a risk she wished to take.

So she paused.

"Your Grace."

She bobbed into a curtsy and then waited, a step or two below him.

He ignored her formality. Instead, he leaned against the wall, and smiled like he was just a man flirting with a pretty girl and said, "You didn't stay to say goodbye."

"Pardon me if I am not certain of the etiquette of such a situation that we should never speak of. In fact, we should pretend it never happened."

"I gathered as much. But I don't want to pretend it never happened," he said. "In fact, all I want is for it to happen again and again and again."

She looked away, and her lips curved into the slightest, saddest smile as she remembered his kiss, his touch, the sweet things he'd whispered. Memories, that's all.

"You have a lot to learn, Your Grace."

"What happened to Just James?"

"It never happened. I never knew him. And you certainly do not know me. We never happened."

"All right, I understand. But why?"

"Dukes do not marry mere companions,

and mere companions cannot risk compromising their reputations. One does not court scandal," Meredith said, explaining the fundamentals of the haute ton. "The duchess does not condone scandalous behavior, and as her faithful companion, I don't dare disobey her wishes."

"I don't care about scandal."

"You will, Your Grace."

"Forget this talk of marriage — what of pleasure?"

"I am merely a servant, but I'm not the kind that exists for the whims of the master of the house."

"I would never think that. Or act thusly," he said, eyes flashing. He was not that kind of man and was offended she'd even considered it.

The truth of their situation was dawning on them both. Whatever had transpired that night in Southampton could not happen again. There were intangible, but real, barriers between them. His position was high and permanent; hers low and forever uncertain. This wasn't exactly news to her, but she'd never *felt* it so palpably before.

Meredith took one, two, three, four steps up so that she could look him in the eye.

"I owe everything to the duchess. Everything," Meredith said in a low, strong voice, thinking of the situation from which she'd been rescued long ago and the unbelievable chances she'd been given. "I will not forget that. Not for you, not for anyone. I am determined to keep my position as her companion secure. I have saved enough of my allowance that I could leave with some independence, but know this, Duke, *I will never leave the duchess.*"

"I just wish to know you better. To know you more. I like you. I like what we shared. I would like to share it again." His fingers anxiously tugged the buttons on the ridiculously fancy coat someone insisted he wear. It didn't suit him; he seemed uncomfortable in all that finery. "If it should please you."

"The night we met, I didn't know who you were," she said. "I didn't know until you stepped out of the carriage. Otherwise, I would have never smiled at you across that crowded room."

"I see," he said grimly. Her heart did ache for him — what a day he must have had and how his whole world must have turned on its head. She had an inkling of what he was going through: giving up freedom for wealth and duty, restraining one's true self in order to follow protocol, stifling passion for the "wrong" person because of the rules.

"As long as I have my reputation, I have a chance at security," she said. "If you care for me at all, you won't take that from me. You, Your Grace, will never have such worries. But I had one night, Duke. One. Just one, Just James. That's all it will ever be."

Chapter 2

A duke is often the most high-ranking, the most powerful, the most handsome, and the most wealthy man in the room. He ought to keep this in mind and conduct himself accordingly.

— The Rules for Dukes

The next day
In a drawing room

"The first rule of being a duke is to remember, at all times, that you are the master of high society," the duchess declared. "Only a few people outrank you — the king and queen, of course, plus the royal dukes. As such, you are likely to be the most powerful high-ranking person in any given room."

And so it began. Duke lessons.

They were in a drawing room — not *the* drawing room where he and his sisters had been yesterday, but a different one, because there were multiple ones. It seemed excessive.

His sisters were still abed, still exhausted from their travels. He was the only one up, and so James was trapped in this chamber alone with the duchess.

And Miss Green.

She was demure and pretty in that blue frock as she sat beside, and a little behind, the duchess. She hardly seemed like the kind of woman who had a passionate encounter with a man she'd only just met. He couldn't reconcile the girl he'd met in Southampton with the lady who sat primly before him.

This only had the effect of intriguing him more.

Of course he stole a glance or two with the hopes that she'd changed her mind about maintaining a distance between them. But no, she was deliberately avoiding his gaze. Those doe eyes of hers would not connect with his.

He understood that they were to pretend not to know each other.

He understood that she was very aware of the differences in their stations, even if he hadn't accepted that yet, because he hadn't accepted that *he* was a duke.

And he idly wondered just why she was *so* loyal to the duchess.

I owe everything to the duchess. Everything, she had said last night, in a fierce whisper. What long, secret history existed between them that would make her forgo the attentions of the highest-ranking and most powerful person in the room?

"So I am the highest-ranking and most powerful person in this room?" James confirmed.

"Yes, Your Grace."

"So my word is as good as command."

"Yes." The duchess pressed her lips into a thin line indicating that she did not care for the direction in which he was taking the conversation. She was eyeing him sharply, but her hands and posture gave no indication that he was rattling her. She was good.

Miss Green, on the other hand, looked nervous. Very nervous.

"So if I were to insist that we remove all the furniture and fetch some musicians so I might dance around the room with Miss Green, everyone would have to obey my orders."

Miss Green looked horrified.

The duchess didn't bat an eye.

"Of course you *could* do that, Your Grace. It is well within your rights. But it is deliberately misunderstanding your role. Such power is not bestowed so one might act like a petulant schoolboy or licentious rake."

She paused to give him a sharp, reproving look.

One that made him feel like a petulant schoolboy.

Miss Green gave him a similar look.

One that made him feel like a licentious rake.

Again, he became acutely aware that he was no longer Just James and she was no longer just a beautiful woman he met in a tavern one night.

He might have been the most powerful man in the room, but he wasn't sure how to wield that power.

He just knew he didn't want it.

"Then I suppose it is also within my rights to declare that this session is over. As duke, I should like to inspect the stables and ensure they meet my standards."

The duchess pursed her lips, but otherwise made no outward show of exasperation. They both knew he wished to escape and go muck around in the stables, with the horses, where he might pretend this duke business wasn't happening and where he might feel like himself, if only for one blessed hour.

"Your Grace, it is vitally important that a man of your station set an example to others. People will be watching you for clues as to how to conduct themselves. If you disregard your station, it indicates that those below you may as well."

In other words: the perpetuation of this archaic British aristocratic system rested on his shoulders. His reluctant, provincial, American shoulders.

"Once you enter society, all eyes will be on you, and they will be watching for the slightest misstep."

"I take it going outside to see the horses is a misstep. The things that interest me, that I care about, are missteps." Here he couldn't resist another look in the direction of Miss Green. She held her head high, but looked away.

"A duke does not muck around in the stables, though if one wishes for a ride, one might request a groom to saddle a horse and bring it around," the duchess said.

"And how does one do that?"

"One does not when one is engaged in important estate business."

James felt his temperature rise. His valet, one Mr. Edwards, had tied his damned cravat too tightly, in spite of James's requests to do otherwise. So much for being the most powerful man in any room. He stood swiftly, nearly knocking over his chair as he did so.

"So the first rule of being a duke is that I am not truly the most powerful person in the room. I am to devote my life to service of the dukedom, which I may or may not want, and set an example for people I may or may not give a damn about."

He was irate. Self-righteously so.

James knew he sounded like a petulant, ungrateful brat. It seemed impossible for him to explain that he wasn't ungrateful, just scared of failing in such a supposedly sacred mission, in which so many relied upon him. The only example he'd had of interacting with the dukedom was his father happily leaving it all behind and never speaking of it again.

He wasn't certain that he was the man for the job, and yet it now all rested upon him. Perhaps he never should have come to England.

"Most people would consider it lucky indeed to be a duke. Many come to understand it as a great honor to be tasked with stewarding tradition, family, and prosperity from one generation to another."

Yes, but . . . it was just a circumstance of birth. It wasn't because he was worthy, or qualified, to say nothing of whether or not he wished to. James had a hunch he wasn't worthy or qualified. The idea of even trying

61

to become worthy or qualified had him running for the stables.

"Regardless of what you may think of the situation — and I can see that you think very little of it — you are the duke now. It is done. You may flee and shirk your responsibilities, or you may remain and make a valiant effort to uphold the Durham estate for another generation. It depends upon the kind of man you are. And given that you have so diligently cared for your three sisters, I think we both know you are capable of rising to this occasion."

The duchess had to bring up his sisters. She had to bring up the three reasons he was here and the three reasons he *would* have to try. She was good. And she, clearly, was the most powerful person in this room.

The duchess rose to her feet. And even though he towered over her, she still managed to look down at him. Quite a feat, that.

Without another word, she quit the room.

Miss Green followed, though she paused before exiting. For one blessed second they were alone together. His heart lurched.

"The bell pull," she said, giving a tug on a gold, corded rope hanging near the door. "It will summon a servant, who will honor your request."

■ ■ ■ ■

The duchess had kept her cool with the duke, but once the doors closed behind Meredith, her frustration revealed itself in a sharp huff of annoyance and the brisk pace with which she walked down the corridor. Meredith didn't have the luxury of revealing her feelings.

Tap tap tap. The duchess's shoes clicked along the marble tiles.

Thump thump thump. Meredith's heart was still pounding from the anxiety that, at any second, the duke would give her away with one of his smoldering glances or an offhanded remark. In her defense, she hadn't known who he was then — but that excuse would hardly hold sway with Her Grace. Especially when she was in a mood like this.

"That was more of a trial than I had hoped. It was not unexpected, though still exasperating," the duchess said. "Any man in England would be beside himself to inherit a dukedom, but no, the title must go to an American who could not care less."

"He may just need time to adjust to this dramatic change," Meredith replied.

She spoke from her own experience. Meredith remembered being a young girl coming from a simple life to live with the duchess and suddenly being expected to dress, speak, and behave a certain way. She was supposed to learn French and embroidery and a dozen other things that girls like her were never expected to know.

She hadn't been sure if she could do it and had been overwhelmed by the prospect of even trying. The duchess was so *exacting.*

She suspected ~~James~~ the duke felt the same way.

The difference between them was that he had the liberty of rejecting the lot of it. He could go back to America, an ocean away from all of this.

Of course, Meredith was free to leave at any time, too, but her alternatives were far less alluring — and she had confirmed that on her recent trip home. She recognized that staying with the duchess as her companion was her best opportunity for a secure, comfortable, and interesting life.

"We don't have time for him to adjust," the duchess continued sharply. "The estate needs a firm hand and guidance *soon.* The gossip columns are already rife with speculation about him and his sisters."

"Never mind the gossip columns, Your Grace. This is only his first day. Perhaps you'll make more progress with him tomorrow, or with his sisters this afternoon. We have a modiste appointment with them shortly. Soon they'll look the part of perfect English ladies, and you have said that is half the battle."

The duchess sighed. "I fear your optimism may be misplaced, but I do like how you hope for the best."

The duchess paused, troubled, as she considered something. Meredith could read her well. She waited, patiently, for Her Grace to speak.

"I will need your assistance, Meredith."

"Of course, Your Grace."

"He seems like he responds to you," the duchess said.

Thump. Thump. Thump. No one was supposed to notice or to know. But nothing ever escaped the duchess, now did it?

"And Lord knows his sisters will keep me occupied," she added with a sigh. "I need you to help me turn him into a proper duke. I've taught you well, Meredith, and now it's time for you to help me teach him."

Thump. Thump. Crack.

Heart, still pounding. Heart, starting to break.

Meredith, who had vowed to avoid him, found herself saying yes.

CHAPTER 3

Being the highest-ranking, most powerful, and probably the most handsome and
charming man in the room, the duke
should always take the lead. Including, but
not limited to, dancing.

— THE RULES FOR DUKES

Days passed with Meredith catching only
glimpses of the duke. He spent his hours
behind closed doors in the study, consumed
with the demands of solicitors and estate
managers, and some of the late duke's colleagues in parliament.

Was he coming around to the idea of this
duke business?

Perhaps.

Perhaps not.

These sessions were inevitably followed
by a visit to the stables, doing whatever it
was that one did in the stables. She learned
from his sisters that he would spend an hour

or two brushing down horses or saddling one up himself and going for a ride and then grooming the animal afterward. In other words, servant's work.

In spite of the duchess's request that Meredith work closely with him, she hadn't had the chance. For this she was glad, because it also meant fewer encounters to tempt her.

His Grace had obeyed her wishes not to say a word about their night at the tavern and to not even try to seduce her once more. No heated glances, no secret half smiles, no brushing of hands as they passed on the stairs or in the hall.

This was good. Excellent. It proved that he was a decent gentleman. It kept her free to focus on attending to the duchess, and assisting her with the duke's sisters because oh . . . Lud . . . the duke's sisters were something else entirely.

On Tuesday, they had spent hours learning to curtsy. Well, moments learning and hours practicing, until Bridget snuck off to the kitchens, Amelia wandered off to find her, and Claire shrugged at the lot of them and retired to her room to focus on her studies. That one was always studying.

There were trips to the modiste in order to outfit the girls with complete wardrobes as befitting their new rank. There were trips to the milliner as well, the bookshop, the apothecary, et cetera, et cetera.

And there were lessons in pouring tea and table manners, pianoforte and letter writing, elocution and English geography.

Meredith remembered her own crash course in becoming a lady. She'd been merely twelve and had gone from keeping house for her parents to standing with books on her head and reciting all the kings and queens of England in chronological order until her accent was more like the duchess's and less like her mother's. She, too, had learned to quiet her inner wild spirit girl and learn to look and act Like A Lady.

Today the lessons for the Cavendishes continued with dancing.

This time, the duke was there, too.

"Will you play one more time, Miss Green?" The duchess sounded only slightly exasperated to make the request. Again. She didn't look nearly as frazzled as Monsieur Bellini, the dance instructor, a small spritely man, supposedly from Paris.

Meredith gave a pleasant smile that gave no indication of her fatigue at playing the same bars of music again and again. And again.

She dared a glance at the siblings over the

pianoforte. James was taking turns leading each of his sisters; each one was a disaster in her own way. Bridget stepped on toes in spite of staring at her feet, Amelia was too jubilant in her movements, Claire was too stiff. James was too wooden.

Meredith longed to have someone else play, so she might have a spin around the ballroom, feeling pretty, weightless, and glorious with her skirts swirling around her and her heart racing. She wished to put her hours of dancing lessons to use. But she rarely had an opportunity to dance, even when she attended balls. Because dancing was courtship and impoverished companions of duchesses were not courted.

And so Meredith had been stuck on the sidelines, being a companion.

Or, today, stuck on this bench, plunking out the same chords and melodies again and again. And again.

At least the duke was a terrible dancer. That was her only comforting thought. Her visions of being swept around a ballroom in his arms would not happen. At least, not anytime soon, and not without hours and hours of practice.

But the memory of being in his arms . . . she remembered the soft click of the door shutting behind them, the rustle of her dress as she lifted it off and dropped it to the floor, the heat of his body against her bare skin as he enveloped her in his arms and found her mouth for a kiss . . .

"Miss Green?"

"I'm sorry. I missed the chord."

"Try again. Everyone." The duchess paused. "Actually, Miss Green, why don't you demonstrate with the duke as your partner? Monsieur Bellini, you can play for this one."

"Of course," Meredith murmured.

Thump. Thump. Thump.

Her heart was pounding as she stood and stepped from behind the pianoforte.

Thump. Thump. Thump.

James's eyes locked with hers and he stepped toward her.

His eyes were blue. A deep, dark blue like the sea or the night sky. She remembered the thrill that had coursed through her when their gazes first locked across that crowded tavern and the thrill at the way his eyes sparkled when he looked at her. He had thought her pretty. He had thought her special.

He saw her. For a woman who lived in the background, it was like stepping into the sunshine after weeks spent indoors while it rained.

"Now, girls, watch their steps," the duchess said. "And watch how Miss Green comports herself with restraint and elegance."

Restraint: not throwing herself into his arms and demanding that he carry her off to bed so they might start up where they had left off.

Elegance: maintaining the proper placement of hands, steps of the dance, moving with grace, and observing all the rules.

James reached for her hands.

"No, you mustn't forget the protocol," the duchess cut in. "Though it may seem like an unnecessary extra step, it is all part of the ritual. One wouldn't just pounce on a woman, would one?"

"The answer to that better be no," Claire remarked with her sisters giggling in the background.

Like the perfect gentleman, James bowed before her. In spite of his longish hair and informal dress, it didn't take a stretch of the imagination to envision him resplendent in evening clothes, bowing to a beautiful, gently bred woman at a ball. She felt a pang of longing.

She foresaw hearts beating faster, flirtations, and swoons. There would be a run on smelling salts.

Meredith curtsied in return. She had but

this moment, in an empty, day-lit ballroom, wearing a simple morning dress, with an audience of family and an exasperated dancing instructor looking on.

"May I have the honor of this dance?" His voice was low, and strong. And in the wrong accent, but one that sounded pleasing to her ears.

"I would be honored, Your Grace," she replied politely, in the correct accent.

Monsieur Bellini struck up the chords. James clasped her hand and pressed his other palm on the small of her back.

"Stronger," she urged in a low voice. She felt his muscles engage. He stood taller, chest out, shoulders thrown back. "You must hold me tighter."

His grip tightened.

"Yes," she said breathlessly. "Yes, like that."

His eyes flashed.

The music played: *one, two, three, one, two, three.* He held her like a man claiming his possession — keeping her close, his grasp strong. Together they moved, but she still controlled the direction.

"As duke, and as the man, you must take the lead," she said. But then she remembered his resistance to all that. So, dropping her voice lower so the others wouldn't hear, she added, "Do with me what you will."

Her words had the desired effect. James took the lead, determining where the steps of the dance would take them. Her own movements softened as he took more control of their direction and she let herself get swept away.

It was like that night . . . *she remembered falling back onto the mattress. His arms, tense and strong as he lowered his weight onto hers. He took the lead in their lovemaking, nudging her legs apart and settling between them. She had softened, giving herself up to him . . .*

"Don't look down, Your Grace. Your eyes can't guide you. You must feel the rhythm of the music and move to that. A strong, steady, relentless rhythm."

James's eyes darkened.

She wasn't talking about waltzing and he knew it.

"Look at me. Drink me in."

He did, oh, he did. And she almost lost her own footing, except his had become sure, steady, and relentless. His grip on her was strong, his command of their performance complete. Every touch, every movement let her know, in no uncertain terms, that she could surrender, and he'd catch her.

But this was just a waltz. Just a practice spin around the ballroom. Even if it felt like they were on the verge of making love. Even if it felt downright indecent to have an audience.

"That is quite enough," the duchess declared sharply. Her eyes were narrowed. Her Grace was no fool, and that made Meredith nervous. "Excellent demonstration, thank you. Monsieur Bellini, do stop the music."

She and James dropped their hands. Stepped back away from each other, creating distance between them. They parted, and as they crossed the ballroom to join the others, she remarked softly, "Dance like that, and look at the London ladies like that, they'll all be throwing themselves at you."

His response was quick and sure: "And what if I only want you?"

Impossible. It was all kinds of impossible.

Just because a duke is often the highest-ranking person does not mean he is excused from learning the order of precedence and all the ways to address (lesser) peers.

— THE RULES FOR DUKES

The duchess had assembled the lot of them in the drawing room for more lessons. To say the Cavendish siblings were not enthusiastic was an understatement. Lady Amelia slouched on the settee like a sulking young girl, and Lady Claire looked frightfully bored. Only Lady Bridget seemed to be making an effort to sit upright and pay attention; in that, she reminded Meredith of herself years ago.

As for the duke — he was seated in a chair that was entirely too small for his frame. His long, muscular legs, clad in fawn-colored breeches, were stretched out before him. His strong arms were crossed over his chest. Meredith could see, and practically feel, all the tension coiled in his limbs.

His gaze flitted in her direction, resting on her face for a brief second. It wouldn't do to be caught staring and in this intimate setting — especially after that dance lesson had raised some eyebrows — and she must take care to hide what happened to her heart and her nerves when he was near.

She schooled her attention on the bored Cavendish siblings. Meredith couldn't entirely blame them for finding these sessions tedious; today's lesson was one of the more frustrating and maddening topics, but it was required learning if one were to mingle with the haute ton.

"One of the most important things to know is the order of precedence," the duchess began. Claire lifted her eyebrow skeptically. "Making a mistake with this can be perceived as a grave insult. For example, in 1818, the Countess of Delmar accidentally sent Lord White into dinner before the Marquess of Thorne. Their families have been feuding ever since. The countess's reputation has never quite recovered."

"What does the countess's reputation matter to me?" Lady Amelia inquired.

"That is entirely beside the point."

"It's like with horses, Amelia," James cut in. "The leader of the pack must go through the entryway first. The others follow. It keeps the whole pack calm and orderly."

"A very apt analogy, Duke, though one I will thank you not to make among the haute ton," the duchess replied dryly.

But Meredith was biting back a smile, imagining the haute ton as a pack of ponies and finding it quite made sense.

"I can't believe there's an order for going into supper," Bridget muttered. This drew another quick smile from Meredith, one she took care that the duchess wouldn't see.

"Rest assured, Bridget, I bet as sisters to a

duke we'll get in first," Claire said, patting her sister's hand consolingly.

"It will depend upon who else is in attendance that particular evening," the duchess added. "For example, if the king or queen or one of the royal dukes were present, you would certainly not be first. But at soirees at one of our country estates, it is likely that you would."

"Glad this title is good for something," James said dryly. "Wouldn't want my beloved sisters to starve at a party."

That earned him scowls from all three beloved sisters.

"Now, who can tell me the rankings of the peerage?"

Amelia was staring out the window longingly. Bridget was flipping through the fat volume of *Debrett's Book of the Peerage.* Claire looked as if her thoughts were elsewhere. James closed his eyes. The duchess emitted the slightest sigh of frustration.

Or despair; it might have been despair.

Meredith needed to rescue everyone.

"I know this is not the most scintillating of subject matters, but it is important," she said. "If only so you know when you might go into supper or so that if you insult someone it is at least deliberate."

She wanted to add, *at least you are as-*

sured attendance at the balls. At least your station is at the top of the list. Hers was barely on the list at all.

"Thank you, Miss Green. Please, do tell us the order of precedence."

"The king and queen, of course. Princes and royal dukes. Then it's duke, marquess, earl, viscount, and baron. Their wives are duchess, marchioness, countess, viscountess, baroness. And then there is the landed gentry . . ."

She continued on.

And on.

And still did not get to her place on the list. Commoners taken in by duchesses were near the bottom.

She glanced at the duke, asking him with her eyes: *Do you see now, what separates us?* Titles, money, land of one's own, and the strict separation of those at the top of the list and those at the bottom.

Whether one was listed in that fat volume of *Debrett's.* Or not.

He held her gaze. But did he see?

"Excellent, Miss Green, thank you. Next, let us review how to address a peer when speaking versus when one is writing. For example: a duke is addressed in speech as Your Grace, whilst his social equals might merely address him as Duke. In formal correspondence one would write *My Lord Duke,* though in social correspondence it would be *Dear Duke of Durham.*"

"And his sisters might address him formally as My Lord Annoying Older Brother or informally as Annoying Brother," Amelia added.

"I have a name," James said, through gritted teeth. But everyone ignored him.

"Why are spoken and written forms of address different?" Lady Bridget asked.

"Because it is," the duchess answered.

That reply was met with a peevish purse of Bridget's lips — as if she were learning from the duchess already.

"Just think of what other, more useful things we might spend our time studying," Claire remarked to no one in particular. "Like calculus or geometry."

"I'm not sure which would be more tedious," Amelia muttered. "I honestly cannot decide."

"Now tell me, how might one address the younger son of an earl?" Her Grace asked.

"I would say 'Hello, sir, won't you tell me your name?'" Amelia replied.

"No, you wouldn't say anything unless you were introduced to him by a mutual acquaintance. At which point you might say 'Hello, Mr. Younger Son. I am honored to make your acquaintance.' "

"Hello, Mr. Younger Son, what are the chances you stand to inherit?" Claire added dryly.

"But we don't have any mutual acquaintances," Bridget pointed out.

"I shall perform introductions to eligible suitors for you, ladies, and potential brides for you, Duke."

There it was: a sudden statement of the obvious and inevitable that still managed to knock the breath from her lips. It was not shocking news that he would have to marry, and marry a woman with her family in *Debrett's,* perhaps even with pages devoted to her lineage. He would have to wed a woman who was addressed differently whether on paper or in person.

And she, Meredith, would have to watch it all, until she accompanied the duchess to the dower house, eventually. Her youth would fade, along with it her prospects. Eventually the duchess would pass on, and Meredith would be alone in the world, with just the memories of that one stolen night of passion. The world would carry on with everything and everyone in their rightful places.

But what if it could be different?

All those questions the Cavendish girls

asked — ones she had never considered, always accepted — made Meredith want to ask some questions of her own. There was something about the way these American siblings refused to find all these rules and titles impressive, to say nothing of the protocol holding the aristocracy together.

Lady Claire stubbornly refused to hide her passion for mathematics; it made Meredith wonder what talents of her own she might have discovered had she not been dedicated to embroidery and letter writing.

Lady Amelia hungered to see the world, or at least London; it made Meredith wonder what she was missing by always hovering in the duchess's shadow.

And each day, Meredith watched Lady Bridget try to shrink herself into the little box of Perfect Lady, and she wanted to put a stop to it.

Their questions, their interests, their spirits, all combined to plant a seed in Meredith. That little question, *what if it could be different,* had taken root in her head and heart. Who knew what it might bloom into?

"If you'll excuse me," the duke interrupted, "there's an urgent matter I must attend to in the stables."

"Miss Green, do go have a word with him while I continue with these ladies. See if you can make him see sense and reason."

Despite being told that dukes didn't do such things, James did indeed spend time mucking about in the stables. Of course there was no need for him to do so, as the grooms and stable hands were more than competent. The horses were fine and well cared for.

But there was a deep, driving need for James to be in a space that felt like home. He needed the company of creatures who didn't care about his fancy title, newfound wealth, whether his boots were dirty, or if he addressed an earl correctly.

James needed to be in a space where he knew what he was doing. He'd been unsure of himself during the dreaded duke lessons, unsure of how to conduct himself with estate managers, and unsure of how to act when being presented with a formal dinner setting of more cutlery than any reasonable man needed.

James was excruciatingly aware of being watched by all the servants.

He also needed to do something with his hands, even if it was just the tremendously soothing activity of brushing a horse's coat in preparation for a hard and fast ride around Hyde Park. It didn't compare to galloping through the Maryland countryside, but it was better than being caged in a drawing room.

It was easy enough to listen to the duchess lecture him on the rules and his new role in life. He was American, not a moron. He just couldn't bring himself to embrace the lot of it. The only reason he could see to bother being all ducal was to attract Miss Green, but she'd made it clear that was impossible. Instead, he just wanted to escape. So he lifted a saddle onto the horse's back in preparation for a ride from which he may or may not return.

As companion to the duchess, Meredith spent her time in the company of Her Grace, who, it should go without saying, had not once found important estate business to conduct in the stables.

While she was as happy as a Cavendish to escape the drawing room, it was with some trepidation that she approached the stables and thus, the duke.

They shouldn't be alone together. Not

when he looked at her the way he did — like he had seen her unclothed, laid bare, crying out in pleasure. No matter who was around, he looked at her like that. It was almost enough to forget her place.

They especially shouldn't be alone somewhere as elemental as the stables — away from the supervising eyes of household servants, away from the finery of the house reminding them to behave and remember their places.

Meredith recognized Johnny, one of the grooms, and nodded to him as she stepped inside. The stables were dimly lit, and the air was thick with the scent of hay and horse and earth.

"Have you seen His Grace?"

"Last stall on the left, Miss Green."

"Thank you, Johnny."

She walked down the center aisle, past large horses standing in their stalls. Some stuck their heads out, curious as to the new person in their midst, while others were more interested in eating or sleeping.

She found the duke, right where the groom had told her to look.

James was brushing down a big white horse. He probably knew the proper name for its breed, and the correct way to describe its height (it wasn't feet; was it hands?), and all the little details about its demeanor, and how it related to all the other types of horses.

In other words, exactly what the duchess had been trying to teach them earlier, except about a certain type of people instead.

James paused when he saw her. She had to stop thinking of him in her head as James, or Just James. It would raise too many questions if she were to accidentally address him that way in front of others.

He straightened upright slowly. There was muck on his boots, his shirtsleeves were pushed up to his elbows, and there were damp patches of sweat on his white shirt. His hair was a bit shaggy, falling forward into his eyes.

He was a mess.

An undignified, elemental mess.

She'd never found him more attractive.

Especially when he gave her a lazy smile and drawled, "To what do I owe the pleasure, Miss Green?"

"I am to have a word with you."

Something shuttered in his expression.

"Don't waste your breath on that. I believe that knowing the hierarchy of those in society is tremendously important. Everyone knowing their place and the rules to the game keeps things running smoothly. It's the same with horses. And I know a man of my position" — and those words were said with some distaste — "has a duty to uphold the lot of it. I know."

"So you were paying attention."

"It so happens, Miss Green, that I'm not just a pretty face."

James gave her a smoldering smile that she weakly returned. Aye, but he did have a pretty face. Strong features, a firm mouth, and those eyes . . . they were sparkling at her again.

"Excellent. Perhaps you might endeavor to reveal your brilliance to the duchess."

"Why would I do that?"

"Why not?"

"Should I tell you a story?"

No. Yes.

"I trained a horse back home, a filly named Athena. That horse could run faster and with more power than any other horse I'd seen — as long as no one was looking. The minute you put a saddle on her and took her to the starting line at the track with all the shouting and hollering, she refused to even trot. That girl *walked* around the track, coming in dead last. On purpose. Do you know why?"

"Why?"

"Because she wanted to run for the joy of it, to feel the wind in her mane, to express her truest natural self. As soon as running became a high-stakes race, a competitive sprint in a circle for a prize she'd never see, she lost interest."

"That's a good story, but what does this have to do with anything?"

"The minute the duchess realizes I know how to address the daughter of a marquess or can do a bloody quadrille with my eyes closed is the moment she decides to take us into the ring and show us off, like show ponies. Do you see?"

"You want to be a duke when no one's watching?"

"To be honest, I'm not certain I want to be a duke at all."

"Then why are you here? You've come a long way to not be a duke."

"Because how do you say no to all this?" He gestured to the stables, yes, but she knew he meant the grand house beyond it, and the vast estates beyond that, and the adventure of it all. He shrugged his shoulders, then fixed his gaze on hers. "How do you say no before you've seen it, experienced it, tasted it, stayed up all night with it?"

"Your Grace . . ." she murmured, fearing

he was no longer talking about the dukedom.

"And frankly, how do you say no to my
three sisters?"

This brought a smile to her lips. Meredith
was starting to know them — the way they
teased and chattered and loved each other
fiercely. Part of her yearned to be a part of
their pack, but part of her hung back, afraid
of being swept away by their exuberance.
And, of course, forgetting her place.

"You know, my father never spoke about
this. All those hours we spent together, just
us and the horses, and he never mentioned
it. We had no idea about any of this."

And with that, Meredith began to understand. He was as surprised as anyone that
he was now Durham. At least a small part
of him was here to try to understand his
father, to try to get close to a man he had
lost and, in some ways, the man he had
never known.

It wasn't greed or a hunger for power or
glory that drove him. Just a son, wanting to
know and stay close to the father he'd lost.

Meredith thought it sad and sweet and
wonderful all at once.

"I understand," she said softly. "So
wouldn't you want to see and experience all
this life has to offer, so you might know the

life your father led? All the soirees, and elegant conversation. And you haven't even seen the ducal seat yet — the stables there are marvelous. The envy of many."

"You mean, the life he gave up?" There was that. He continued. "What I've seen so far are rules, each one more stupid than the last."

James — how could she think of him as anything but James in environs like these? — set down the brush and took a step closer to her.

And then one more.

And then they were oh, so close together because there was only so much room for two people and a horse in this stall. "The only thing that excites me about London is you."

They stood nearly toe to toe. She imagined she could feel the heat pulsating from his body. Or maybe that was herself, heated with wanting this man.

It was the damndest thing — here she was trying to convince him to make himself so far out of her orbit that nothing could ever happen between them. But they were standing in the stables, speaking as equals, with a thick undercurrent of desire pulsing between them, all of it tempting her to dreams she shouldn't even dream because they would never come true.

Because like it or not, he was the duke.

"Pity, that."

"Now why is that a pity?" He leaned against the wooden wall of the stall, like he was settling in for a lengthy and detailed explanation of why he shouldn't fancy her.

Reasons. She had them. She would explain.

"I can't really be the most interesting thing you've experienced in London —"

"Southampton," he corrected.

Her lips pursed at that. Or maybe they puckered, like they were ready for a kiss. And they were, just thinking about that night.

She recalled the soft sound of the door clicking shut, followed by the rustle of her dress. His mouth claiming hers. The sound of her sigh, the touch of his hands. She remembered like it was only last night.

But she'd been sent here on an errand and it wasn't to reminisce.

"You really ought to get out more. See more interesting things. Meet more women. Eligible women. Marriageable women. The type of women who have noble bloodlines and adjacent estates."

She blinked. He blinked.

"Well then. I suppose I should stop thinking about kissing you, and I should certainly stop getting close enough to do so."

He was close enough to do so. Meredith hadn't even been aware of the distance closing between them; it seemed like space just evaporated.

"And I probably shouldn't be in the stables," he murmured. "We probably shouldn't be alone."

"That's right," she whispered.

"You probably shouldn't be here, either. This is no place for a refined and elegant woman like you."

And didn't that make her heart beat faster, too.

People didn't take much notice of her. And if they did, most saw her as a pitiable relation, not quite a servant and not quite a lady. Then they stopped looking.

They never saw that she was a living, breathing woman with a head full of thoughts and a beating heart. It escaped their notice that she was as refined and elegant — as much as any lady at a great house — because she'd been taught and cultivated by the best of them all.

The duchess. Meredith owed her everything; the least she could do to repay her was *not* forget everything she'd been taught and, instead, to press her body against the duke's — sweat and scent of the stables at all — and kiss him senseless, right here with a big white horse looking on.

"I should go," she said softly. Her lips, still inches from his.

"Before I get us both into trouble," he replied.

"I should hate to keep you from important estate business," she replied with a slight smile. Reluctantly, she stepped away from him. There was nothing more to stay for.

Meredith found herself liking him more now — he was handsome, humble, conflicted, and real. Pity then, that she had to help turn him into a Proper Duke.

CHAPTER 4

Just because most women will swoon at merely being introduced to a duke does not mean that he is excused from flirtation. Any man worth his salt knows how to flirt.

— THE RULES FOR DUKES

If Meredith needed a reminder that she and James could never be together in any lawful, meaningful, socially acceptable way, the duchess provided it the next morning in another one of those duke lessons.

Once again, Meredith joined James and the duchess in the south drawing room, a small and informal chamber. Relatively speaking, of course.

"As the duke, you have many essential tasks," Her Grace began, "but the most important one will be siring an heir."

"My pleasure," James murmured in a rakish way.

Meredith half smiled.

The duchess was not amused.

"And by heir, I mean a legitimate son. To do that, you must wed."

"I am aware of how it all works," he drawled and, Lud, if that didn't make the color rise in her cheeks. "When a man and a woman love each other very much . . ."

"Love has little to do with it," the duchess said bluntly. "This is the haute ton now. You cannot wed just anyone. A duke's bride must possess prestigious bloodlines and impeccable behavior. She must carry herself in a manner that is at once refined and assured. Good breeding is essential."

"Tell me, Duchess, are you talking about a horse or a woman?"

"Given your previous profession, I shouldn't need to convince you of this."

"Given my previous profession, I never imagined that *I* would be the stud horse," he muttered.

The duchess pursed her lips in her expression of I-disapprove-of-what-you-are-saying-but-will-not-dignify-it-with-a-response.

"You must also consider the lady's connections, particularly her ties to other prominent families who might prove to be useful allies in society."

"What happened to the duke being the most powerful man in the room? Besides the king, that is."

He said the words *the king* as if they tasted bitter in his mouth.

Meredith watched this back-and-forth with no small amount of fascination. When she'd had lessons with the duchess, she hadn't even thought to question anything she was told; she'd just been so grateful for the chance to rise up in the world, let alone to escape what her home life had become. Then again, she'd been a twelve-year-old girl.

In all those years since, she'd never seen anyone challenge the duchess, or challenge the very way of things. She had never thought to question the ways of the haute ton.

But here was James, Just James, just asking questions that managed to puncture the aura of perfection and elegance of the haute ton. It was so rebellious, so uncivilized, so *American* of him.

A woman or a horse, indeed.

"Your title will take you far, Duke, and it will certainly open doors for you. But everyone needs connections in society, especially should you, or members of this family, need to weather any storms or scandals. Given your . . . American manners . . . I do confess that I don't expect an entirely smooth entry into society."

What an ominous, foreboding thing to say.

The duchess sipped her tea.

James glanced at the clock.

Meredith wondered why she was present for this. She might be more useful with the sisters at their dancing lesson. Today they were learning the quadrille, one of the more complicated dances.

"We will attend our first ball soon. I will introduce you to an assortment of suitable women. I hope you will consider making one of them your duchess."

"I assume you wouldn't introduce me to any that didn't strike your fancy?" James replied with a lift of his brow.

"Your current heir, one Mr. Collins, leaves much to be desired when it comes to his abilities to manage something as complex as the estate, relationships in society, or holding multiple thoughts in his head concurrently. The sooner you are wed and delivered of a son, the better. Thus any young woman I introduce you to will indeed be suitable. We don't have time for unsuitable women."

There was a beat of silence. His gaze landed on her.

Don't say it. Don't say it. Don't say it.

Then he said it.

"You have introduced me to Miss Green."

"I have also introduced you to the house-keeper," the duchess replied, so quickly and easily that it stung, even though Meredith knew she meant well enough. "Miss Green is like a daughter to me, and I wish for her happiness. I know she has many fine qualities and will make some man very happy one day."

But . . .

It didn't need to be said to be understood that she wasn't considered duchess material — the circumstances of her birth, her common parents and ancestry, and her lower-class background all took care of that. These were all things that could not be changed, not even by an act of God.

"And what about love?" James asked.

Love. He had to go and mention *love* in that low drawl of his.

The duchess laughed.

"How romantic of you. Young people these days, with their notions of romance and sentiments trumping all practical considerations. I encourage you to have the good sense to fall in love with a suitable woman."

"And what if I don't care to wed?"

"That is what all the rakes say," the duchess said with a laugh. "But they all find themselves leg shackled in the end, mark my words."

This went over as well as to be expected, which is to say, not very well at all. The duke's expression darkened.

Meredith nurtured her own feelings of disappointment in her heart. Just because she knew and accepted the ways of the world didn't mean that she didn't harbor little sparks of hope deep down. But the duchess spoke the truth.

"Now, in anticipation of this upcoming debut ball, we must practice the conversation between a gentleman and lady in such circumstances," the duchess said, getting to the heart of the day's lesson.

Flirting. Elegant, proper flirting. The first step to wooing an elegant, proper wife. Nothing said *flirting* and *romance* like a lecture from one's aunt.

"I'm not sure it's necessary to practice this," James replied, grinning. "Haven't had much trouble talking to women before."

He gave Meredith a glance as if to say, *isn't that right?*

"I'm certain that you were quite the charmer, and that you had all the local village girls swooning," the duchess replied.

"But this is London and the haute ton. Charm and seduction require more finesse than leaning against a wall with a lazy smile and a mug of ale in your hand."

How did she guess? How did she know?

And how had Meredith been such a ninny as to fall for exactly that?

In her defense, one really had to see him lean against a wall with a lazy smile.

"Well, for the sake of seducing ladies . . ." James stood. "Let's practice some high-class wooing."

"Miss Green, please, stand in. Let us pretend that you are an earl's daughter. Let's say, the daughter of Lord Wyndham. Duke, how would you address her?"

James and Meredith stood, as if at a ball.

"What is a beautiful woman like you doing alone in a place like this?" James asked. Just like he had that night. Just like that night Meredith's heart had skipped a beat.

"No proper lady would be alone," the duchess huffed, and Meredith felt her cheeks grow hot. "Try again. And with a less ridiculous line, please."

"I'll have you know that line works," James replied. Meredith felt her blush deepen. What was worse: that she'd ruined herself or that she fell for such clunky attempts at flirtation? Honestly, it was a question that didn't need answering.

"I do not wish to know," the duchess said. "Carry on."

"My lady, you are a queen among women." Then he bent over and kissed her hand dramatically. Meredith couldn't help but laugh and roll her eyes.

"Now, for the introductions. Duke, may I present Lady Wyndham. Lady Wyndham, this is His Grace, the Duke of Durham, newly arrived to town and eager to make your acquaintance."

James bowed, elegantly enough.

Meredith curtsied with all the elegance of a woman with twelve years of training from the Duchess of Durham.

James reached for her hand, and she slipped her palm in his.

Suddenly the air changed between them. His devil-may-care attitude vanished and he became serious. Meredith was able to pretend — too well — that she was Lady Wyndham, daughter of an earl and a suitable match for a duke. She decided to throw herself into the role.

"Good evening, Lady Wyndham," he murmured, a mischievous sparkle in his eye at the ridiculous game they were playing. "It is a pleasure to make your acquaintance."

"Your Grace, I am honored."

"Now you must ask a question, Duke, especially if you find yourself with a wall-flower type," the duchess cut in. "Though a gently bred woman with an ounce of pluck will be skilled in the art of conversation."

"Shall we find some place private to converse? You can tell me your story," he murmured. Then, with a knowing grin, just like that night, he added, "I bet you have a story."

"An inappropriate question," the duchess cut in.

And one delivered in a most inappropriate and altogether too sensual voice.

"Your Grace, you forget yourself," Meredith, as Lady Wyndham, reprimanded him. Because a lady would *never, ever* steal off with a man to whom she'd only just been introduced.

Lud, but she'd been rebellious that night. That one time. And now her one indiscretion was here haunting her. Flirting with her.

"You also set yourself up for some cutting remark on savage American manners," the duchess added. "Instead, you might ask how she is enjoying the social event or remark upon the weather."

"How are you enjoying this party, Lady

Wyndham? Does the music please you? Have you had enough champagne?"

"Very well, Your Grace. It is far more amusing than I had anticipated, now that I have made your acquaintance."

"Excellent. Some light flirting." The duchess nodded approvingly, which hardly fanned the flames of romance. But then again, she and James didn't need help with that. This something sizzled between them, even in this game of pretend, and even with the duchess looking on.

"I am sorry to hear that you have low expectations, but I'm glad to have given you pleasure," he murmured to Meredith.

"Well, it's not every day that one meets an American-born duke. One can't help but wish to know you."

"And it's not every day a man meets a beauty such as yourself."

"You flatter me, Your Grace."

"You enchant me, my lady."

For a moment, she faltered, suspended between her pretend fantasy that she was Lady Wyndham, earl's daughter, at a ball, being romanced by the dashing young Duke of Durham, and the truth, which is that she was just a stand-in for another, better woman for him.

She was his *practice*.

But he didn't look at her like she was practice.

He looked at her like he meant Every. Damn. Word.

"Light flirting within the bounds of propriety is appropriate and will be appreciated," the duchess said. "Indeed, it is an art one should cultivate."

Light flirting?

Did the duchess not see? Could she not feel the magnetism between her and James? This was no mere light flirting. This was passion restrained, seeping out in whatever little cracks it could, even if it was playacting in the drawing room with the most fearsome chaperone in the land.

"It might now be suitable to invite the lady to dance, or promise to call upon her if you are so taken. But I should also note that at this point, it is imperative that you don't show excessive favor to any one lady; you must meet all your options, Duke. And there will be many."

"But only the ones that are suitable," Meredith added softly.

Because of, not in spite of, his lofty position in the world, it is a duke's responsibility to consider those who depend upon him.
— THE RULES FOR DUKES

A few days later
Breakfast

Meredith's lips were just so kissable. Deep red, plump. James liked to think of her as Meredith, now that he knew her name. None of this formal Miss Green nonsense — at least, not in his thoughts. Now if he could only kiss those kissable lips once more, twice more. Such were James's deep thoughts at the breakfast table.

She sat at the opposite end of the table, at the duchess's right hand. That was her place, literally and figuratively, on nearly every occasion. Whether at mealtimes, or during duke lessons, or teatime, she shadowed the duchess. How, he wondered, had Meredith come to occupy such a position? There had to be a story there. He thought about knowing her enough to know.

One would think they'd have every opportunity, living under the same roof, in a vast house where one might steal away and not be discovered for hours or days. But life here was so regimented, roles so strictly prescribed, that it was nearly impossible to deviate from the routine.

For example: every morning the family took breakfast together in the breakfast room, which was not to be confused with the dining room, and the formal dining room, or the morning room. The duchess always had a stack of freshly ironed newspapers by her plate.

Each morning James watched from the far end of the table as she skimmed past everything — parliamentary reports, news from abroad and such — until she reached the gossip columns.

"The papers are already speculating about all of you," she said, pursing her lips. This was a feat, as she had kept the Cavendish siblings hidden quite away, or as much as one could in London. They weren't "ready" yet, whatever that meant.

"Of course you knew that they would, Your Grace," Meredith chided softly, as only she could do.

"This pack of Grub Street hacks has nothing better to do than speculate about people and matters of which they have no firsthand knowledge."

"The haute ton is also clamoring to know all about our Cavendish siblings," Meredith pointed out. "The arrival of an American duke has to be one of the most exciting things to happen during the past few seasons."

The American Duke. They spoke of him the way he spoke of a fine racehorse or prized heifer at an auction. In other words, as if he were nothing more than a show pony or a stud horse. A novelty.

"I suppose they're also hacks with nothing better to do," James remarked, followed by a sip of his coffee.

"The life of a peer is not merely one of leisure," the duchess replied crisply. "At least, not if one takes the responsibility and duty to the title seriously. The peer must manage the estates, see to the welfare of the tenants, attend to matters in parliament, and secure relationships with other families, as well as serve as the head of his own household."

Here, she gave James a pointed look. The hint was taken.

"And the ladies have the sole task of getting themselves married," Claire added, not without some disapproval. Somehow his sister had a brilliant mind for mathematics; she studied extensively and was excited to be in London where she might meet other minds at her level. Marriage would be a waste of her brain. But tell that to the duchess, who spoke of little else.

"The peeress must also manage the households, engage in charity work, assist her husband in seeing to the tenants' welfare, to say nothing of birthing and raising children to be worthy of their station," the duchess continued.

Marriage. Babies. Responsibilities. James would much rather be pondering the kiss-ability of Meredith's lips. And her earlobes — he remembered kissing and nibbling that sensitive spot, drawing a gasp from her lips. God, he loved that sound and longed to hear it again. He might even trade this dukedom for it.

"It is a lot to prepare for," Meredith said. "The newspapers — and the ton — are wondering if you are all ready. That is all."

She glanced from sibling to sibling, smiling so sweetly. As if she really believed that a pack of half-wild Americans might assimilate seamlessly into the world of English high society.

It defied belief, given how their lessons had been going.

James glanced at each of his sisters.

Bridget had her elbows on the table and was hungrily eyeing more food — the duchess had her on a reducing diet, which he thought was stupid.

Amelia was slouching in her seat, munching on a piece of bacon in her fingers, and taking great pleasure in doing so.

Claire had that faraway look in her eyes, like she was performing some complicated calculation in her head.

In contrast, both the duchess and Meredith sat with their spines straight and took impossibly small bites of toast and little delicate sips of tea. They somehow radiated elegance and refinement.

For the first time, James began to genuinely worry about his sisters fitting in here. Or rather, what it would do to their spirits if they didn't find friends and acceptance, and if the newspapers made cruel comments about them for all of London to read. He'd never forgive himself for subjecting them to English society if it broke their spirits.

"Your Grace, the sisters have been attending to their lessons, and I'm certain they'll be ready by the time of Lady Tunbridge's ball," Meredith said. But she didn't mention him — why didn't she mention him?

"Will this ball be our debut?" Bridget asked eagerly.

"Will we finally get to go out?" Amelia added, eyes lighting up at the prospect of leaving the house for something other than a shopping trip.

"I have accepted an invitation on our behalf," the duchess said. "It is to be your first introduction to society."

"If we're ready," Bridget said nervously. "I still don't know the correct way to address the younger brother of a marquess."

"And we haven't exactly mastered dancing," Amelia added.

"To say nothing of all the other little rules that keep cropping up," Claire added. "Such as fans. Who knew fans could be so complicated?"

James furrowed his brow. What the devil was she even talking about? And, damn, he didn't know how to address the younger brother of a marquess, either, or how to do all the steps to a quadrille. And a million other things, probably.

He glanced at Meredith, feeling something like despair, and surely, there was a plea for *help* in his eyes. She seemed to know all the same things as the duchess, and yet he'd rather hear it from her lips. Her kissable lips. With her in his arms, he could learn all and any dance steps. With her, he felt like he could, maybe, possibly, try to pull this off.

"You will be ready," Meredith replied evenly, holding his gaze.

His anxious heartbeat eased up.

"And if we're not?" Bridget asked, worry plain on her face. He couldn't recall the last time he'd seen her so worried — except, perhaps, when their mother was ill.

"How ready do we really have to be? One

hundred percent ready?" Amelia asked. "Must we have memorized all of *Debrett's* already or is it enough to just be prepared to reply properly when we meet this mythical brother of a marquess?"

Claire looked over at him, and they exchanged the sort of glances that older siblings responsible for younger ones did. *They're nervous. They're worried. But I am, too. How can we console them?*

"You *will* be ready," the duchess declared, not mincing any words or even tempering her tone to soothe their nerves. "There is no other option. Society is already aghast that a family from the colonies has inherited one of England's most prestigious titles."

Former colonies, James corrected silently to himself. He saw Claire mouth the words as well.

"They would closely watch anyone who came into a title or wealth," she continued. "That you all have risen so high from so . . . far . . . only intensifies the attention that will be paid to you. One misstep and —"

She paused. Dramatically.

There was a quick intake of breath. Waiting.

Her words hung in the air, like a sword hanging over one's head.

What would their fate be, should one of

them make one misstep?

"Once lost, you will find it difficult to recover their good opinion," she finished. "Everything you do will be watched. Every interaction will set a precedent. All of it will determine whether you succeed or fail. And it should go without saying that failure is not an option."

Right. Great. Thanks to the blunt prophecy of the duchess, his sisters had all gone pale.

Amelia straightened in her seat.

Bridget set down the piece of toast she'd finally given in and taken a bite of.

Even Claire was paying attention. He noticed her hands fidgeting in her skirts under the table, but her attentions were on the conversation and not sums in her head.

Just like *that* they had changed. And just like *that* James felt a spark of anger.

It was one thing for him to come and assume all the responsibilities of the title. It was another thing entirely for the duchess to set about extinguishing the spirits of his sisters: to make them sit up straight and still, to make them go hungry to fit into ridiculous dresses, to use their brains on fans and forms of address instead of real topics of importance.

They were already starting to change and

he didn't like it.

"Remind me again why we are supposed to care what anyone else thinks," he challenged, as his sisters all turned their heads to face him. "Are we not wealthy? Do we not have a prestigious title? Am I not one of the highest-ranking men in any given room in this whole blasted country? Surely that must count for something."

In perfect synchronicity, his sisters swiveled their heads away from him to the other end of the table for the duchess's response.

"Of course it counts. But it isn't everything." And then the duchess's gaze focused sharply on him. "You wouldn't like to compromise your sisters' marital prospects, now would you, Duke? Any hint of scandal or uncivilized behavior will lead to questions and gossip and diminished prospects."

Three familiar brunette heads turned back to him.

"I thought we were clear that there was no rush to marry them off."

Heads turned back to the duchess.

"And if they should meet someone who would make a fine match? What if one of your sisters falls in love? Will you really have such a reputation that would make a respectable gentleman think twice about aligning his family with ours?"

His sisters now all turned their heads to face him, with nearly identical expressions, all asking him the same thing with their eyes, *what will you do for us, dear brother?*

The answer, of course, was *anything*.

He would do anything to see them happy.

He had promised their parents to love and protect them and ensure that they were happy. But even if he hadn't been beholden by a deathbed promise, there was nothing he wouldn't do for them.

But that meant . . . he ruthlessly shoved a handful of his hair back from his face . . . fuck . . . that meant . . .

He felt the walls closing in. His chest tightening.

"What the duchess is trying to convey is that our reputations are all connected. We shall rise — or fall — as a household together," Meredith explained.

And he was beginning to understand that whatever there was between them would never be just about them — Just James and a girl he met in a tavern one night. His life would never be that simple again. And his life would never just be his own.

He would have to *try* at this duke business. That much was plain.

Not because he wanted to, or because it mattered to him. He couldn't ruin the future happiness of his sisters because he refused to be bothered with some paperwork, learning to waltz, or knowing how to properly address people, second sons of marquesses or whatever they may be.

James swallowed hard.

"So tell me, Duchess, what are the papers saying about us already? What must we overcome?"

She smiled, like a general who'd just won a pivotal battle in a war. Like she could taste triumph and it was sweet. She snapped open a newspaper and began to read aloud.

"This author has it on excellent authority that the Cavendish family arrived more than a week earlier, though they have yet to make an appearance, however informal, in society. The Duchess of Durham is keeping the Cavendish siblings hidden away — one wonders what she is hiding. Though given that they hail from a remote outpost of civilization, one must marvel at the task she has in civilizing this pack of Americans.

"That was from *The London Weekly*."

She cleared her throat and selected a different newspaper to read from.

"The Cavendish sisters were finally spotted! The Duchess of Durham was seen escorting three dark-haired women of marriageable age to Madame Auteuil's salon, where they spent

six hours being outfitted for new wardrobes. One presumes their attire from the former colonies is unsuitable — one imagines bear-skins and Chieftain headdresses, plain home-spun gowns and buckled shoes. The duchess will have quite the task of polishing these rocks into diamonds of the first water.

"That was from the *Morning Post.*"

"That is hardly fair to my sisters."

"You will learn, Duke, that the London press — or society — is hardly fair or kind. And they have not ignored you, either."

Relentlessly, she picked up yet another news sheet to read from.

"My spies report that when the new Duke of Durham is not busy learning estate business, he is to be found mucking about with horses like a common laborer. One hopes that one will not detect the whiff of the stables on the person possessing one of England's most prestigious titles. What a harbinger of the downfall of English society that would be."

"That's enough, Your Grace," he said sharply.

He had begun the meal thinking of nothing more than Meredith's kissable lips. And what opportunities might come his way to kiss, nibble, taste, and savor them.

By the time he strode away from the breakfast table that morning, the kissable lips of Miss Meredith Green were the least of his concerns. Though they still might be the stuff of his dreams, his waking hours were now to be consumed with Becoming A Duke.

A title is not enough. It is essential to look the part as well.
— THE RULES FOR DUKES

The duke's private chambers
Merely possessing the title was not enough to truly make one a duke. Neither was learning the orders of precedence or familiarizing himself with the business of his various estates.

Something had to be done about his hair. Something also had to be done with his wardrobe, from his cravat to his muddied boots. And his fingernails — something needed to be done about those, too. What man bothered overmuch with his fingernails?

This was the opinion of the duchess, of course, not necessarily one James shared. But apparently hers — and his valet's — were the only opinions that mattered. So much for being the most important, most high-ranking, and most powerful person in any given room. In matters of style, his opinion mattered not at all.

James stood still, annoyed, as the duchess and his valet, Edwards — a spry, well-dressed man in his thirties — appraised his appearance. An appearance, James would like to note, that never drew complaints from women.

"My dear Mr. Edwards —" the duchess began, while looking critically at James. And then she was at a loss for words. This was rare and thus hardly encouraging. James scowled.

"Yes, Your Grace."

"Something must be done about His Grace." She waved her hand in the general direction of his person.

"Indeed." Edwards murmured his agreement.

Duke and valet shared A Look because the Good Lord knew that Edwards had *tried.* But James, the reluctant duke, had brushed off his efforts. This, then, was revenge or vindication or something of the sort. Honestly, James felt a quake of fear at the eagerness in his valet's eyes, to say nothing of the scissors in his hand.

"I have tried to make adjustments to his appearance, Your Grace," Edwards said, throwing James under the carriage wheels.

"I know you have, Mr. Edwards," she said,

consolingly. "He is a stubborn one."

"You do realize that I am right here, in attendance, with my hearing intact," James pointed out.

"I trust you to make the necessary improvements, Mr. Edwards. The future of Durham depends on it."

Well now, that was laying it on a bit thick, was it not?

One look at Edwards confirmed it was not. It did seem that the state of his fingernails and the length of his hair would have serious consequences for the future of a dukedom that had lasted hundreds of years and survived *actual wars.*

"I would be honored, Your Grace," Edwards said gravely, as if entrusted with a sacred mission.

"I trust that His Grace will be amenable to your efforts," she said, leveling a stare at James, as if he were a mucky schoolboy who hadn't washed behind his ears. That wasn't fair; he was a clean person. He just happened to favor simple clothes and hair that was a bit longer than fashionable, apparently.

The cutting commentary from gossip columns was still echoing in his brain, which had something to do with why he was submitting himself to this frank appraisal of his person and whatever else would come next. Wouldn't do to have the future happiness of his sisters ruined because there was something wrong with his cravat.

"Best get to work then," James said with a sigh, pushing his hair back from his face.

"I'll start with the hair," Edwards said.

"Excellent idea," the duchess replied.

Until then, James had been able to order his valet to back off, in so many words, when the man made suggestions as to how he might better present himself. But now, with the duchess's explicit orders and James's reluctant determination to Become A Duke for the sake of his sisters' happiness, the man was given free rein to take this horse trainer from America and turn him into a proper duke.

His longish hair was the first to go.

Edwards sat him down and came at him with a pair of scissors. Each snip was followed by a wince as locks fell around him. It was just hair. He wasn't Samson and Edwards wasn't Delilah. But damn, if it didn't feel like his old self, his real self, was being cut away with each lock that fell to the floor, to be swept away and thrown out with the cinders from the fireplaces.

"This cut is more fashionable," Edwards explained.

"One must be fashionable," James said, because it seemed like the thing to say.

"It is vastly preferable to being unfashionable."

Snip, snip, snip. Locks of hair fell around him. So much that James worried there wouldn't be any left.

Finally, Edwards set down the scissors. James ran his fingers through his hair, relieved to find some still left on his head. It felt so strange.

A shave was next. While Edwards readied the accouterments, he caught James looking around for a mirror to see what the damage was already.

"Not yet, Your Grace. I suggest that you wait until the transformation is complete before taking a look. Now please, lie back and remain still."

James did as he was told; it was the thing to do when a man had a razor at your throat.

Edwards's ministrations didn't stop with the haircut and shave. The duke's hands were next. James didn't quite see the point of that, given that they would be so often clad in gloves.

"You like to work with your hands," Edwards observed. It was quite obvious — James's hands were strong, and tanned by the sun, calloused from gripping leather reins and lead ropes woven from hemp, and nicked, burned, and scarred from a lifetime of doing things. For instance, there was a round, silver scar near the base of his thumb, a relic from the day he'd helped his father build a fence in the south field.

"You could say that," James replied.

"We must hide evidence of it. A man of your station would never have the hands of a common laborer."

"Of course not," James said dryly. The worst a duke's hands might suffer were ink stains from all the damned correspondence and whatnot that piled up on the desk in the study. But then again, he had a secretary to do the writing for him, if he wished it.

"Fortunately there are things we can do. Crèmes, gloves, treatments, and such," Edwards said as he worked, filing his nails.

James exhaled the breath he'd been holding. He was proud of his strong, beat-up hands that accomplished things and knew how to touch a woman. If he had to hide them — fine. He would hide that part of himself, though he couldn't bring himself to stop doing those things completely. And maybe that was the key to surviving this duke business — he could continue to be himself on the sly.

And now Edwards was massaging his

hands, rubbing in one rough potion to smooth away callouses, another to lighten his sun-browned skin, and something else entirely to moisturize. Everything stank of perfume and flowers and girl. And now he would, too.

"Voila! The hands of a gentleman."

James held up his hands for a look and was relieved to see his scars remained. There, something of his true and former self that couldn't be erased.

"Your first set of clothing from the tailor has arrived," Edwards continued. "I took the liberty of ordering jackets, waistcoats, breeches, shirts, and other items of necessity. The rest of your new wardrobe will be arriving in the coming days. I daresay we selected very well."

By we, Edwards really meant himself. James's sole contribution had been standing still enough to be measured.

Eventually the transformation was completed. James had been bathed. His hair shorn, his face shaved, his hands manicured. He donned his new, ducal clothes, all polished, pressed, and starched.

When he was finally permitted to stand before the mirror, he had one thought: show pony. He was all done up like a show pony.

As such, James hardly recognized himself.

This man, with his pale breeches, silk waistcoat, snowy white linen, and expertly tailored jacket, did not clean out a horse's stall. These manicured hands did not clean hooves. This man did not sweat, or labor in the hot sun, or make love to women he met in taverns after just one night.

This man was refined, mannered, restrained.

"What do you think, Your Grace?"

"It's not me."

"Yes, but it's the man you must become."

CHAPTER 5

Tonight society is on tenterhooks awaiting the debut of the new Duke of Durham.
His Grace and his three sisters are expected to make an appearance at Lady
Tunbridge's ball, which promises to be a
crush.

— FASHIONABLE INTELLIGENCE,
THE LONDON WEEKLY

After assisting the Cavendish siblings with
their lessons, Meredith would not be present to witness their first foray into society.
The duchess had no need of a companion
at balls now that she had her nieces and
nephew.

Instead, Meredith watched from the stairs
as they all prepared to depart, a last-minute
flurry of activity involving the gathering of
hats and gloves and quick peeks in the mirror.

The ladies were beautiful, dressed in the

first stare of fashion: high-waisted white dresses made with layers of silk and lace, delicate beadwork and intricate embroidery. Their dark hair was curled and styled with strands of pearls.

The duchess had even dipped into the vault to find a piece of jewelry from the family collection for each of the girls — sapphire ear bobs from the previous duchess, a diamond necklace passed down for ages, an emerald brooch.

If Bridget, Claire, and Amelia stood very still and did not speak, they could certainly pass as perfect English ladies.

The duchess herself looked as commanding and elegant as always in a dark green satin gown decorated with silver embroidery. But tonight, Meredith noticed something else enhanced her look: pride.

The duchess never had children of her own, and Meredith knew it had long been a source of private anguish, but now she had four to shepherd through society. This was the task she'd been born and raised to do.

While her flock might not be exactly one hundred percent ready for the onslaught of the haute ton, they had come so far in their dress and manner. They at least looked the part, which was half the battle.

And then there was the duke.

James now looked every inch the part of His Grace, the Duke of Durham. From the tips of his highly polished shoes to the intricate and crisp knot of his cravat and the royal blue of his jacket, the man had been transformed. His hair had been shorn, his simple attire exchanged for clothes of the finest quality, all declaring that he was a man of great significance and importance. Meredith could scarcely find traces of the man she'd met in Southampton, which only exacerbated the distance she felt between them.

Whether it was the clothes or he was simply coming into his role, there was something different in the way he held himself. Almost like . . . a duke.

The ladies were all going to swoon.

Meredith was glad she wouldn't be there to watch it.

Or so she told herself.

James stepped aside to let the ladies exit the house first, and they did, bustling out to the carriage in a flurry of ruffled hems and girlish chatter.

James paused and turned to look at her. Her heart ached because there was real longing in his eyes, and she was sure she couldn't hide her own.

"I wish you were joining me," he said softly.

Not us. *Me.*

She wanted to say, *I as well.* But there were footmen in the foyer and ladies' maids bustling about, any of whom might hear and gossip about a moment suggesting intimacy and tenderness between the mere companion and the lofty duke on the night his bride hunt officially began.

James stepped outside, into the night, and toward his future. One that certainly wouldn't include her.

The butler shut the door behind him.

All the servants carried on with their duties.

Meredith was left alone.

Lady Tunbridge's Ball

James had never felt so alone as he did now in this crowded ballroom. There was more wealth on display than he'd ever seen or imagined. Towering chandeliers of beeswax candles hung from the ceiling, everything was gilt in gold, servants glided through the throngs of people carrying trays of crystal flutes full of champagne. The crowds were full of formally dressed men and women decked in silks and satins, dripping with jewels. Somewhere, an orchestra played.

And here he was, just a horse farmer from the former colonies.

"The Duke of Durham," some distinguished gray-haired gentleman announced in a booming voice, followed by the announcement of the duchess and his sisters.

The people fell silent, save for the rustle of those silks and satins and the clink of champagne glasses, and some soft notes of the orchestra, hidden somewhere.

The crowd turned to get their first good look at them.

Discovery: *Fancy people gawk, too.*

Oh, they did so elegantly, with lips pursed instead of mouths gaping open, like carp. Eyebrows were arched. They tried, at least, to be discreet about gossiping to their neighbors by hiding behind their fans. But it was plain to see that he and his sisters were objects of fascination.

He flexed his gloved hand, wanting to reach for Meredith's in order to feel some measure of comfort and security. He would have to face all this without her by his side. Correction: *now* he'd never felt so alone.

He had his sisters instead, and it seemed they were as awed and terrified as he.

"We're not in America anymore," Amelia said quietly.

"Definitely not," Claire agreed.

"Remember what I taught you," the duchess murmured.

The four Cavendishes exchanged expressions of *oh hell and damnation.* It was probably safe to say they hadn't learned half of what the duchess had taught them, and at least half of *that* had fled their brains at the moment.

He remembered one thing, though.

One thing that Meredith had taught him, impressed upon him, reminded him time and again, in all those duke lessons. *You're the duke now.*

It was what she'd been trying to tell him that night on the servants' stairs; he'd thought it was just a rejection, but it was also a gift. *He was the duke now.*

Everyone present — from the fancy folks gawking at them to his sisters fidgeting nervously by his side — was counting on him to play the part of powerful, high-ranking, and supremely self-assured duke. The truth of it was a weight on his chest, impressing on him how he had to conduct himself. In other words, stifling his urge to turn on his heel and flee.

He imagined that if Meredith were here, she would give him A Look. The kind that said, *I know you know how to take charge. I know you know what to do. Think of them as a pack of horses and be* you.

He straightened his shoulders and said, "I'm sure it will be fine."

"Now that they've had a good look at you, it is time for introductions," the duchess said, smiling graciously at the crowd before her. With that, she swept forward with four Cavendish siblings trailing in her wake. The night had only just begun.

Meanwhile at Durham House . . .

There was nothing but silence in the house. Any activity was taking place below stairs, where Meredith wouldn't hear it from her modest bedchamber in the family's wing.

It weighed on her, that silence, as she closed her eyes to imagine the luscious sounds of an orchestra, the sparkling of women's laughter, and the clink of champagne glasses and all the other sounds of a ball.

Meredith wanted to belong.

She wanted to be herself, but still belong. As it was, she didn't quite belong anywhere.

Meredith opened her eyes and, for the first time, looked around her chamber with the point of view of James. She saw not the luxury and privilege that she was lucky to experience, but something akin to a cage. As long as she inhabited this world, she had to abide by its rules — rules that cared little for the contents of her heart or aspirations. Rules that kept her quiet and in her place at home, not whirling around a ballroom.

Just as James had to follow the strict rules set out for dukes. He had a duty to his family, the title, the dukedom, and those who relied on it for their livelihood. He was never to be hers.

She had her duty to the duchess. Meredith reminded herself of this as she sat at home, alone, while the family was out at a ball and she was left behind. She was never to be his.

It could be worse: she could be shut away in that little cottage in Hampshire, tending to her mother, and lacking other company. It was almost funny — she was considered "too lofty" by the townspeople she'd grown up with and not sufficiently suitable for the haute ton, both because of her position.

She didn't belong anywhere except here, in a position that she didn't dare lose. A position that kept her tantalizingly close to the man she shouldn't love.

Meredith couldn't sit still. A novel lay open on her bed, flung aside when she couldn't concentrate on Pamela's repeated efforts to rebuff Lord B's advances. Her embroidery was left unfinished, with needle and thread dangling precariously.

The reason, of course, was James.

No, His Grace.

It was excruciating to think of him flirting and dancing with fancy ladies while she sat at home reading silly novels about servant girls snaring the master of the house.

All the fancy, *suitable* ladies.

The ones with titles and lofty ancestry. The ones with vast tracts of land and hefty dowries. Meredith knew her education and manners rivaled any of theirs — the duchess had seen to that. But as the daughter of commoners, she didn't have status or pedigree.

She would never be considered a suitable bride.

And as long as James was still his authentic, humble, and honest American self, who didn't care about such things, she might have a chance.

But Meredith saw him transforming before her eyes, learning the ropes and learning the rules of being a duke. Tonight he was stepping more into the role.

She may have looked and acted the part of devoted lady's companion, but tonight, the cracks started to form.

They may have looked the part of wealthy, powerful duke and his family, but James could tell their manners and knowledge of the rules still left something to be desired. The pinched lips hiding smirks of disapproval proved it.

The duchess performed introductions, and at least one of the Cavendishes managed to bungle it. Every time.

"And this is the Marquess of Ives."

"I thought we already met the marquess," Bridget whispered a touch too loudly. "Or was that a different one? How many marquesses are we going to meet anyway?"

"How charming," said marquess remarked dryly.

Or they all failed another conversation:

"And how are you finding London?" some lord inquired politely, a well-dressed and coiffed lady hanging on his arm. The correct answer was *It's splendid! It's incomparable!*

Amelia did not provide the correct answer.

"I'd like it more if we might visit the sights instead of learning how to pour tea and address all the fancy folks here. Say, are you the second son of a marquess by any chance? I did look up how to address him, whoever he is."

"I'm keen to visit the Royal Society to further my study of mathematics," Claire said. "That is one area in which America does not yet compare to London."

Her attempt to be diplomatic and offer some sort of compliment failed.

"How funny! She wishes to study math!" Lady Whoever said, laughing. "You both must take a visit to Bond Street. Such shopping is unrivaled anywhere in the world, perhaps even Paris!"

"Duchess, didn't you say there were three sisters? Where is the other one?"

They all turned, looking around the ballroom for Bridget, whom they had apparently lost in the crush, only to watch her slip and fall right on her backside, in the middle of the dance floor.

James winced and started toward his sister.

"No, wait." The duchess held him back, and they watched as two gentlemen — young, presumably titled and suitable gentlemen — rushed to her assistance.

Matchmaking at its finest.

It is a truth universally acknowledged that ladies love dukes. LOVE THEM.
— THE RULES FOR DUKES

James Cavendish never had much trouble

attracting women. He had the hair that fell forward into his sparkling blue eyes, a mouth that tipped up into one hell of a smile, and a kind and charming manner. As the new Duke of Durham he had even less trouble.

The haircut and fashionable clothes didn't hurt. Neither did his young age, or the fact that he had all of his teeth — which could not be said of many other eligible lords. Taken all together with his title, and the promise of prestige and riches that came with it, and the women swarmed.

They swarmed like flies around horseshit.

There was Lady Isabella Bradford, a petite blonde with flushed cheeks and bright blue eyes, who seemed *very* eager to meet him.

"Good evening, Your Grace. I am delighted to make your acquaintance."

She batted her eyes prettily. Her fat, blonde curls shook as she giggled and tilted her head . . . prettily. Unfortunately, she reminded him of one of Bridge's toy dolls from ages ago — before Amelia took it on an extended camping adventure. That thought put an end to any potential romantic inclinations.

But her brother, the Marquess of Wickham, was overheard to say, "Well, he cleans up better than expected."

"I'll pass your compliments to my valet," James murmured, leaving Lord Wickham red-faced.

There was also Miss Nigella Banks, a statuesque brunette beauty with full red lips, a striking contrast to the white gown she wore. All the debutantes wore them to signal their virginal status.

"Good evening, Your Grace," she cooed. "I look forward to properly welcoming you to London."

Nigella bit her lip and gazed at him. For a mere second James was almost taken in by the combination of virginal innocence and minxish flirtation. Almost. But he knew women like that were nothing but trouble.

As James walked away, he overheard someone laugh about catching "a whiff of the stables in the ballroom."

He *wanted* to say the stench was actually a big, stinking pile of bullshit, which is what this whole societal farce was, in his mind. But he knew better; there was no eau de anything wafting through the ballroom.

Just one American who happened to outrank them, and who happened to think this ranking business was stupid.

He also happened to be swarmed by all the eligible ladies in the ballroom.

It was clear to anyone and everyone that

James could have his pick of these women. And by God he would, if the duchess had anything to do with it.

Since the duchess did have everything to do with it, he danced.

There was the girl who peppered him with questions about America. There was another girl who kept making faces at her friends. When he pointed out that he could see her, she turned a bright, beet red and he was sorry for embarrassing her. Some ladies were flirty, and a few were excellent demonstrations of that English reserve he had heard about.

None of them were Meredith. None of them brought out the duke in him, or made the waltz into a devastatingly erotic and frustrating dance around the room, as she had done.

He was dancing with a horse-faced girl when he caught his sisters laughing at him from the sidelines of the ballroom. Frankly, he couldn't blame them.

He should probably say something to this girl.

But he could feel her noxious mix of disdain for him (dancing with a horse breeder, how crude!) and wanting (a duke!).

James Cavendish never had any trouble attracting women, and when he did, he knew they wanted him for *him*.

James the duke knew why these women were after him: the title, and only the title.

CHAPTER 6

The fate of the dukedom often rests upon how His Grace conducts himself in society.

— THE RULES FOR DUKES

Later that night

It was late when the family returned home and Meredith went to see to Her Grace, carrying a glass of sherry on a tray. It was their evening ritual. Tonight, she half wanted, half dreaded to hear a report on the evening.

She saw immediately that the duchess wore her expression of I-would-despair-if-it-weren't-such-a-low-class-thing-to-do. Meredith knew right away that the evening hadn't gone well.

"I can take over now, Betsy," Meredith told the duchess's lady's maid.

"How was the ball, Your Grace?"

"It was a disaster."

Somehow, the duchess managed to sip sherry through tightly pursed lips.

"It could not have been that bad," Meredith replied. The duchess had exceedingly high standards; to fall short of them was still to do well. But Her Grace gave a sharp look in the mirror to indicate that it was, indeed, that bad.

"Lady Bridget fell and lay sprawled upon the floor. Lady Claire could not hide her boredom if her life depended on it, which it does, though I cannot seem to impress it upon her. She already has a reputation as a bluestocking, which will hardly serve her well. Lady Amelia mentioned riding astride on their farm, so now everyone thinks her a hoyden at best. That one will be the death of me, I am sure of it."

This did sound bad. And it did, to be sure, sound like the Cavendish siblings as Meredith had come to know them: exuberant, straightforward, refusing to dissemble.

But much as she admired the sisters, Meredith was less interested in their evening than a certain someone else's.

"And the duke . . ."

"What about the duke?"

Curses. Her breath had hitched at the mention of him. The duchess leveled another look at her in the mirror, and Meredith truly feared that Her Grace could tell that Meredith had spent the hours of this evening in a pointless pastime: mooning over the duke. Feeling covetous, jealous, and a half dozen other petty feelings.

"You'd think he was being led to the gallows, not waltzing with the finest young women in England."

"And how was the dancing?"

The duchess took another sip of her sherry. One might have been tempted to describe it as a swig, but everyone knew that duchesses did not swig.

"They were adequate. They were not ready for society, but if we delayed their debut, everyone would think the worst. Of course now they already know the worst."

The good opinion of the ton mattered, especially with regard to the Cavendish sisters making suitable matches. It was essential when it came to finding a new duchess, who would ensure the dukedom carried on for another generation.

Meredith had an inkling of what was really troubling the duchess. She had long ago resigned herself to having failed at her one purpose in life — continuing the Durham family and legacy. Meredith had been too young to understand, at first, why she seemed to see the duchess in tears every month or so, and it was only later that she understood the duchess's despair at not being able to provide an heir. While Meredith could be the daughter she never had, she still didn't satisfy that need for an heir.

When the duke died, all hope was lost — until the Cavendishes arrived. Now the duchess had another chance. Her one and only.

"They still must be better than Mr. Collins," Meredith pointed out.

"The less said about Mr. Collins, the better."

"There is always tomorrow for more lessons with the girls. And there is always you to teach them."

"Thank you, Meredith. If anyone can mold them into perfect lords and ladies, it is I." This was the truth; no one was more perfectly and impeccably behaved than the duchess. Meredith had witnessed this firsthand and had heard stories of Her Grace as a young girl. She never made a misstep. "Though I fear for the future of the dukedom if even I cannot manage it. I have had one task in life and it was to secure the Durham dukedom for another generation. Failure is simply not an option I shall consider."

And that was precisely why nothing,

absolutely nothing, could happen between Meredith and James. Because after all the duchess had given her, Meredith could not take this chance from her.

Meanwhile, in a bedchamber down the hall
James knocked on the door to Claire's bedchamber and pushed it open. His sisters had a habit of gathering together at night to talk, tease, and gossip — to be, well, sisters. After a night of being fawned over and dissembled to, James wanted the company of those who would not be impressed with him at all.

Sisters.

"Are you all decent?"

"Yes, do come in, Your Grace," Claire called out.

"Oooh, it's the duke," Amelia teased. "We'd better bow and curtsy."

Giggling, she and Bridget slid off the bed to stand and greet him with overdramatic bows and curtsies. Bridget, never the most coordinated or graceful person, accidentally smacked Amelia in the nose.

"Ow!"

"Good evening, Your Grace," Bridget said.

"We are *so* honored to have you grace us with your presence, Your Grace." Amelia tried to curtsy and hold her nose at the same time, which resulted in her tumbling to the floor.

"Do shut up, all of you," James muttered. He'd hoped to avoid this kind of fawning behavior; at least he was comforted by the fact that they were deliberately teasing him and didn't actually mean it.

He pulled up a chair next to the bed and took a seat, stretching his long legs out before him. He wore plain breeches, boots, and only a shirt — all those fancy ducal clothes had been discarded as soon as he returned home.

"We were just discussing what a disaster this evening has been," Claire told him.

"Living through it wasn't enough? You have to discuss it, too?"

"Was it so bad dancing with all those women?"

"Aye." James grimaced.

"What is it with gentlemen who do not like dancing?" Bridget wondered.

"It's not so much the dancing as it is having everyone watch you do it," James said with a shrug. He didn't dare mention it, but one's partner did make all the difference. Tonight, he'd gone through the motions, but it hadn't been like that for his practice waltz with Meredith . . .

"I cannot believe Father never mentioned any of this," Amelia said. As the youngest, she was just ten when their parents died, one after the other. First, their mother passed away after contracting a wasting disease. Their father followed a few days later. Everyone said his cause of death was a broken heart.

"Sometimes he spoke of life in England before he came to America," Claire said. She was the oldest and remembered more than the rest of them. "He spoke of fox-hunting, cruel schoolmasters, and his time in the cavalry."

"He spoke about Messenger," James added with a tender smile.

James had fond memories of the family's prized horse, may he rest in peace. Legend had it that their father had absconded to America with the prize stallion — owned by his brother, the duke, Josephine's late husband. He'd fallen in love with an American woman his family forbade him to wed, so he left England and never looked back. When their father needed to find a way to support his new family, he bred Messenger and raised and trained a series of champion racehorses on their farm.

James followed in his father's footsteps when it came to raising and training horses. Now that they were in England, he wondered if he might follow in his father's footsteps when it came to ditching the dukedom and running hell for leather for freedom in America.

"But he never mentioned any of this, did he?" Bridget asked softly. She waved her hand at the bedroom, and the house, and all the other houses scattered about the countryside that the duchess had mentioned.

"He occasionally referenced his brother the duke but he did not say much," James said, thinking back to all the hours of companionable silence he'd spent with his father around the farm. If they talked, it was about which horse needed new shoes, or a new training method. "He certainly never mentioned that he or I were in line to inherit. Probably wasn't the best topic of conversation back home, if you think about it, with all the anti-royalty and anti-British sentiments."

"Vastly preferable to all the anti-American sentiments we encountered this evening," Bridget said.

"I wonder if there is a portrait of Father somewhere in this great big house," Amelia mused. "I'd love to see what he looked like as a young man."

"We can ask Josephine tomorrow," Claire said, affectionately patting Amelia's hand.

"Oh, good. Perhaps it can distract her from more deportment and etiquette and torture lessons," Amelia said.

"No, we *need* those," Bridget said. All eyes turned to look at her. "If we are going to stay . . . we need to fit in."

"Bridget, that is all part of her nefarious plot to marry us off. We'll be separated," Amelia said, anguished.

"I'm not going to let her marry the lot of you off," James said. Then, just to tease, he added, "Much as you plague me and I sometimes consider it."

"I hate to point this out, but Bridget does have a point," Claire said thoughtfully. "If we are going to stay, we ought to make an effort to fit in."

"This is not a temporary situation then, is it?" Amelia asked.

An uneasy quiet settled over the group. Of course they should stay. James was a duke, for Lord's sake, and he was apparently *needed* here. His sisters could return home and find husbands there, but . . . they would have a better chance of finding decent husbands in England. And while they might end up in different households, they should at least be on the same continent.

They were a pack, he and his sisters. A herd of Cavendishes. They stuck together

— no matter what.

"I don't want us to be apart," Claire said softly.

"So we stick together," James said, leaning forward to look earnestly at his three worried sisters. Leaving the dukedom behind wasn't out of the realm of possibility for him. After all, he was his father's son. But leaving his pack of sisters was unthinkable. "We either all stay in England. Or we all return to America. Together."

Just because a dimly lit and empty corridor is conducive to a romantic interlude doesn't mean one should take advantage of the situation to engage in a romantic interlude.

— THE RULES FOR DUKES

Even later that night
After seeing to the duchess, Meredith left for her room. The door clicked shut softly behind her as she stepped into the dimly lit corridor.

And of course, there he was. Strolling her way with those long, muscular legs. His untied cravat tangled around his neck, the vee of his shirt open to expose a patch of skin. But otherwise he was still dressed for the ball. He was part elegance personified,

148

part rake, part pure man. A tempting combination indeed.

Meredith paused, her hand still on the knob behind her. She considered returning to the duchess's room on the pretense of having forgotten something. But really, she'd be fleeing from temptation.

Then he saw her and there was no turning back.

Instead she walked toward him, putting some distance between them and the duchess's door.

"Miss Green . . ." His voice was low, so as not to attract attention. But she heard it. Felt it, the vibrations of his throat carrying all the way to the center of her chest.

"Were you going to run away from me, Miss Green?"

"I was thinking about it," she admitted.

"Are you afraid of me?"

I'm afraid of me around you.

"No. I'm not afraid of you."

And she wasn't. She had given herself to him. Given him a secret that could wreck her, and he'd been a perfect gentleman about all of it.

Which meant she could trust him.

Which made her want him more.

But, oh, the way he looked at her was hardly gentlemanly at all.

Something in his gaze sparkled when his eyes fixed on hers, and it had to be a dead giveaway that there was something between them. Thankfully there was no one around to see it — this time anyway.

"You really must stop looking at me like that."

"Like how?"

Like that! His eyes sparkled again, this time mischievously, like he knew exactly how. She dropped her voice to a low whisper to answer.

"Like we have been naked in each other's arms."

"But we have."

"Shhhh . . ."

She looked around, fearful that someone was near enough to eavesdrop — a sister cracking open her bedroom door, for example. But there was no one, the hour was late, they were alone. Just her with Just James. After the lonely and anxiety-riddled hours of this evening, she couldn't bring herself to do the right thing and quit his company immediately.

She wanted to bask in his nearness, like a cat in a patch of sunlight.

"Can you blame me if I can't stop thinking about that night?"

Meredith gazed up at him. He wasn't flirting so much as speaking earnestly now, hinting at late nights and stolen moments when his thoughts wandered to that one magical night. Just like her. And didn't that make her heart start to pound hard in her breast.

She wasn't alone in this wanting.

Heart. Pounding. Stuff. That.

"It was just one night."

"One I'd like to repeat," he murmured, a lazy grin playing on his lips. "Repeatedly."

"You are mad."

"Mad for you, maybe," he said easily. Then, on a different note, he said, "I met so many women tonight, Mer."

There was the intimacy of calling her Mer, instead of Miss Green or even Meredith. And then there was the sad fact of what he'd said: he'd met many women. Proper women. Ones with the right birth and dowries and that lot. Ones he would have to marry.

Best to stop this thing between them now . . .

Before he starts courting.

Before he takes a wife.

Before she has to watch all of it from the sidelines.

"None of them were you," he said. "They were all so . . ."

"Suitable."

"Depends on how you define *suitable*. I found them wanting. You see, Meredith, none of them kissed me like you did."

"You shouldn't be kissing ladies at balls."

"Of course I wasn't kissing anyone. Except you. Your lips are the last ones I've touched."

"Oh."

"And when I looked in their eyes, I didn't feel this pounding in my chest, like I do when I look into your eyes." He put his hand over his heart. Aye, she knew that pounding. The heart, reminding them that they were alive and this was real and wasn't a dream.

"And I didn't want to know them, Mer, the way I want to know you."

For a girl who lived in the background, it was one thing to even be noticed. And it was quite another to be seen and known and wanted.

There was a lot to know about her, and she had half a mind to tell him so he'd understand why they could never be together as man and wife. She could explain how she ended up with the duchess. Why she'd been away recently, and what had brought her to that inn at Southampton that night. Why she could never betray the duchess's faith and trust, especially when it came to the duke.

Or little things, like how many times a day she thought about James.

Or how she was rereading the novel where the servant girl wins the hand of the lord of the house.

Ladies didn't burst forth with a deluge of intimate information, though. Ladies didn't spill all their secrets, all at once.

But after a long, lonely night, she wasn't quite ready to relinquish his company, especially when he was leaning against the wall, looking for all the world like he wouldn't want to be anywhere else but in this moment with her. So she asked him, "What do you want to know?"

"What's your favorite color? What was your childhood like? What do you do when you can't sleep at night?"

She smiled.

"When I can't sleep at night, I read novels. My childhood was good, until it wasn't, and that's when the duchess took me in and changed my life for the better. And blue. My favorite color is blue."

"Me, too. My favorite color is also blue. See, we have something in common." He leaned in closer to her. "It's a sign."

"A sign of what?"

"That we belong together."

She laughed softly.

"But that doesn't mean we can be together."

"Shhhh." It was his turn to shush her.

"I don't know about you, but I've had enough of thinking about could and should and proper matches for one evening."

"Yes," she whispered.

"I don't know about you, but I'm dying for one moment, just one moment, of bliss. Of feeling your lips, full and soft, against mine." He pressed the pad of his fingertip against her lips gently, indicating the spot where he'd want to kiss her.

But he didn't actually kiss her. Because she'd told him not to and he respected her wishes.

"Breathing you in." And here he leaned in, closing the distance between them, and inhaling deeply. She felt the warmth of his nearness, like sitting too close to the fire on a cold night.

But he still kept a few precious, vexing inches of hot air between them. A respectful distance, she supposed.

"Finding all the places I could kiss you. Here and here and here."

James traced his fingers along her collarbone, dipped low along the edge of her bodice, teased at going lower.

Her breaths became quick and shallow.

Her imagination did what he wouldn't do: fill in all the blanks, take those suggestions, pretend it was happening for real and not just in her head.

And then his fingers moved back to her lips, tracing the bottom lip, then the top. She was tempted, so tempted, to whisper, *kiss me. Come with me. Just one more night.*

But she couldn't. Just couldn't.

Instead, she took his fingertip between her lips, sucking for a second before biting down. Just to show him how quickly pleasure could turn to pain.

CHAPTER 7

Until His Grace has found a suitable bride, it is his duty to make the acquaintance of as many suitable young women as possible.

— THE RULES FOR DUKES

A week later
Lady Waterford's Musicale

When it came to social events, James had learned that balls and soirees were one thing, and musicales were quite another. At a ball, one might move about the room, step onto the terrace, play a spot of cards, or find a respite from conversation during a dance.

But at a musicale, one had to sit idle for hours, left alone with one's thoughts.

James wasn't the sort who was moved to paroxysms of emotion at the sound of a beautiful melody. He was a man of action, not a daydreamer.

And lest he forget, he was also in urgent, desperate need of a wife. He wasn't exactly opposed to marriage in general, as an institution. He wasn't even opposed to marriage himself. He was opposed to the way the duchess was going about it, though. How she found a steady stream of "suitable" women without Meredith being one of them was beyond him.

He would have thought he'd met everyone in England by now. But no, these suitable ladies kept coming out of the woodwork and damask-papered walls, one after another, with their posh accents and practiced remarks, all with the purpose of snaring a husband like him: young, rich, and titled.

James had learned that those in possession of the least desirable characteristics, such as an unfortunate lack of conversational ability or a deplorable tendency to giggle, were often those who *just happened* to have dowries that included hundreds or thousands of acres of land that *just happened* to abut one of his own estates.

He still wasn't accustomed to thinking of "his own estates." Plural.

All the suitable ladies were suitable in the way a business transaction was — as per calculations performed on paper, with no regard to love, intimacy, attraction, or passion.

Thus, when the duchess insisted there was someone he simply must meet, James had no expectation of anything more than a polite conversation with a female who wouldn't even come close to supplanting Meredith in his heart.

"May I present His Grace, the Duke of Durham. And this is Lady Jemma Winston."

James was presented with a woman who was not unattractive. Her light brown hair curled around a pleasing face. Her complexion hinted at time spent out of doors — he noted a faint smattering of freckles, and a flush that didn't flare and fade when presented with a human of the male persuasion. When she smiled, he noted one slightly crooked tooth, which seemed to enhance rather than detract from her appearance.

"It is so good to meet you, Your Grace."

"I am pleased to meet you as well, Lady Jemma."

"How are you finding London thus far?" Gah, that question again.

"I am becoming more accustomed to it each day." He gave his standard answer.

"I shall leave you two to chat whilst I tend to Lady Amelia," the duchess said. "She is standing alone near the instruments. I fear the worst."

And with that, the duchess took herself off, leaving them alone in an obvious setup. It should have been awkward. And for a moment, it was. He still hadn't gotten used to this forced mating dance, and he was still far too aware of other people watching him and discussing him. James already knew this would be in the papers by morning.

And then she said something he didn't expect.

"I hear you like horses," Lady Jemma began. At his grimace, she quickly added, "Oh, no, that wasn't meant to be a cutting remark. I do as well. Frankly, I'm hoping that you'd rather talk about horses than music or the weather or what everyone is wearing."

She smiled. A genuine, artless smile.

James was stunned.

"I see I've shocked you speechless. My mother despairs of me. I've never quite managed the art of simpering. But I do know how to spot the distance to a jump eight strides out. And you should see me at a hunt."

James blinked. It was a moment before he could form words.

"I confess I am shocked that someone wishes to discuss something of substance and that I have been introduced to a lady with whom I shared a mutual interest. But happily shocked. And impressed. Many men I know couldn't manage that, and I didn't think ladies were encouraged to hunt. But then again, that never stopped my sister, Lady Amelia."

"They aren't encouraged, of course, but I do it anyway. It's either that, or go slowly, quietly mad while arranging flowers and paying social calls. But enough about my shortcomings when it comes to being an earl's daughter."

James could only stare. She was pretty, with a face that was too quirky to be conventionally beautiful, but was all the more captivating because of it. Though she didn't hold a candle to Meredith's beauty, in his opinion.

And she was like him. A kindred spirit, Bridget would say.

She was the last woman he had expected to be introduced to. He wouldn't look now, but somewhere in the room, he was certain the duchess wore her expression of I-am-right-and-will-outsmart-you-yet.

"You are looking at me queerly," Lady Jemma said.

"I am just surprised to meet a woman like you. Well, surprised that we have been introduced. The duchess seems to throw a different sort of woman in my direction."

"Yes, the ones with prestigious relations, a plethora of boys in the family, or adjoining lands."

"Or all of the above, by some miracle."

"Tell me about your stables in Maryland. I've only heard scurrilous gossip about them, and, as someone who manages our estate's stables, I am keen to know more about your practice and methods."

And with that, something twigged in James. He didn't fall in love, or even in lust. He just relaxed. And began to enjoy himself. Thus far, he hadn't met a single person at society events that he could have a real conversation with about a mutual interest, and here was one, in female form. One considered suitable, too.

He told her about his stables.

"We usually kept a dozen horses. I bred and trained them, mixing a heavier draft horse with the Thoroughbred stock in an effort to create the perfect sport horse. I was also experimenting with breeding some mustangs, too."

"I don't suppose your program has any-thing to do with that famous stolen horse the papers are always reporting on?" She referred to Messenger, and the horse his father once stole. "It's old news, I know."

James debated, quickly, and decided to ignore her references to the gossip in the newspapers. He had yet to meet someone in London who hadn't read them. This was no reason not to engage in an interesting conversation with a charming and *suitable* woman.

"Yes. It's true. A dastardly tale, too."

"I am shocked. Simply shocked."

"You wouldn't be if you met Messenger, and knew a bit about my father. It's a good story."

"Do tell. Otherwise I shall have to suffer through a conversation with my mother and her friends about the fashion choices made this evening."

"We can't have that," James said in all seriousness. But maybe there was a smile tugging at his lips. "The story it shall be. My father was stationed in New York City during the Revolutionary War."

"You mean the War of Colonial Aggression?"

She smiled. Her eyes sparkled. She was flirting with him.

"While he was stationed there, he met my mother, and they fell in love. After the war he returned to London . . . to all this . . . but it didn't hold the same appeal it once

162

had. Or so I presume. His heart was in America now. So he started plotting his return. Knowing he'd need to support himself and his bride, he cast about for something to do. The only thing he was good at was horses. And his brother, the duke, had horses. Lots of horses."

"Don't tell me he stole a horse from a duke. Even if the duke was his own brother."

"He stole a horse from a duke. Not just any horse, either. Messenger was known to win races by a full ten seconds ahead of the next horse."

"Obviously he could never return to England after that," Lady Jemma said with a voice full of awe. Not only was it against the law, but it was against common decency. One didn't take a man's horse. Especially his lucrative, prize-winning racehorse.

"I think he was well aware of it." Repeating the story now, James realized what it meant for his father to steal from his brother, a duke, and to know with utter certainty that he could never return to England.

He would have known that he was leaving this forever.

Love mattered more.

More than family, more than duty to the estate, more than a title.

"So he stole a horse and absconded to America for love, knowing he could never return? I'm not very romantic, but even that makes me think about swooning."

"I don't think one *thinks* about swooning," James replied.

"Are you an expert?"

"I do have three sisters . . . although none of them are the swooning sort. So perhaps not."

"Well it's a very romantic story."

"I suppose it is."

"And you are following in your father's footsteps?"

Would he marry for love and throw away the dukedom? That couldn't be what she meant. That couldn't be something he discussed casually at a social function.

"I took over the farm when he passed on," James answered. "Except for the part where I ended up here, assuming the fate my father ran away from."

James swallowed a lump in his throat. What would his father have done if he'd lived and the duchess had come for him? Would he have returned to assume this role, or would he still be lounging against the old oak tree, watching the horses graze in the field, under that big blue sky?

"But you must be curious about the

duke's stables," Lady Jemma continued. "The ones from whence Messenger came."

"They're kept at one of the estates, Durham Park. But I haven't had a moment to attend to it."

Jack, the head groomsman, had told him about it. There were fine stables for two dozen horses. The estate contained vast expanses of land, rolling hills, and riding paths cut through forests. It was, by all accounts, idyllic.

"Durham Park is not far from London and well worth the journey. I do know there is some very fine stock in the stables. The land is beautiful. The house is impressive as well, but I suppose it goes without saying that all ducal residences are impressive."

"How do you know all that when I do not?"

"Because I have gone to visit on numerous occasions and had been corresponding with the late duke about it. Discreetly, of course, because I am a woman, and if word got out that I was horse mad and actually competent at something other than household management, my mother fears that she would never marry me off. I am taking a great risk with my reputation with you tonight, Your Grace, in revealing this scandalous aspect of myself to you."

He took a step closer. An infinitesimal step. But it closed the distance between them just a little bit.

"I promise, your secret is safe with me."

And just like that . . . they had a secret. He had a friend. He had met another woman who didn't terrify him, or bore him. One who was *suitable.*

James was struck with the desire to tell Meredith. He wanted to return to Durham House, climb the stairs to her room, slip inside, and lie down on the bed beside her. He wanted to talk in the dark and tell her about this evening, and finding a friend, and then stop talking for the rest of the night. Nothing happened in his life now that he didn't want to share with her. Nothing made him feel lonely quite like having to keep his distance from her.

But he knew something about women, being experienced, in addition to having listened to three sisters grow up, so he knew better than to tell Meredith, *guess what! I met a suitable match!*

Not that he wanted to make presumptions about her feelings for him. He didn't want to be one of those men who just assumed any woman must want him, especially now that he was this supposedly lofty duke. She had made it plain that because of his title, nothing could transpire between them.

The musicale was set to begin, and the hostess busied herself with ushering everyone to their seats. James returned to his family — though he was surprised to see Claire sitting with what one would call a Suitable Prospect. Judging by the astonished and gossiping reactions of those around them, it seemed he was a Very Suitable Prospect.

If she was making an effort . . .

And, come to think of it, Bridget was, too, what with her fawning over some bloke named Rupert, whom she always sought out at balls. Amelia told him about it, after reading her diary.

And if Bridget was making an effort . . .

His sisters were *trying* — trying to fit in, trying to find matches. That meant something. That meant they were thinking of staying, and thinking of making a life here. That meant that if he wanted to stay close to them — and he did, much as he might roll his eyes and lament to the Lord about the trials and tribulations of being saddled with three sisters — he would have to try, too.

Perhaps he would start tomorrow, by paying a visit to the charmingly horse-mad and eminently suitable Lady Jemma.

The gossips will report on anything and everything when it comes to a duke.
— THE RULES FOR DUKES

The following morning
Breakfast at Durham House
"Let's see what the gossips have to say today," the duchess said, opening *The London Weekly* directly to the gossip columns. While she consumed the news, the rest of the family consumed food.

"The new Duke of Durham was spotted engaged in a lengthy conversation with Lady Jemma, the daughter of Earl Winston. His lordship's stables are widely regarded as some of the best in England, and so we can only presume that horses were among the topics of conversation. But perhaps they also discussed things of a more romantic nature?"

Meredith concentrated very hard on bringing the cup of tea from its saucer to her lips without a shaking hand or the slightest tremble revealing that she cared.

Caring was silly.

This was bound to happen, she told herself.

It was inevitable that his name would be linked in the papers with a suitable woman, like Lady Jemma. But that wasn't what stung.

It was that they had something in common. Something more than just one night of pleasure at an inn in Southampton.

Meredith tried to tell herself it was only gossip. The papers got things wrong all the time. It didn't really signify. There was no point in trembling hands or tumultuous feelings.

"You did seem to enjoy your conversation with her," the duchess said, looking at the duke.

"You were talking for quite a while, actually. And you didn't even notice when I made faces at you across the room," Amelia added.

Meredith's heart sank.

"I noticed when you did that to me," Claire muttered.

"Perhaps you should pay less attention to other people's business and more to your own, Lady Amelia," the duchess admonished. "It would be an excellent match, Duke. Will you pay a call upon her?"

Don't look. Don't look. Don't look.

Meredith didn't want to look, but there was no way to stop herself from lifting her gaze away from a small spot of tea on the tablecloth and up to him. Just James. Sitting at the head of the dining table.

Like the head of the household.

The head of the family.

Like the duke.

She saw his gaze shift to her. Then to his sisters.

She saw his jaw tighten.

There was a long, agonizing pause before he said anything.

Her heart beat hard. Her skin felt hot and cold and clammy. She set down the teacup before she could no longer hide the tremble in her hand.

This was happening. This was beginning. It was inevitable.

But logic failed to comfort her, and the truth of the situation did little to ease her heartache.

Matters were not helped when he said, "Yes. I am considering it."

A duke must know the proper etiquette of courtship. He shall find it useful when pursuing a suitable bride.
— THE RULES FOR DUKES

Later that morning

Meredith had survived the inevitable revelation that James would be properly courting a proper lady. Was it wrong that it felt so soon, so sudden? Nevertheless, she believed that she had not only survived, but did so discreetly, so as not to reveal the turmoil of her heart.

Meredith's hopes and dreams to further avoid the duke that day — out of desire for some emotional self-preservation — were dashed shortly after breakfast.

"I must escort the girls for more fittings with the modiste this morning," Her Grace began. "But it sounds like the duke will need to be informed of the etiquette and protocol surrounding courtship calls sooner rather than later, thank the Lord. Miss Green, do take a moment to instruct His Grace."

The answer was yes. Of course it was yes.

Even if the words on her lips were, *I'd rather stick myself in the eye with a thousand sewing need les.*

She merely had to instruct him on the etiquette and protocol for courting a gently bred lady, with intentions to one day wed her. She had to help him find and woo and win the hand of another woman.

Even if her heart rebelled at the thought.

Fate was cruel like that.

Or perhaps the duchess was the cruel mistress here. Perhaps she noticed that frisson in the air between Meredith and James whenever they were together, and this was a deliberate maneuver to put to rest any daydreams of love Meredith might harbor between her and the duke.

Or perhaps Her Grace felt it was more important to accompany the girls to the modiste, and Meredith was merely experiencing the pangs of a guilty conscience.

She went to the study.

The elegance of their surroundings reminded her of her place even if a look in James's eyes made her forget for just a second. She took a deep breath, willed her heartbeat to steady, and steeled herself to do her duty to the dukedom, just as he must do.

"Meredith." He stood when she entered the room.

"The duchess requested that I speak to you about the etiquette and protocol for a courtship call," she said.

"Did she?" he asked dryly, suggesting he found this uncomfortable as well.

"As you might imagine, the etiquette for a courtship call is as strict as anything else," she began. At his direction, she took a seat, but on the settee opposite him. Distance. She must keep distance between them.

"Meredith . . ."

He murmured her name. He awkwardly reached for her hands, which were elegantly folded in her lap. She wanted to reach for him, she really did.

But the duchess. But the dukedom. But Durham.

"You may call and leave your card in the afternoon," she began, reciting the protocol for a system she never really participated in. Nevertheless, she knew it well. "Or you may drop in during their calling hours. If so, it is likely that you will join others during the visit, which will only amplify the message of your call. Lady Jemma and her mother have calling hours on Thursdays."

"How do you know that?" James asked, awed.

"I have been the duchess's companion for twelve years. There is little about the haute ton that I do not know."

She didn't know much by way of mathematics, Latin, or horses. She had not studied botany, biology, or any other sciences. But by God she knew the right way to address the wife of the third son of a marquess, both in person and in writing. She knew when and where every lady of note held calling hours. She also knew nearly every tenant on each of the estates.

"Depending upon the seriousness of your intentions and how swiftly you wish to pursue marriage, you may wish to arrive with flowers. Is this something we need to review?"

There was a beat of silence. Even her heart paused to observe it.

"No." There was another beat of silence. "But, please, tell me anyway. Just in case I wish to bring a woman flowers. Meredith . . ."

There it was again: a note of longing in his voice when he said her name, accompanied by a searching gaze. All of it made her wonder if he meant her, bringing flowers to her. It seemed like he meant her? What did it matter if he did?

But she could not do *this* and consider such a thing.

"A small bouquet will sufficiently convey your interest at this early stage. A larger arrangement will certainly do more to declare your intentions and presumably to woo her. You'll want to pay attention to the message the combination of flowers states."

"Good God."

"I know." And Meredith allowed herself a smile at the ridiculousness of it all. "This is the sort of thing ladies of the ton are instructed to learn. Boys learn Greek and Latin, girls learn French and the language of flowers. But a servant can take care of this for you."

"What if I wish to do it myself?"

She blinked. Whoever heard of a duke doing such a thing? But he wasn't just any duke.

"How romantic. Perhaps one of your sisters will be able to help you. The duchess is instructing them in the language of flowers."

There was another beat of silence in which they imagined the duchess endeavoring to teach something as frivolous as the language of flowers to his sisters.

They both burst into laughter.

"When you arrive, you will make polite conversation for a quarter of an hour. Appropriate subjects will be the weather, the season, mutual acquaintances, or perhaps a new play. Then you will take your leave."

"She doesn't care for small chat," he said off-handedly.

There was another beat of silence. This one, tinged with awkwardness. That he knew such a thing about Lady Jemma meant things might be more serious than Meredith had wanted to consider. Very well, it was definitely more serious.

"Oh."

"We talked about horses," he said, as if this were any consolation, but it only made things worse. Meredith forced a smile.

"You share a mutual interest. Actually,

175

two: horses and a dislike for idle social chatter. She sounds different from the other women you have met."

Meredith did not share his interest in horses. The great beasts scared her, frankly. They had nothing in common, except for Durham and one night of passion in Southampton.

"Hardly the stuff of a lifetime of marriage," he said, dismissing it, or attempting to. But an acute ache in the region of her heart remained.

"Marriages amongst the ton are built on less."

"That's not what I want."

Again, she was acutely aware of the space between them. Just a few feet of air, and furniture, and whatnot, but it seemed insurmountable.

"What do you want?" Meredith asked in a small voice.

"Love. Companionship. Passion."

"What luxuries. I hope you find that."

"What if I might have found it already?"

"In your wife. I hope you find that in your wife," Meredith clarified. In truth, her hopes and feelings were not that simple. She didn't wish unhappiness for him. She just wanted him to be happy with *her.* But the world they lived in conspired to make that impossible, and so she was left feeling awful and selfish because perhaps she didn't want him to be happy with another woman. *She* wanted to be happy with him.

"What are you thinking, Mer? I can see that you are thinking something."

Ha. As if she could tell him the truth.

"It's important that your call only lasts for a quarter of an hour. Any longer and it will lead to gossip and speculation with regard to your intentions. It will add undue pressure to your courtship. Also, it is doubtful that you will be left unchaperoned."

"Making all of this a performance," James remarked. "It is as if we are all putting on a great play of Life, High Society Style. We have roles to play and lines to recite. Bouquets of flowers as props . . ."

She smiled a little, enjoying his interpretation of life in the haute ton.

"But tell me, Meredith, why are *we* alone? Why is it acceptable for you and me to be alone as we are right now?"

Her smile faded.

"The rules are different for a woman of my position. Of course I must have a care with my reputation — any woman does. But virtue and reputation matter more for women of a higher station, since more is dependent upon her innocence. You could compromise me, and it would not necessarily lead to marriage."

Never mind that her virtue was already gone, and he had already compromised her. And there had been nary a word of a betrothal. And it wasn't necessarily wrong.

This was the way of the world. But now that she spoke about it aloud, Meredith started to wonder: Wasn't she as good or as valuable as Lady Winston or Amelia, Bridget, or Claire? Why did her virtue matter less than theirs? Oh, she had to mind her reputation and such in order to maintain her place with the duchess. But it wasn't the same.

Then again, she had more freedom. As long as she was discreet, she could get away with more than any highborn lady. Then again, she already had. Then again, it all came back to her place with Her Grace.

"I wouldn't take advantage. You know that."

"I do. You are a gentleman in action as well as in station. You are a good man, James."

"I do try."

And that was the thing: he did try. It made him more admirable in her eyes, even if it meant they couldn't be together. It almost made her wish that he were more of a cad so that she would like him less.

"Do you have any further questions, Your Grace? You must have other business to attend to."

"Meredith, I need you to know that it's not what you think."

"I don't know what you mean."

This time he stood, and came around to sit beside her on the settee.

Because he could. Because there was no chaperone.

"With Jemma . . . it's just . . . a formality," he said.

"You are using her given name," Meredith pointed out. "I wonder if that is to suggest intimacy or if it is your stubborn American refusal to learn and adhere to titles and proper forms of address."

"Stubborn American refusal, probably," he admitted. "I don't want you to think that this social call changes things . . . or . . . means something that it doesn't . . . ."

Gah. Now he wanted to soothe her feelings. He reached for her hand, interlacing their fingers — as he was about to court another woman. Heat flared within her, and it wasn't lust or passion.

Did he not know that she needed to relinquish any romantic thoughts or feelings for him? She needed to let him go, to send

179

him out in the world with a bouquet of beautiful flowers arranged in a combination that conveyed the perfect message, to the right house and at the right day and time. She needed to pull her hand away.

"Do you presume to know my own mind, Your Grace? My own heart?"

"Tell me what is on your mind. I want to know."

"I think that you are beginning to accept the requirements of your station. I think you are beginning to try to step into your new role. And we both know that means at least trying to find a suitable bride."

"You do have the right of it, Mer, but it has nothing to do with how I feel about you."

"How do you feel about me?" she asked.

James clasped both of her hands and gazed deeply into her eyes.

"I feel that the night we spent together in Southampton wasn't enough, Mer. I want to spend all my nights with you. And yet I feel that only you can show me how to be Durham, and the man I must become, and as such, a man who should not spend his nights with you. Funny, that." He paused, gave a wry smile. "I know that you are poised and elegant, and I have a hunch that you are stuck in a position beneath you.

There's so much I don't know about you, and I want to know everything. I want to know you, Meredith."

His words flooded over her, drowning her. Coming up with excuses felt like coming up for air. But still, he said more of this heart-wrenching stuff that pulled her under once more, like a strong current she couldn't resist, but had to resist for the sake of her heart and sense of loyalty. For her sense of self-preservation.

Meredith withdrew her hands from his.

"And yet you will go court another woman."

"Tell me not to, Meredith. And I won't."

His words, his blue eyes looking at her like that, all of it another strong undertow tugging her down, sweeping her away. The only thing she could do was close her eyes to his handsome face.

She thought of her mother, instead. She thought of the duchess. She thought about how much these two women needed her. She wouldn't throw it all away, not for just a boy, not for Just James, not even if he was a duke.

Any regrets she might have had of not doing so were abandoned, given the letter she received later that afternoon.

The duchess's private sitting room

Her Grace was not usually interrupted when she and Meredith sat down to tend to her correspondence — an assortment of invitations, letters from far-flung friends, missives from town friends discussing the latest gossip, et cetera, et cetera. It took an hour, at least, each day to read through it all and craft the correct replies.

But this afternoon, Pendleton arrived with a letter on a silver tray. This one was for Meredith as well as the duchess. Meredith accepted it, and Pendleton left the room, leaving the door slightly ajar behind him.

There was only one person who wrote to them both. Meredith glanced warily at the missive — the tattered paper, the blue-inked scrawl, the stamps gathered on its passage from Hampshire to London. Her heart had a strange, mixed-up reaction when she saw it.

"It's another letter from my mother."

The duchess raised an eyebrow, questioning.

"Well, it's from Mrs. Bates," Meredith quickly clarified. Her mother no longer wrote, not even her own name. "Presumably with news of her."

Meredith hesitated for a moment before opening it, turning it over in her hands. She wasn't certain what she hoped the letter would say — she half wished her mother had recovered completely, and a small, dark corner of her heart wished her mother would find her eternal peace and rest. Meredith did hate to hear of her suffering.

The only thing worse was actually witnessing it.

This letter probably contained more news of her ongoing decline.

"Well, do open it up. The contents won't change the longer you linger over it."

Right. Meredith broke the wax seal and unfolded the sheet. She quickly scanned the lines of Mrs. Bates's inelegant scrawl, trying to quickly ascertain the most important thing: Was her mother well? She would read it all more slowly later.

"Her good days are becoming fewer and farther between. In other words, not much has changed since I visited last. But then again, it has only been little over a fortnight."

That meant it had only been little over a fortnight since she met James in Southampton. Meredith had been in a certain mood that evening — all too aware how precarious life was, how it could all go in an instant, or how one could have nothing but their memories in their old age. That night

Meredith thought only of living fully in the moment and of making memories that would stay with her until the end.

"I am glad you had those days with her," the duchess said softly.

"I as well. Thank you for giving me leave to visit her."

The duchess smiled as if to say, *of course, child,* and then she sighed and said, "What are we going to do?"

We. What are *we* going to do? Not, what are you, Meredith, a single woman of little fortune and no connections, going to do about this heartbreaking and expensive and tragic situation? Without the duchess's assistance, Meredith and her mother would be eking out a very mean existence indeed.

This was why she could not dally with James and wreck the duchess's plans for him. Meredith owed her that much.

"What can one do?" Meredith replied, trying, and failing, to keep the frustration out of her voice. She hated not being able to do anything. And while she appreciated the duchess's help, more than anything in the world, there was still the fact that she alone couldn't care for her own mother.

"Write to Mrs. Bates. Tell her carry on as best she can. That woman is a saint."

"Thank you," Meredith said softly. And

just like that, her future and her mother's were assured. They would carry on as they were, for better or for worse.

"Your mother served me well. Above and beyond what was required of a lady's maid. This is the least that I can do for her." With no small amount of bitterness and regret, the duchess added, "Especially given all that has happened on my account."

Meredith bit her tongue. "All that had happened" was not known to Meredith. No one was very forthcoming whenever she tried to ask. Her mother, bless her, wasn't lucid enough to relate stories from so long ago, and the duchess wasn't talking. Like-wise, *all she had done on my account* was also unexplained. When she tried to ask, the answers were always vague and gave no clar-ity to why a duchess supported her former lady's maid so well, after so long.

"On her good days, she is grateful," Mere-dith said. "And I am also grateful, and forever in your debt."

Meredith lifted her eyes to the familiar face of Her Grace: the pale skin, lined, but with a fresh complexion. Her blue eyes were brighter and sharper than ever. Her hair — pale, pale blonde, nearly white — was styled firmly, like a helmet, but prettier. She was a warrior. A major general. Anyone would be a fool to cross her.

She was strong and kind and had given Meredith a life she never dreamed of.

Meredith was forever in her debt.

The truth of it was never far from her mind. Or her heart.

And she knew exactly how to repay Her Grace for a generosity that could not be repaid. It seemed the duchess did, too.

"I know you are appreciative, child. And I am counting on you as everything changes. I need your support. Your steadiness. The circumstances that have brought us together are sad. But I daresay together we can make something positive come of it. We have been blessed with all these years of companionship, of course, and now we must persevere in our efforts to secure Durham for another generation."

Meanwhile, in the corridor

Eavesdropping was not polite on any continent, and yet that did not stop James from pausing outside the slightly open door to the duchess's chamber. It was almost embarrassing how he unabashedly lingered and listened.

His sisters were having a profoundly terrible effect upon him.

But he happened to be walking past the

door, which was already slightly open. And then he happened to have heard Meredith's voice.

It's from my mother. Well, it's from Mrs. Bates. Presumably with news of her.

This piqued his curiosity. James hadn't imagined her having a mother, which was absurd, because everyone had a mother. He hadn't imagined her having a family. He supposed she had just emerged from the duchess's head, like Athena, fully formed and all knowing.

The rest of the conversation he heard only stoked the flames of his curiosity further.

Thank you for leave to go visit her.

At the mention of a fortnight since, James quickly counted the days — or nights, rather — since *that* night in Southampton. He concluded that this visit to her mother must have been the purpose of her journey.

Her good days are few and far between.

Meredith had a mother. And she was ill, possibly dying. And yet Meredith was here in London and not at her mother's bedside. He wondered why.

Your mother has served me well, above and beyond what was required for a lady's maid.

Meredith's mother was a lady's maid. A servant. Which explained why Meredith was so achingly aware of the vast difference in their positions and so adamant that she was not suitable for a duke. But did daughters of ladies' maids grow up to be companions to aristocratic ladies? He had no idea who to ask, besides Meredith, and he hesitated to broach such a personal topic.

James stood there in the dimly lit corridor, feeling like the worst sort of lurker, stitching all the pieces together in his mind. And, not being much of a stitcher, he came up empty — save for more questions. Who was her father, then? What was wrong with her mother? How had she come to live with the duchess?

James meant what he'd told her that morning: he wanted to know her, all of her.

CHAPTER 8

Occasionally, a duke might enjoy the same entertainment as the masses, but only under certain circumstances and with certain appropriate persons.

— THE RULES FOR DUKES

The boxing match

When a most unlikely scenario presented itself — the brawny Lord Fox invited the brainy Lady Claire to a boxing match — James immediately seized the opportunity. He insisted she accept and that he and Miss Green accompany her as chaperones.

He rather fancied spending the day at a boxing match instead of whatever the duchess had planned for the lot of them. He rather fancied spending the day with Meredith, too. They had spent a night together, but never a day together, from morning to night, without the watchful eye of the duchess, or servants, or society.

Until today.

After a pleasant carriage ride — not for a picnic, as they'd led the duchess to believe — in which Lord Fox expounded on the significance of today's match and in which James and Meredith couldn't keep their eyes off each other, and in which Claire either didn't notice or pretended not to, they arrived.

The match took place on the outskirts of London, but first they paused outside of the Bull and Bear, while the groomsmen saw to the horses and carriage. Fox and Claire walked ahead slowly, while James and Meredith stayed a few paces behind, which allowed them something like privacy.

"Do you know what this reminds me of?" James asked.

"One of the many English villages you have visited," Meredith teased, knowing he'd been to hardly any.

"No. Southampton."

"I fail to see how. Southampton is a bustling port city and this is a provincial village, nowhere near water."

"Yes, but it is you and me outside of London, away from all the gossips in society, where no one knows us. All those things together remind me of the night we met," he said.

"I hate to inform you, Your Grace, but this mob is likely littered with peers, and younger sons, and all their scoundrel friends. At least a few of whom are likely to recognize us and retain the memory of it in spite of the massive quantities of alcohol they will consume today. It is a truth little acknowledged that men gossip just as much as women, if not more."

"Are you telling me that we must be on our best behavior even here, in this little village outside of London?"

"Well if not the best, at least not the worst. If the duchess were to learn of this . . ."

Meredith glanced up at him with worry in her eyes. James detected real concern there, and he was reminded about that conversation he overheard. There was more at stake, he suspected, than mere obedience.

"Shhh. Let us not think of any of that," he said. "Let us enjoy each other's company on this beautiful day in this place, wherever we are." Dropping his voice, he added, "Let's pretend that it is the morning after our night together and we have the whole day to ourselves to do whatever we like."

"And you have taken me to a boxing match with thousands of people," Meredith said dryly. But he caught the slight upturn of her lips — she was teasing him. "Oh, the romance."

"Don't tell me you're too fancy for a little sport."

"To be honest, this is my first time at an event of this nature. You might be surprised to learn that this is not the sort of engagement to which I normally escort Her Grace."

"You don't say."

They laughed. He wanted to hold her hand. Just take her hand, interlace their fingers, and carry on . . . but he knew that she did not wish to attract that sort of attention, and he respected her wishes. So he did not reach for her hand.

"I shall tell you what I think after the match," she said. "In the meantime, I shall endeavor to enjoy these half-naked boxers along with all these people. I daresay I've never seen such a crowd."

"If you wanted to enjoy half-naked men . . ." James teased, while pretending to tug off his jacket.

"Don't even say it! Or do it!"

"You're blushing."

She smiled, and laughed, and looked away. "Quick, do change the subject. This is a most awkward topic of conversation."

That, too, reminded him of that night in Southampton. When she would nervously engage with him, but quickly withdraw. It was modesty, to be sure, and merely being sensible. Yet, given what he'd overheard the other day, James had the sense that there was something else, something more to Miss Meredith Green than he knew — a real reason she kept a *duke* at arm's length.

"You know, you never did tell me why you were in Southampton that night."

"I was just passing through," she replied evenly. "Like you."

"From where?"

"Visiting family in Hampshire."

"I didn't know you had family. I mean, that is to say, I hadn't considered it. My apologies."

"Of course I have a family, though I can see why one might assume the duchess was the only person I had. Occasionally I go to visit Hampshire to see . . . them."

Like always, she spoke with care. Her words, so cultivated and deliberate, made her seem elegant and refined. But James couldn't help but wonder if there was more she wasn't saying. Something more between *the duchess this* and *the duchess that*.

"How often do you go?"

"Rarely," she replied.

"Perhaps I will join you on your next visit."

"That is a lovely offer, but it won't be

necessary. You have important ducal matters to attend to. Besides, I'm not certain when I shall go visit next."

He glanced her way and saw that she was looking off in the distance, staying quiet, and content to let the topic of conversation lapse. He decided not to ask more questions — for now.

"Do let me know if you intend to make another trip there. I shall endeavor to be waiting in the common room of a tavern, leaning against the wall, ready to make eyes at you across the room. But not in an uncomfortable manner."

She gave a little laugh. She didn't laugh often enough, he thought.

"An illicit, secret rendezvous," she said in a low voice. "Outside of London, away from the attentions of everyone we know, just me and just you, just James . . ."

Hearing those words, murmured in her low voice, did things to him inside. Got his heart pumping, the blood rushing, and it intensified his wanting. He wanted to be able to touch her, and kiss her, and feel himself inside her once more. He wanted that space where they could just be and breathe together, to hold her hand if he felt like it, to be free with each other, all without fearing the stares and comments of other people. Without worry about what the duchess would think.

This place might do, if it weren't for a massive raucous and rowdy crowd pulsing and shoving around them, spoiling for a fight.

Oh, the romance indeed.

Once they were all settled at the match, James paid barely any attention to his sister, who seemed to be perfectly content with Lord Fox, a fellow James found himself liking more than he expected. Though Fox had a reputation for being concerned only with sport, and excessively so, his explanation of today's match and the boxers was rather insightful. It was a battle, Fox had intimated, between logic and passion, the head and the heart.

Today, for James, the heart was winning.

It had something to do with being out of London, away from the attentive eye of the duchess and the curious glances of servants. He felt more at ease knowing he wasn't being watched so closely.

It certainly had something to do with Meredith being near; he might not have been able to hold her hand or otherwise demonstrate affection, but he didn't have to force his gaze away or observe some restraining protocol. As a result of all those things, he felt himself sliding into the old version of himself: relaxed and happy with the simple pleasures of a beautiful woman and a pleasant day. He hadn't a care in the world.

Then the fight began. The two boxers circled each other, fists raised. Minutes passed, then a half hour, then more, as the opponents swung and missed and jabbed and connected.

It was all so base. And elemental.

Yet studied and practiced all the same.

The crowd was riveted, cheering and groaning and roaring with each move.

James was aware of it all: the energy of the crowd, thousands strong, the hot sun beating down on them all, the sweat of the boxers and those watching. The fighters went too long without a hit; the crowd grew restless as they clamored for more action.

All at once, it seemed the thousands of them surged forward in a hot mass of humanity, lifting people off their feet. Some stumbled and others fell.

Meredith glanced at him, eyes wild with panic.

He pulled her close, using his size and strength to protect her and keep her steady on her feet.

She melted against him. Her body fit against his perfectly.

Wanting rocketed through him.

Lust and desire and the rightness of this feeling.

All of a sudden he was taken back to that night . . .

. . . *holding her against him, feeling her breasts against his chest, his arousal hard and pulsing against the vee of her thighs. Her face, tipped up to his so he could kiss her. And kiss her deeply he did, sinking his fingers into her hair to hold her close. All the while holding her, never wanting to let her go* . . .

This memory, this feeling was followed by an overwhelming sense of helplessness. He didn't know how he was supposed to forgo this, or her. And by all accounts he must.

He couldn't go back to that night, but he couldn't go on as things were in London. He couldn't take bloody courtship lessons from Meredith, lessons he was supposed to apply to other women.

No, it was intolerable.

"Is everything all right?" Meredith asked.

"I should be asking you that," he replied.

"I'm fine." *With you,* her eyes seemed to say. Or was that just wishful thinking?

"Are you all right, James?"

His name on her lips. Like it should be.

No, he wasn't fine. He was in an untenable position of wanting what he couldn't have — a romance with a certain girl — when anyone would think he had everything. No one wished to hear his laments. He couldn't bring himself to completely disregard the rules, either, given that his sisters' happiness depended in part upon how he conducted himself.

The lot of it just made him so damned lonely.

Even here, holding her, in a crowd of thousands.

"As long as you're safe," he answered.

"And Lady Claire . . ."

"She has Lord Fox to watch out for her."

James glanced over just to make sure that was correct. And clearly, she had Fox, who held her protectively and possessively. Her cheeks were flushed bright pink — the heat, probably.

One thing was plain: his sister was finding a match. A proper match.

This prompted a selfish thought: If his sisters were properly settled, would he be more free to marry whom he wished, or less? Would he sacrifice their happiness for his? What kind of person was he for even considering it?

But one more glance from Meredith's big

doe eyes, the slightest upturn from her lips and the slightest caress of her hand against his, and there was no way he wasn't thinking about it.

Later that night

They arrived at Durham House much later in the evening to find that the duchess had taken Amelia and Bridget to some ton function. Claire pleaded exhaustion and retired.

That left James and Meredith alone, at the top of the stairs, lingering in the corridor.

Meredith knew why she delayed: she didn't want this day to end. This day, which had been different than all the others before. It wasn't the boxing match, or the travel or any of that. It was feeling equal, all day long, to her company: a duke, his sister, and a marquess. She acted as a gently bred lady, as she'd been raised to act, and the others treated her as if she was. There were no little tasks requested of her, however benign, to remind her of her place.

Today, she didn't feel any *less*.

Today, she felt *more*.

She felt like a girl, just a girl, flirting with a handsome man. One she'd given herself to and who still wanted her, plain as day.

So, no, she wasn't in any hurry for the

day to end, which is why she lingered with James at the top of the stairs. He didn't seem to be in any rush, either.

"I'll walk you to your room," he offered.

"Thank you, Your Grace. Though my room is just there."

They both looked in the direction she pointed — her door, one of many in the family wing. *Just right there. So close.*

"One never knows what dangers might befall you on your way. Pirates, murderers, highwaymen . . ."

"Rogues and scoundrels," she continued. And then, because she was feeling daring and different today, she added, "Or handsome, tempting dukes."

He grinned at her and leaned against the wall.

"You think I'm handsome?"

"Are you scrounging for a compliment?"

"From you, yes."

Lud, but the man's blue eyes had some sort of sparkle. Even in the dim light of the sconces above, she could see that mischievous, flirtatious glimmer. And it was directed at her — and, she had noticed, often *just* her.

Since he was so unabashed in showing his feelings to her — if one knew where to look — Meredith, emboldened by the day, decided to flirt right back.

Just this once.

"All right. I think you're handsome. And tempting. But I can't believe you need to hear me say it to know it."

"Maybe I didn't *need* to. But what man wouldn't want to hear a beautiful, intelligent, and sensual woman complimenting him?"

What woman wouldn't want to hear herself described thusly?

"So you're just like any other man?" Meredith replied. She took a step toward him, closing the distance between them.

"I'm nothing special," he said, his voice husky. A little vulnerable, even.

"You are, but not for the reasons you might think, and not for the reasons anyone will tell you."

And then she touched him. Just a small, gentle caress along his jaw. At this hour, it was a little rough with stubble. If he hadn't cut his hair, she would have pushed a lock of it away from his face.

He caught her hand. Held it against his cheek. Then his heart.

When he said, "I don't want this day to end, Meredith," she was undone.

She was done.

Done resisting. Done denying herself.

Done feeling second-rate. At least for to-night.

"Maybe it doesn't have to?" she whispered.

"What are you saying, Meredith?"

"One kiss can't hurt, can it?"

He tugged her darker into the shadows, where they wouldn't be seen. He tugged her right into his waiting arms, which folded around her, holding her close to the warmth of his chest.

Meredith tilted her head back, waiting for and wanting his lips on hers. She had only to wait a second before his mouth claimed hers.

This. Like souls connecting with each touch and taste and back and forth and give and take. This, passion fusing them together in binds that were invisible but that felt unbreakable.

This was not just a kiss.

"I wanted to hold your hand all day," he whispered, interlacing his fingers with hers. "Just hold your hand. Like I was yours and you were mine."

I want to live a life and live in a world where we can, she thought. But words were beyond her now, so she just squeezed his hand to let him know she wanted nothing more than to hold his hand, too.

There was little talking after that.

Just lips touching and tasting.

Hands roaming and caressing.

Hearts beating, hard and steady.

Soft sighs, sweet exhalations of bliss.

Closer and closer they became until there was no space between them, nothing but stupid layers of fabric and fashion.

Meredith threaded her fingers through his hair.

James cupped her cheeks in his hands.

Her back was up against the wall, her world reduced to her and to him, to this little universe they created out of shadows and kisses.

She couldn't think of *should* and *should not* when he lovingly caressed the curve of her jaw, pressed a kiss on the curve of her neck, or when his hands skimmed along the curve of her thighs, ruffling the fabric, and swells of her breasts.

The whole house, the whole city, the whole damn country ceased to exist when she felt his weight against her, and felt the evidence of his desire of her pressing at the vee of her thighs.

When he sighed "Oh, Meredith," nothing else mattered. Nothing.

Until it did.

Until the illusion that they were alone was

shattered.

Until the duchess and the sisters entered the house and climbed the stairs, leaving just enough time for their entry to pierce their little world, just enough time for them to reluctantly part, putting a suitable distance between them.

"Ah, good evening," the duchess said, eyeing them both.

Meredith, foolishly, pressed her fingers to her lips, full from kisses.

The duchess's eyes narrowed.

James was breathing hard.

The duchess's lips flattened into a thin line of disapproval.

Meredith discovered that, yes, one kiss could hurt.

CHAPTER 9

A duke will occasionally encounter the consequences of his actions.

— THE RULES FOR DUKES

The next day
The drawing room

When one's very existence was at stake, there was really only one thing to do: pretend everything was absolutely normal and focus on one's embroidery. The next morning found Meredith, the duke, his sisters, and the duchess in the drawing room.

She and James locked eyes immediately.

What do we do about last night? she asked, wordlessly.

He shook his head as if to say, *don't worry about it. Act normal.*

Then he picked up a newspaper. He leafed through the sporting section while the duchess continued her perusal of the gossip columns.

Lady Bridget was writing in her diary — if Meredith was curious about the contents, she need only to wait until Lady Amelia read it and informed the rest of the family, as she was wont to do.

Lady Amelia was browsing through her London guidebook, occasionally folding down a page or circling something that struck her fancy. Meredith admired her optimism that she would have a chance to explore the city, beyond the ballrooms and drawing rooms. She stuck the needle through the fabric, and pulled. When had she given up on her own adventures?

Lady Claire was busy at work on a mathematical problem — she was a genius with numbers, as Meredith witnessed when she chaperoned her to lectures at the Royal Society.

The lectures were, as one might expect, frightfully tedious to one who was not passionate about that sort of thing. But they gave Meredith a chance to wonder at what talents she might have and what she might do with her brain besides merely being a companion, if such an opportunity ever presented itself. As a young girl of limited means, she hadn't been encouraged to dream.

Life with the duchess opened her eyes to the possibilities that existed in the world. Through conversations with worldly people at soirees and calling hours, or books, newspapers, and nights at the theater, Meredith was exposed to a wealth of possibilities. But through a steady stream of subtle reminders of her place — a request to fetch something, say, or never being asked her opinion on the ideas in a book — she was reminded that it was not her place to dream of them. She was here to be a loyal and faithful companion and nothing more.

Meredith kept stitching, pushing and pulling the needle and thread through the fabric. She was *good* at being a companion, though. She knew all the rules and etiquette. She knew the ways of the haute ton, even if she didn't quite belong. Perhaps one day she might write a book or start a school: *A Commoner's Guide to High Society.*

Rule number one: do not dally with the head of the household, especially if he is a duke.

Despite her inner turmoil, Meredith did adore how the family had the entirety of Durham House at their disposal, but still sought out each other's company to sit in a companionable silence, each engaged in their own pursuits. It would be a lovely, relaxed scene of family harmony if . . .

What happened yesterday wasn't discovered.

What happened last night was ignored.

Meredith, knowing the duchess as she did, was not optimistic. The woman was sharp and missed nothing.

She stabbed the needle and thread through the sampler she was working on and then tugged it back again. Stitch after stitch kept her hands busy and steady, even if her nerves were frayed and mind bleary from a night spent fretting rather than sleeping.

Thus far, she had made it through breakfast unscathed.

But the day was young.

And the duchess was nobody's fool.

And Meredith was positive that any second now the duchess would say something.

Meredith took no satisfaction in being right.

"How was yesterday's picnic outing?" Her Grace asked, innocently enough. Meredith and James exchanged a fleeting, heated glance.

"It was quite nice, actually," Lady Claire replied, absentmindedly, as she continued her work, doing things with numbers that went far beyond multiplication and division.

"I should have liked to have gone," Amelia added morosely. "Instead of more social calls."

"But Lady Whoever We Visited served some very delicious cakes," Lady Bridget replied. "I would enjoy calling hours much more if every hostess served such excellent cake."

Meredith kept her head down and prayed. *Don't ask me. Don't ask me. Don't ask me.*

"Miss Green," Her Grace said. "What did you think? Did you enjoy the picnic?"

She couldn't lie. But she also couldn't tell her that they had gone to a boxing match instead and had deliberately misled her — all in addition to whatever Her Grace witnessed in the corridor last night. It was all a tremendous betrayal of trust, and now, the morning after, Meredith couldn't even believe she had done it.

In a panic, she glanced to James, her gaze crying, *help!*

"We had an excellent time," he replied smoothly. "The weather was fine, the company charming, and the events of the day were entertaining."

Only a mischievous sparkle in his eye belied that, while everything he said was true, it was also terribly misleading.

In that second Meredith caught a glimpse

of him as a rascally young man, causing trouble and charming his way out of it. Such a vision was almost enough to make her smile. Almost.

"I don't suppose the day might also be described as raucous, scandalous, or violent," the duchess said dryly.

"Now that sounds like a picnic I might enjoy," Amelia said, grinning fiendishly.

Lady Claire dropped her pencil and looked to her brother, alarmed. Meredith fought the urge to do so as well.

Keep stitching. Keep stitching. Keep stitching.

"Duchess, what *are* you imagining?" James feigned shock.

"My sources informed me that you were spotted at some boxing match. Some low-brow fight, attended by thousands of the great unwashed."

Meredith concentrated very, very hard on her stitches, ensuring they were perfectly small, tight, and straight. Because she had a feeling that, in spite of James's charm and bluster, things were starting to unravel. What seemed to be innocent conversation was, with the duchess, an interrogation that would trap and doom them all.

"We were chaperoning Lady Claire with her suitor, Lord Fox," James replied. "The marquess invited us."

"You did say to encourage him, Your Grace," Claire added, her voice trailing off as the duchess, being brilliant and ruthless, shifted her focus to the one person in the room who could not lie to her.

"Miss Green, as my devoted companion, I am surprised that you would allow me to persist in believing a deliberate untruth."

"Uh-oh," Amelia said softly under her breath.

Bridget reached for a biscuit.

Meredith took a deep breath and summoned her courage. All of it, every last bit. There was no point in denying what was known and true.

"I do apologize, Your Grace. I seem to have forgotten myself."

She *was* sorry, she thought, as she resumed stabbing the fabric with her needle and thread. Sorry that they had to hide and mislead the duchess to assist Claire's courtship. Sorry that she had taken advantage of the opportunity to be near the duke. Sorry that her heart yearned for him so much that she even considered things that, until recently, were inconceivable. Meredith was sorry that she was torn between loyalty to the duchess and the desires of her heart.

She was sorry that the world made her choose.

But she was not sorry they had all gone.

"I told her I would take care of informing you about our plans," James cut in to protect her, just as much as he did yesterday in the crowd. "I apologize for being remiss in that. The good news is that Claire and that Fox fellow seem to have gotten along. Perhaps they might make a match, given more opportunities to spend time together, as they did yesterday."

"Um, maybe . . ." Claire said halfheartedly. Or maybe even 1/4-heartedly.

"If I had known courtship involved excursions to violent and raucous boxing matches, I might take it more seriously," Amelia said. "Really, Josie, you should have told me."

Only Lady Amelia could get away with calling the Duchess of Durham *Josie.*

"Josie" ignored her.

"Ah, so you are coming around to the idea of your sisters making matches and settling down in England?" The duchess arched her brows, more challenging than questioning. "Do you mean to encourage them? Lady Claire has Lord Fox, Lady Bridget has Mr. Wright. We'll just need to make arrangements for Lady Amelia, and soon they'll be settled and out of your hands."

Meredith watched James tense, then shift uneasily. His sisters stopped what they were doing and watched him carefully.

His sisters were the one point of leverage the duchess had with him, and Her Grace knew it. They all knew it.

"I want them to be happy," he said.

"And if it means chaperoning them to various outings with suitors?"

"Well, yes . . ."

"Except for my math lecture," Claire said pointedly. "You missed that."

"Let's not go too far," he replied. "It was the same day as the Exton races, and I couldn't very well miss that."

"But a boxing match . . ."

"The things a man does for his sisters."

This was punctuated with his usual sigh and eye roll heavenward. And yet . . . it felt as if they all knew that yesterday hadn't entirely been about Lady Claire's courtship. It had been an excuse for something else — whether it was time with her or merely an escape from the dukedom, Meredith knew not, but either way the duchess would disapprove.

"I must commend you, Duke, on a valiant attempt to convince me that yesterday's outing was nothing more than an unconventional excursion which both you and Miss Green were supervising. But it has not escaped my notice that you have been exchanging loaded glances with Miss Green all morning." The duchess paused. "Perhaps even longer."

The clock ticked loudly in the silence.

Lady Bridget stopped writing.

Lady Amelia closed her book.

Lady Claire looked up from her work.

Meredith's heart was pounding.

This. *This* is what she'd been afraid of. Discovery.

"Now, Duchess . . ." James drawled, attempting to charm her.

She would not be charmed.

The duchess silenced him with just one look: the one that conveyed what-kind-of-fool-do-you-take-me-for?-I-expected-better-than-this-from-you.

And as for the look she gave Meredith — well, a little corner of her heart might have turned black and withered away. The guilt. The anguish.

At this, Meredith accidentally stabbed her finger with the needle, drawing a tiny drop of red blood.

"I have decided that it's time for you, Duke, to visit one of your estates," the duchess said in a voice that would brook no disagreement. "We'll go to Durham Park first — it's a short drive from London, so we shan't miss too much of the season. We wouldn't want to miss out on *proper* courtship opportunities, now would we?"

"That sounds wonderful," Lady Amelia exclaimed. "I'm ready to go immediately."

"A trip to the country does sound lovely," Bridget mused.

"Shall I make arrangements for packing?" Meredith inquired.

"Please. And it will just be the duke and me."

"I think my sisters would like to see the country estate as well," James said.

"This is not about your sisters, Duke. It is about your duty. And how you have been distracted from it by" — the duchess paused and looked at Meredith — "London."

CHAPTER 10

A duke must take time to visit all of his properties. Visiting multiple vast estates around the country may prove to be a strenuous and lengthy endeavor for which many will feel no pity.
— THE RULES FOR DUKES

There were worse things, James supposed, than spending a few hours alone in an enclosed carriage with the duchess for a trip he had no wish to embark on. He spent the first portion of the journey listing them privately to himself: a trip to the dentist, bloodletting, enduring a mathematics lecture with Claire, being separated from Meredith . . .

She had stayed behind to supervise his sisters.

That was the polite excuse anyway.

It was understood that the duchess had seen them in a somewhat compromising position. Perhaps she had also witnessed that invisible, intangible, passionate something between them.

He shouldn't be kissing anyone the way he kissed her. It was one thing when Meredith told him not to — that, he could respect. It was all those rules and expectations forbidding them from being together that he found intolerable.

But he couldn't say he was surprised by it. Meredith had let him know that she wasn't suitable, and thus that the duchess wouldn't approve. Yet he hadn't quite been prepared for the extent of her disapproval. It radiated from her like rays from the sun on a cold day — bright, cold, relentless.

Even now, a few hours into a carriage ride.

"Well, it is nice to leave London at least," James remarked, finally done with his list of greater tortures and eager to thaw out the duchess. "I confess I do miss greenery. And open space. And fresh air."

"You will like Durham Park. The house is very fine, of course, but I suppose it is the grounds that you will find most enticing; there are many rolling hills and a forest thick with game. The stables are fine, too. I imagine that you might wish to spend the majority of your time at Durham Park, once things are settled."

"You mean my sisters are settled."

"And you. When you are all *properly* settled." There it was again — a pointed little reminder that she knew, or suspected, or at any rate disapproved that the one woman he fancied was not considered an acceptable candidate for the role of wife and future duchess. "We can always retire there when the season concludes."

"And when does that blessed event occur?"

"In midsummer."

"I shall count the days," James said dryly.

The duchess opened her mouth to say something and quickly thought the better of it. Was it a lecture on how *lucky* he was to have to suddenly assume more responsibility than he wanted? Or was it another lesson on how to succeed in society? Perhaps she even had a reason why he should prize the good opinion of the haute ton over true happiness with Meredith.

James braced himself. She ought to have a go at him now, when he was a captive audience. Instead, she pressed her lips in a firm line and looked out the window.

"C'mon now, Josie, what were you going to say?"

"You'll see, Duke." The duchess gave him a smile that made him nervous. "You'll see."

Durham Park

When the carriage turned in the drive, something clenched in James's chest. That tight squeeze in the region of his heart felt something like love. The land was beautiful with lush green fields dotted with grazing sheep, massive trees, all set against an endless blue sky. It reminded him of home, in America, and it made him wonder if his father had picked their land to settle on because it was so achingly familiar to this beautiful ancestral estate.

It made him wonder if perhaps he could be happy *here.*

The house was, as she described, very fine and imposing, and he wasn't too bothered with it. Not when he was so taken with the grounds.

As with his London arrival, the servants lined up to greet them. There were so many that James didn't have a prayer of learning their names or faces.

The butler, who, like the London butler seemed to be hundreds of years old, inquired if James would like to start with a tour of the house. The duchess answered before he could reply.

"I think the duke would prefer to tour the grounds and stables first, Rutherford," she said. "We should also like to pay a call upon the tenants this afternoon. Please, see that baskets are prepared for us to bring them. His Grace has been learning about the social aspects of his title, and today I should like to show him another side of this duke business."

The stables were what one might imagine for a duke — large, well-constructed, with every amenity for both man and beast. James whistled softly, reverently, under his breath as he strolled through the center aisle, looking into each stall as he went by. They were stocked with fine specimens of horseflesh for every purpose — great animals for racing, breeding, or merely riding around the estate. He could tell.

Lady Jemma was right that these stables were enviable. He would have to tell her about his visit. When he called on her. *If* he called on her.

James could imagine working with these magnificent creatures. *If* he stayed.

James could also imagine his father sneaking in here in the dead of the night, stealing away with Messenger, escaping with the horse all the way to America, where he used him to establish his own stables.

It was a story he'd heard a thousand times: a story of a moonlit night, of a young man determined to make his own way in the world. The whole plot threatening to go awry, thanks to grooms stirring awake — but thankfully drifting off to sleep. All that whiskey they'd drunk with his father earlier in the evening saw to that.

It was the story of a midnight ride, through this very countryside, with his father knowing, every step and hoofbeat of the way, that he could never, ever return.

James wondered, again, if his father would have returned to assume the title had he lived to inherit it. He wondered, too, how he was supposed to return to the place his father had fled and call it *home.*

A duke must become acquainted with his tenants, for it is their labors that support his livelihood. He will do well to keep this in the forefront of his heart and mind.
— THE RULES FOR DUKES

The afternoon was spent paying calls upon the tenants. James was happy for a ducal duty that didn't involve sitting behind a desk.

He and the duchess took an open carriage, filled with heavy baskets full of gifts and foodstuffs. The duchess didn't say much — which surprised him. He had come to expect rules and protocol to learn or instruction on what to say and how to stand.

Instead, she smiled and took in the scenery.

"It's beautiful, isn't it? This is where the duke and your father were raised. The main country seat is in Hampshire, but the family has always preferred this place."

"It is very picturesque," James agreed. But inside, he was awed by the beauty and taken with imagining his father here. How could he not have spoken of this more? There had been fleeting mentions — fishing in the lake, a rope swing in an old oak tree, that story about absconding with Messenger. Perhaps he'd have time on this visit to seek out all those places, and understand his father a little more — like why he left only to seek out a home that resembled this.

James turned his head and fixed his gaze on the scenery, as a way to dissuade the duchess from more conversation. He was afraid that if he were forced to speak, he would confess to the emotions bubbling up inside him: curiosity about this place, wanting to understand his father, wanting to understand why he now felt some connection with this land.

The carriage rolled to a stop in front of a small and quaint stone cottage, surrounded by some other small buildings, presumably other houses and accommodation for animals.

A man strolled forward to greet them — he could have been thirty or fifty. He could be James, in twenty years' time, if he kept up his life of tending to horses outside in the sun.

"This is Mr. Simons," the duchess said. "His family has been farming this land for four generations."

"We're hoping it'll be five, Your Graces."

With that, a small-ish boy with flaming red hair dashed over and lurked shyly behind his father.

"And who is this?" James asked.

"My son, John. He's just ten years old. My oldest." The boy wore plain, well-lived-in clothes that bore evidence of adventures and work. There was a smattering of freckles across his nose. "The missus and I have a few more."

"Sisters," the boy muttered. "A lot of bloody sisters."

"John! Mind your manners in front of the duke and duchess. I'm so sorry, Your Graces, but —"

But James only laughed.

"I have three sisters myself, so I feel your pain, young man. They're nothing but trouble and constantly plague a man. But it's a brother's job to tolerate them and look out for them."

The boy wore a skeptical expression. His father, one of thanks.

"We brought something for your family," the duchess said, motioning to the footman stationed with the carriage to bring one of the baskets over.

"Thank you, Your Graces," Mr. Simons said with an incline of his head. "The missus and I do appreciate it."

"If there is anything else we can do . . ." James said.

"There is one thing. Sprock, my neighbor, and I have been having some trouble with the drainage ditches in the north fields . . ."

A conversation on drainage ditches ensued, during which the duchess went inside to visit with Mrs. Simons. James had an inkling of the issue, having helped some neighbors back home with a similar problem, and promised to discuss it further with the estate manager and read up on it, if necessary. Marriage and addressing marquesses were problems he didn't care to bother with, but drainage ditches — now this was something he could handle.

Being a duke is not all soirees and games.
— THE RULES FOR DUKES

The scene was repeated with each family they visited. It was always a family that had been farming this land for three generations, or four, or five. There were young mouths to feed and more on the way. There were leaky roofs, sick cows, and fences in need of repair.

"These people need help," James said quietly to the duchess as they settled into the carriage to return to the house. "The estate manager has said nothing to me of any of this. I had no idea of any of it."

"They all need you," she said. "You see, James, being a duke isn't all about attending the right parties or idling away the hours at some club. Families like Simons, Sprock, and the rest rely on your careful management of the estate for their livelihood. Good people rely on the lord of the manor to help them flourish, and in return, they support our lives."

"I thought the estate manager took care of all this." James had a few meetings with the man, Spicer, in London, but he hadn't mentioned any of this. "Which begs the question of what he has been doing instead."

"An estate manager will do as much or as little as required. They will serve as directed, or they will not serve at all. But they will never care overmuch about families that have been intertwined and supporting each other for generations. That is why we need you."

It was one thing to be needed as a stud horse, to provide an heir for the dukedom, which, until this visit, was how James felt.

It was another matter entirely to know that good, honest, hardworking families relied on him for the management of the whole operation for their continued existence. He had to pay attention to their needs, and it was essential that he use his position to advocate and act on their behalf. It was also clear that real, honest lives would suffer if he left them at the mercy of this estate manager.

Fleeing was still an option, but now there was a real, human cost attached to it.

It also was clear now that a "quick jaunt" to the country and a tour of the stables were just an excuse.

This is what she really brought him to see: the real duties and responsibilities of a man of his position.

This was the *why* he'd been arrogantly asking about.

This is what she'd wanted to tell him in the carriage, but she had learned it was better for him to experience it than to listen to another lecture. She was right. Something about the plight of these families and the beauty of the land had hooked him.

He was *needed* — as more than just a show pony, but as a workhorse, too.

And the only way he'd see this was to experience it, fully, in the flesh — without Meredith nearby to distract him.

"I'm glad you understand," the duchess said.

James just shrugged, like an obnoxious youth. But the truth was, he was too choked up to speak. Because this path was calling to him now, appealing not to his vanity, but his sense of decency. And that was harder to deny — while still possessing a modicum of respect for himself.

Well played, Duchess, well played.

It is important that a duke be able to cultivate an imposing or even terrifying air.
— THE RULES FOR DUKES

The following morning
The duke's study at Durham Park was not unlike the one in London. With its soaring ceilings, tall bookcases, and large windows

and heavy furniture, it was designed to impress. Thus far, James was the one intimidated by it, and he hadn't yet appreciated how it could serve him by intimidating his caller.

Today he would see Spicer, the estate manager. The one who had apparently neglected to, oh, manage the estate.

James would have to question the man about things he didn't quite understand, demonstrate a sense of authority he didn't feel, and display a knowledge he didn't possess.

Hence, he chose as his setting the study that could make a grown man feel small. James started to appreciate it now, and started to make sense of these big, grand houses.

The butler announced Spicer, a short, balding man in a neatly pressed, though illfitting, suit of clothes.

"Thank you for taking the time to meet with me," James said, feeling that was far too polite and even deferential to a subordinate. It wasn't as if the man had a choice in the matter.

"Of course, Your Grace."

James took a seat behind the large, intricately engraved oak desk, then indicated that Spicer might sit on one of the chairs opposite.

Then he waited a moment before speaking. A long moment. It was a trick James had learned from his father, who would give a lengthy pause whenever James was in trouble and about to receive a lecture. That moment of silence was always more terrifying than anything he could possibly say.

"I had the pleasure of visiting with the tenants yesterday."

"A time-consuming endeavor, one a busy London man such as yourself needn't concern yourself with regularly."

"On the contrary, it was apparent that I do need to concern myself with it." James paused. "Regularly."

Spicer paled, slightly.

"Now that I am aware of your interest, Your Grace, I can provide you with regular reports."

"That would be excellent. I should like them weekly."

"Weekly?"

"What were you thinking?"

"Er, seasonally."

"I should like them weekly. Having visited with many of the families yesterday, I learned of many issues requiring more immediate attentions. A seasonal update will not suffice. Are you aware of the situation with the drainage ditch in the north fields?"

Spicer nodded, barely.

"Or the Joneses' fence. Or Mr. Thayer's roof."

"I'll see to them," Spicer said meekly, which was the only thing he could say, really.

"Thank you." James realized that was probably too soft. He imagined Meredith, whispering in his ear: *Take charge. Be confident. You know what to do. Fight for your tenants.* He cleared his throat and tried for something more confident, more authoritative, more ducal: "See that you do. I'll expect to see your plans to fix these things in next week's report."

"Will that be all, Your Grace? I should like to get started."

"The account books," James said. "I should like to take a look at them to familiarize myself with the running of things."

And to see what else you have been mismanaging.

In truth, James would have Claire look them over, since she had an eye for numbers and figures and that sort of thing. He could muddle through it in a day, but she'd comprehend it within the hour and actually enjoy the process.

Not that Spicer needed to know that. James gave him a firm stare.

"I'll have them sent to you in London," Spicer said.

There was an awkward moment where both men just sat there in another excruciating silence — until James realized it was up to him to bring the interview to a close.

"That will be all, Spicer."

"Good day, Your Grace." Spicer bowed, and shuffled out, and only when the door clicked shut behind him did James allow himself to deflate — and wonder how a man was supposed to act thusly *all the time*.

A duke ought to put the estate first, above all.

— THE RULES FOR DUKES

Later that afternoon
Having tackled some important estate work, James took advantage of an opportunity to make his way down to the stables.

In spite of the protests of the grooms, he saddled a horse himself — a spirited mare that one of the grooms, Peter, said had been cooped up too long. She reminded him of Artemis, one of the few horses he'd raised and couldn't bring himself to sell. He got a lump in his throat even now as he remembered saying goodbye to her.

Another groom, Henry, told him which

way to go: "Follow this dirt road down to the old barn, then cross over Sprock's field. You'll come across a thicket of trees and a nice, cold stream. After that, you can ride up the hill and get a bloody good view of the place."

James and the mare, Cleopatra, set off along the dirt road, quickly came across the old barn (the one needing the new roof), and at Sprock's field — a wide expanse of green fields, dotted with rabbits and a flock of sheep — he took a long look at the drainage ditch situation, which still didn't make much sense to him, and then urged the horse into a gallop.

Oh, damn, did she fly across the wide, open space.

Hooves thundering. Heart pounding.

This.

The wind in his hair. The blue sky above. The ground below. Lungs heaving.

This.

This was the feeling he'd been missing. The simple connection of man, beast, earth. Feeling his heart pounding, blood pumping, lungs heaving, all shouting at him that he was alive. Hearing the horse's hooves on the ground echoing the beat of his heart.

Perhaps the problem wasn't England or the dukedom, but the city . . .

He and the horse slowed at the thicket — a cluster of trees and bushes, home to warbling birds and buzzing with insects and teeming with small little critters. Back home, he would have known the names of all of them. Learning the names, purpose, and connection between these creatures was a task he would enjoy.

He and the horse stopped at the cold stream to drink water and rest in the shade.

It was quiet, compared to the city.

But it was country quiet, in that the air was loud and thick with the sound of nature: birds singing, bees buzzing, wind rustling through tree branches, water skipping over stones.

This.

He lay back on the earth, arm under his head, and stared up at the sky. The only way this could be better, he thought, was if Meredith were here to share it, lying on the earth beside him, her head on his shoulder, and staring up at the sky with him. He wanted to tell her about his interview with Spicer — both the moments he felt he'd blundered and the moments he felt he'd succeeded. James knew she would encourage and advise him. He knew he could ask her questions about the estate and the tenants and she would probably know all the answers.

And then he would kiss her.

Kissing her was why he was here. Alone.

Kissing her was why they were separated.

Because apparently he couldn't do this ducal business and be with her. He would have to choose.

Eventually he continued on his ride, up along the ridge with the "bloody good view" which gave him the sight of many of the tenants he and the duchess had visited yesterday.

Smoke rose lazily from chimneys, revealing all the work occurring within and without the houses. Women were cooking, cleaning, and minding babies they hoped would stay on this same land. James saw men outside, chopping firewood, feeding animals, repairing things. Somewhere down there was Spicer, working on his report, if he knew what was good for him.

All of it, right down to the horse he was sitting on, was due to their hard work — along with the clothes he wore, the roof over his head, and the dowries for his sisters, that would allow them to marry the man of their choice, and not wed for money. The fine food they ate, the wine they drank, the life they lived were all due to these people's labors.

Aye, James hadn't asked for any of it. But it was all his now not just to have, but to steward. And in return, the families had only asked for help with easily fixable things: ditches and roofs, medicines and foods. Things it was within his power to give.

Things he would be cruel to deny them, if he were to, say, leave everything to the various estate managers and return to raising horses in Maryland.

James settled deeper into the saddle, his thoughts circling the obvious conclusion but not wanting to land on it.

And then, a rustle in the bushes nearby spooked the mare. She darted off to the side, intent on running, but James quickly soothed her. He turned toward the bushes, where a boy emerged, his face and fingers stained from the berries he'd been snacking on.

"Hello there," James greeted him, recognizing Simons's son from the previous day.

"Your Grace." The boy bowed.

"Just call me James."

"My father says I must address you as Your Grace."

James did not want to be formally addressed by anyone, let alone a ten-year-old boy, eating berries fresh from the bush.

Which was probably his.

Which he probably shouldn't allow.

But which he most certainly *would* allow.

"Well, I guess you better do what he says then," James said with a shrug. Then, with a grin he added, "At least, when he's around."

"Are you going to stay, Your Grace?"

"We will return to London today."

They had parties to attend. This, he could not say aloud.

"No, I mean are you going to *stay*? My father says you can't escape being the duke, but my aunt read in the London papers that some people think you and your sisters will pack up and return to America. So, we're all wondering, are you going to stay?"

It was a good question, a fair question, and one with significance for many people, James now realized. More than just himself, and Meredith, and his sisters, or the duchess's ambitions to see the estate secure. These people's livelihoods depended on it.

Another good question: How do you lie to a ten-year-old boy with berry on his face?

Because until this moment, he'd assumed he would leave. The option to flee, just like his father before him, was always there, as an emergency escape route. It meant he had a choice in being here.

But after seeing the land, and meeting Simons, Sprock, Spicer, and this small, nervous-yet-hopeful boy, something had changed.

James's heart was heavy now. He knew what he had to do. He was torn and tugged between two directions. There was the selfish desire for his own pleasure, happiness, and freedom. He wanted nothing more than to take Meredith and his sisters back to Maryland and pretend this duke business never happened.

But there was a sense of duty that he couldn't quite shake. It tugged him here, to this land and these people. It tugged him away from his father because now he wondered how an upright and devoted family man like his father could leave all this behind. Then again, when his father had left, the duke and his new bride had been young, with every expectation of siring an heir and a spare. Things were certainly different now.

The boy stared up at him, expecting an answer.

James knew then it wasn't a sense of duty, obligation, or responsibility he was feeling.

It was compassion. It was a feeling of empathy in the face of struggle. And it was the knowledge that he alone was in a position to do something about it.

James nodded to the boy. And as he rode

away he thought once again, *well played, Duchess, well played.*

CHAPTER 11

A duke's most important task is siring an heir. To do that, he needs a suitable bride — one who is similarly titled, wealthy, and preferably with assets that will enhance the duke's own estates. Sharing mutual interests is merely a bonus.

— THE RULES FOR DUKES

Upon his return to London, James paid a call upon Lady Jemma Winston, the only proper and suitable woman he'd met whom he could tolerate. The trip to Durham Park made him realize that he could not leave the dukedom. He still had no interest in the flashy, fancy, London-based aspect of being a duke. But the land and the people tugged at his sense of decency, integrity, and responsibility. He could not turn his back on them.

Unfortunately, this meant that whatever he felt for Meredith — and he felt oceans and oceans of feelings for her — had to be pushed aside. This is what she'd been trying to tell him.

He had a duty.

He had to at least *try*.

And so, he would call upon Lady Jemma.

His valet, Edwards, was thrilled to dress him up for the occasion, taking extra care with every aspect of the process. The man went through four lengths of starched fabric before his cravat was deemed perfect enough to be viewed by the eyes of the potential future Duchess of Durham.

James also reckoned flowers were in order. Women loved flowers, he'd been told.

"Just a small token of a bouquet. Nothing serious," he requested. He could not bring himself to care enough to pick them out himself. "And make sure they don't communicate any secret message about feelings or intentions."

He was glad Meredith had warned him.

James was immensely relieved for all the instruction she had given him, when he finally strolled up to the Winston residence on Berkeley Square and into the drawing room of their home. Knowing a little of what to expect — and what was expected of him — was the only thing steadying his nerves.

That, and the thought of that boy with berry on his face, worried about his family's future all because of James.

"Your Grace. We are delighted to see you. How good of you to call," Lady Jemma said as she greeted him. She flashed him that charming smile with her slightly crooked tooth as he handed the bouquet of flowers to her — which she promptly passed along to a servant.

"It is a pleasure to see you again," he said, bowing.

"What has kept you occupied ever since the musicale?" she asked, resuming her place on the settee. He took a seat nearby and declined her mother's offer for tea.

"You might be interested to know that I have visited the stables at Durham Park."

Her eyes lit up. Her mother groaned and said, "Oh, Lady Jemma doesn't care to discuss stables, Your Grace."

"Yes, she does," Lady Jemma replied, smiling at him and utterly ignoring her mother. "And we all know it. Tell me, what did you think? How did it compare to your stables in Maryland?"

An animated conversation ensued. James actually enjoyed it, and even expressed genuine interest at her invitation to visit their stables at their estate in Kent. James

241

nodded, as if he knew where that was.

Lady Winston looked increasingly distressed as her daughter and the duke spoke of such unglamorous topics as horses, stable design, and training methods. That is, until it dawned upon her that rather than her daughter boring the duke, she was engaging and holding his attentions. And then, oh then, did Lady Winston smile. The sort of plotting, machinating smile that made a man fearful for his freedom.

Frankly, it made him nervous, as if he'd unwittingly walked into a trap. But it was merely a polite social call, during their calling hours, and he'd brought only a paltry bouquet that he was assured communicated nothing more than *I recognize that you are alive in the world.*

The whole visit was nothing more than that. Never mind those cunning smiles from mother and daughter alike.

Wasn't it?

A duke's courtship is breaking news and will be reported and widely discussed.
— THE RULES FOR DUKES

The next day
It was not. At least, not according to the newspapers which his sisters had apparently

taken to reading, as he learned the next day when Bridget burst into his study, with Amelia in tow.

"Dear brother, you didn't tell us you were courting someone," Bridget declared, waving a news sheet in the air.

"I cannot believe your own, dearly beloved sisters had to find out like anyone else. In the gossip rags," Amelia added. "I am shocked."

"I am hurt." Bridget pouted.

"My feelings are wounded," Amelia said.

"This is not about either of you," he said, which, of course, was completely insignificant. If anything, that only made it more interesting to them. "In fact, I don't even know what you are talking about."

"Read this." Bridget thrust the news sheet in his face. He swatted at the thing, then grabbed it, then read it.

Lady Winston is telling anyone who will listen that the Duke of Durham has taken a particular interest in her otherwise on-the-shelf daughter, Lady Jemma. It seems like these two horse-mad people might have found their perfect match.

Oh, dear God. James grimaced. *Horse-mad people?* Really?

But more urgently, what would Meredith think or feel when she saw this? He had not yet reconciled his desire for her with his newfound sense of duty to the estate. He wasn't even sure they could be reconciled, but he knew he at least had to try at this duke business. Still, his heart ached for her and for them, and he wasn't sure what to do or say when he faced her next. Suffice it to say, this was not how he wanted her to find out.

"What does this mean for Meredith?" Bridget asked bluntly. For a second, James was taken aback. He hadn't realized anyone had known about them. One thing that was clear: this was not a topic of conversation for him and his sisters.

So, he replied evasively: "What do you mean what does this mean?"

"We all see you gazing longingly at each other across the breakfast tables, the drawing room, et cetera, et cetera," Bridget said. "Don't be surprised that anyone noticed."

"You mean *everyone,*" Amelia added.

"I should think you have more important things to pay attention to than whatever or whomever catches my eye in any given room in this house. Or otherwise."

"Dear brother, what could be more important than your romantic happiness?" Amelia mused.

"If I felt that you were actually concerned

about it, I might be moved."

"I could be actually concerned," Amelia said. "Something to do, I guess."

"I am beside myself with concern for the state of your heart," Bridget said. "If you could just tell us everything, it would help tremendously. I fear I'm getting worry lines and we can't have that."

Sisters.

Dear God, sisters.

They were relentless and impossible. And exhausting and frustrating. And tenacious.

And he would do anything for them.

Except explain that he was confronted with denying his love for Meredith, potentially breaking her heart, and marrying a fellow *horse-mad person* just so his sisters could be happy and have no scandal or constraints when it came time for them to wed whomever they wished.

And as he looked at his little sisters — somehow, all grown up and now ladylike, but still as spirited (and annoying) as ever — he knew what he had to do. Bridget and Amelia had their mother's eyes and mouth, and to look at them now reminded him how he promised their parents he would always, *always* watch out for them and fiercely protect them.

He knew.

He knew what he had to do.

He'd known all along, he supposed.

But that didn't mean he was ready to declare his intentions to his plague of sisters.

"This is all none of your business," he said, trying out his new Ducal Voice.

"Your point being . . . ?" Bridget inquired.

"I don't see what that has to do with anything," Amelia said flatly.

Very well, new Ducal Voice needed work. Or a more obliging audience.

"Can't you see that I'm trying here?" James asked, now annoyed.

He was met with two blank stares.

"Trying to, er, be ducal," he explained.

"Ah. I see, Your Grace." Amelia swept into one of her ridiculously elaborate curtsies with all sorts of hand flourishes and swishes of her dress.

"Don't do that," he said. "Don't call me Your Grace or curtsy or any of that."

"But now you are acting ducal," Bridget said. "You are courting a suitable woman. But you really fancy Meredith. Who for whatever reason is not suitable. At least, not according to the duchess."

"I think she's lovely. I'd love to have her for a sister," Amelia remarked.

"Which only makes everything more tragical," Bridget sighed.

"I don't think that's a word," James said.

"Shakespeare made up words," she replied.

"You and Shakespeare. I get your writings confused *all the time,*" Amelia retorted. Bridget snatched the newspaper from James and swatted her sister with it.

"If you'll excuse me, I have important estate matters to attend to," he said, trying again with this Lofty Duke Voice. To reinforce his point, he opened the account book on his desk and made a point of studying it intently.

"What is that? An account book?" Bridget asked.

"Yes. From Durham Park."

"Would you like us to send in Claire to have a look at it?" Amelia offered.

James scowled and grumbled his response of "Yes."

And with that, they finally took their leave, apparently having accomplished what they had come to do. He was alone with a boring account book and his newly awakened sense of duty.

A few days later
When another letter from Hampshire arrived, Meredith hesitated in picking it up from the silver salver Pendleton offered to

her. She was never quite sure what she wanted the news to contain, and that made her feel like a wretched daughter and heartless human.

She has been asking for you, Mrs. Bates wrote in her sharp, slanting script. *On her good days, anyway. She has had just three this month.*

Her mother hardly remembered her.

It didn't matter whether she was there with her in Hampshire or London. Something had happened to her mother's mind that she forgot her own flesh and blood. Imagine that — to be forgotten by one's own mother. What prayer did she have to be remembered by anyone else then?

I fear the worst may be near, Mrs. Bates wrote.

But she was wrong. The worst was already here — this endless suspension between living and death. Being forgotten by one's own mother except for a few days or mere hours, here and there, which Meredith may or may not be present for, hardly seemed something to be happy about.

She was sitting by the window in the library, the letter in hand, trying to sort through all her conflicting feelings when James strolled into his library, in his house.

Her heart did a little pitter-patter thing.

He was the last person she wanted to see now, and yet, he was the only person she wanted to see. The trip to Durham Park had changed him — he was finally becoming more . . . ducal. He'd even called on Lady Jemma, which Meredith learned about from servants' gossip and read about in the newspapers.

"Meredith. My apologies if I am interrupting. I didn't realize you were here."

"You're not interrupting. Don't mind me." She turned back to look out the window at the garden, but was still aware that he crossed the room to sit beside her.

Don't look. Don't look. Don't look.

"What has you so melancholy?"

"Oh, nothing."

She could not share this with him. Not now. Her conflicted feelings about her mother's illness were something she'd never confided to anyone. The last thing she needed now was to share more intimacy with James. A distance was growing between them; she ought to respect it.

"Nothing? I don't suppose that has anything to do with your mood." He gestured to the paper, once folded and now crumpled, in her hands. When she finally stood, she would burn it. But until then, she would read it a few more times, just in case she'd missed a glimmer of good news.

"It's just a letter. From my mother. Or rather, about my mother."

"How is Mrs. Green?"

"She is not well."

"I'm sorry."

Meredith shrugged, as if to say, *me, too.* And she was sorry, but she'd long ago accepted that what afflicted her mother was not her fault. There was nothing she could do, other than watch. And wait. And not give the duchess cause to withdraw the funds that paid for her mother's care. And not give cause for the duchess to send Meredith away because once her mother was gone, she would have no one.

"There is nothing to do, other than ensure she is comfortable."

"If you wish to visit her, arrangements can certainly be made. I'll accompany you. I can keep you safe from rogues, scoundrels, and highwaymen on the journey. I shall endeavor to be a comfort to you while we are there."

Meredith knew it was not a hollow offer — he truly would drop all his responsibilities here to go with her. They would stay the night at that inn in Southampton on the way . . . This only made her heart ache more.

"Thank you, but it's all right. I was just with her recently."

"I suppose this is your family in Hampshire you were just visiting, on a trip that took you through Southampton."

"How observant of you." She smiled, a little. Because he noticed her and listened to her and remembered. It was wonderful, if a little bittersweet.

"Only when it comes to you."

His blue eyes were doing that thing they did — gaze at her with a loving sparkle, like he was the luckiest man in the world just to be able to look at her.

She smiled, halfheartedly, because it hurt too much to smile all the way.

"See — and now you're smiling. I think you might need me, Meredith, for whenever you are feeling melancholy."

Truth be told, she thought she might need him, too.

As long as her mother was alive, in this wretched state, both she and Meredith were dependent upon the duchess's largess. It was her support and duty to her former lady's maid that kept her mother in comfort and dignity, instead of in a madhouse. It meant Meredith had a home. It also meant that the burden of caring for her mother was lifted from her shoulders. It was as much a relief now as it had been when she was just twelve and the duchess swooped in to take care of the situation.

"The duchess ensures that my mother is well cared for."

"How noble of her."

"You may only see her determination to see you all married against your wishes, or to see that the estate succeeds. But she is tremendously kindhearted and dedicated to the people in her life."

"I am beginning to see that," he said softly. "I saw it when we visited Durham Park."

"I am forever indebted to her, James, for the care she has shown my mother and me. Especially when no one would have faulted her for turning us out, or discreetly providing some necessary funds. Instead, she has taken me in and raised me as a daughter."

He didn't say anything, but she could see that he was adding everything up in his brain. He was beginning to understand. But Meredith needed to make sure he understood completely that she was sorry for tempting him and would be keeping her distance from now on.

"I forgot, for a moment there . . ." That moment being when they kissed. "But this letter has reminded me. So if I am melancholy, it is because I regret that kiss. And that we were seen. And that she has cause to question my loyalty."

He had his duty and she had hers.

CHAPTER 12

A duke MUST have a legitimate heir, preferably one with some sense and decency.

— THE RULES FOR DUKES

For all of the duchess's talk about the necessity of James siring an heir, it so happened that James already had one — some distant cousin, from a remote country village, in some nearby shire. One Mr. Collins.

They were at breakfast when James learned he would be visiting — a particularly torturous breakfast in which Meredith would not look at him, not that he could blame her after their painful encounter the previous day.

"Tonight we shall dine at home as a family before attending Lady Belmont's ball, as we will have a very important guest with us," the duchess announced from her place at the head of the table.

"Don't keep us in suspense, Josie," James drawled from the other end.

She scowled, as she always did when they addressed her as Josie. But she had at least stopped correcting them.

"It is your heir, Your Grace."

"My heir?"

Bridget giggled at his alarm, but it wasn't funny at all. How he'd managed to sire an heir was beyond him.

Because if he already had a bloody heir then why . . .

James glanced again at Meredith. She was very focused upon sipping her tea.

"Your cousin, Mr. Peter Collins. It's very important that you meet him and perhaps take him under your wing." The duchess took a sip of her tea and said, very pointedly, "Just in case something should happen to you."

"Is my life in danger?" James inquired. "Did this duke business just get life threatening and thus, interesting?"

"I most certainly hope not," the duchess said passionately.

"If we are dining as a family, will Miss Green be joining us?" Amelia asked, innocently enough.

James tensed. He knew his little sister probably had some notion of matchmaking.

He also knew his little sister had no idea the extent of what existed between him and Meredith — or what didn't. Not anymore.

He dared a glance at her; she was diligently avoiding his gaze. Still. He shifted uncomfortably in his chair.

"She may join for a portion of the evening," Her Grace said.

"Not the entire evening?" Bridget inquired.

"It is not customary that a woman of her position would join for the duration of the meal."

"But our guest is hardly of a lofty position himself. A village vicar you said?" Amelia challenged.

She *meant* well. But Amelia's sudden interest in whatever she was trying to accomplish was only making things worse. Meredith had given up trying to sip her tea and was staring intently at an invisible spot on the tablecloth.

"Ah, and what is this sudden interest in the hierarchy of British society?" the duchess inquired.

"I'm interested in including Miss Green. Besides, if we have to suffer through dinner with Mr. Collins, why should she get out of it?"

"There must be some perks to my position," Meredith remarked pleasantly enough, but James winced.

"Who says dinner with Mr. Collins will be something to suffer through?" Claire asked.

At that, both Meredith and the duchess sipped their tea and chose not to comment.

"Ah. I see," Claire replied.

"Mr. Collins is, shall we say, provincial in his attitudes," the duchess said.

"How I look forward to making his acquaintance," James said dryly.

"You shall see why I wish you would put another heir in place," the duchess replied. And why she'd gone through all the bother of tracking down the long-lost American duke.

That evening

They'd hardly completed the first course when James saw exactly why the duchess was so keen for him to wed and sire an heir *and* a spare. Upon meeting Mr. Collins, it became quite clear that any wishes for James's continued good health may have had as much to do with an affection for him as despair at the prospect of Mr. Collins inheriting Durham.

"It is such a great pleasure to meet my esteemed cousins who have journeyed from such a faraway land," he declared.

"Are we cousins?" Amelia inquired.

"Actually, I consulted *Debrett's,*" Bridget said and the duchess beamed. "And we are more like second cousins."

"Then I use the term affectionately," Mr. Collins said grandly.

"I think it's fortunate that you are all not so closely related," the duchess said. "A match between you, Mr. Collins, and one of the sisters is quite possible."

Three Cavendish sisters shot her looks of horror.

It was almost funny.

Almost. But James's hands balled into fists as he watched Mr. Collins obviously appraise each of his sisters in turn. His watery-eyed gaze ogled Amelia, flitted over Claire, and lingered on Bridget.

It was only the duchess's sharp, reproving look that stopped James from an act of intimidation and possibly violence.

"A splendid prospect," Mr. Collins said.

Claire paled and Amelia burst out laughing. Right in his face.

"We would want to keep the dukedom in the family," the duchess said in response to the girls' looks.

"I'm still here," James drawled from where he sat at the head of the table. The duchess smiled like a queen.

"Is this the good silver or the everyday silver?" Mr. Collins inquired, selecting a fork and holding it up to the light of the chandelier.

"Only the best for the duke and his heir," the duchess replied. She gave a tight smile.

James wanted to stab the man with his fork. The good silver fork.

Because he couldn't leave the tenants of Durham Park or any of his estates, plural, at the mercy of this peon who cared about which silver they were using. He couldn't let the duchess match one of his sisters up with this revolting man.

But that meant he had to accept the rules and expectations of his station, which is why he was not supposed to think longingly of Meredith, somewhere in this great big house, dining alone.

"Lady Bridget, I understand you are on a regimen of self-improvement," Mr. Collins said.

"Why and how have you come to understand that?" Bridget asked.

"I have been speaking with Lady Amelia about all of your lessons. I think it's so important for a lady to strive to better herself and to become accomplished in the ladylike arts."

"And which ones do you think are more

important?" Bridget asked. "Needlework? The pianoforte? Simpering?"

"Smiling demurely at idiotic comments?" Claire asked innocently.

James's lips twitched into something like a smile. Sisters. Sometimes their fiendishness was just the thing.

"Well, a woman's duty is to support a man in all things and be a respite at home for a gentleman made weary from his dealings with the greater world," Mr. Collins replied.

"How fortunate for you," Claire said flatly. "And gentlemen everywhere."

"Indeed. It's only fitting, as men are the stronger and more intelligent sex."

"Is that so?" Claire inquired coolly. She gripped her fork tightly and, if James knew his sister, she was probably contemplating violence and doing the man an injury with it.

James couldn't say that he would stop her.

Mr. Collins then changed the subject to quiz James on the status of the various estates — intimating that it was very much his business to ensure that the dukedom was being managed correctly since he stood to inherit it.

In truth, James struggled to answer many of the questions — how much wool was produced here, how much grain was grown there, the condition of the various houses, the placement of paintings and other precious family artifacts, et cetera, et cetera.

To his credit, it was a lot for one man to have learned, in only a few short weeks largely spent learning how to survive in society. Perhaps if he hadn't spent so much time lusting and longing after Meredith . . .

But the more this provincial Mr. Collins questioned him, the more irritated James became. He did not have to answer to this man who quizzed him upon things that were not, in fact, his business. He did not have to answer to this man for anything.

I am the duke.

The thought came unbidden, from some hidden depths of his soul that he'd not yet explored. It was a shock to him to find himself so possessive over the title. It was another moment, one after another, that shocked him with his increasing sense of duty and determination to serve the title and all the people who came with it.

Mr. Collins would think only of the things — the houses and the horses, the good silver and the servants. And in doing so, he would wreck lives, to say nothing of the estates.

The truth was plain, if heartbreaking: he couldn't be the man he wanted or needed to be if he up and ran off with Meredith, or if he even allowed any intimacy between them at all.

Later that evening

While James and Mr. Collins took brandy together in the dining room after supper, Meredith joined the ladies for tea in the drawing room. All the Cavendish sisters could discuss was how boorish and horrible they found their "cousin."

"You had better hope your brother weds soon," the duchess said, pausing in lifting her teacup to her lips. "It would be dreadful if your fates should rely upon the charity of Mr. Collins. No, the only way to assure your security is to marry or for James to wed and sire an heir. Or for one of you to wed Mr. Collins."

Something clenched around Meredith's heart. The pressure for James to wed would only increase — perhaps it would even come from his sisters. Soon, soon she would lose absolutely any chance with him.

Not that she had much of one.

The words of *The London Weekly*'s gossip column from a few days earlier were burned into her memory and, even worse, had made a probably permanent, painful impression on her heart.

Lady Winston is telling anyone who will

listen that the Duke of Durham has taken a particular interest in her otherwise on-the-shelf daughter, Lady Jemma. It seems like these two horse-mad people might have found their perfect match.

Meredith was no fool; she knew what was happening. James was finally embracing the dukedom, and was finally stepping up to do his duty. It meant leaving her behind in favor of a suitable match. And he'd found someone!

It wasn't just the item in the newspaper, either, now that she thought about it. He had changed since he returned from his brief trip to Durham Park. She noticed the difference the minute he had alighted from the carriage. His bearing was different: his gaze more focused, his shoulders more square.

"Ah, and here is His Grace and Mr. Collins now," the duchess said as the gentlemen rejoined the ladies.

"What have we missed?" James asked.

"We were just discussing our dear 'cousin,' " Amelia said with a grim smile.

"All good things, I hope!" Mr. Collins said nervously.

Three Cavendish sisters merely sipped their tea and smiled tightly.

"Of course, Mr. Collins," the duchess

murmured.

Meredith stole a glance at James. His mouth was pressed in a firm line.

She touched her fingers to her own lips, remembering the taste of him, the weight of his body against hers, the sound of his breath catching, the way he looked in the shadows. Most of all she remembered how they felt *so right* together.

Connections like that didn't just come along every day — or night. Meredith's brain spun, considering all the things that had to transpire for them to find one another, to find that connection: his father fleeing England and raising his son in America so that he might be brought up without such a strict view of class that would allow him to actually notice her. The miracle of the duchess taking in a common girl and raising her in the ducal household. The journeys they had taken that led them to that one night in Southampton.

And then, and only then, all it took was a glance across a room and a smile for that something between them to spark to life.

She glanced at him now, expecting to find him looking at her and expecting to catch his eye. But his attentions were elsewhere.

As the family chattered away, the hour grew late, and Meredith's heart grew heavy because suddenly something had changed in James.

He would not look at her.

There were no secret smiles or smoldering glances to let her know that he still felt something for her. She felt cold in their absence.

The minutes ticked by, and still, he would not look at her.

She didn't realize how much she'd come to expect and savor those smoldering glances.

Meredith knew what was happening: the dukedom was getting to him. Soon he would wed, he would have a wife and children and an estate to manage. In time she would be nothing more than just a girl he'd shared a bed with one night.

Her heart rebelled at the thought of being so *inconsequential* to him.

If she had a chance at real love with him, she would have to seize it soon. Was she just going to let it go, or was she going to do something?

As the family conversed about parties she hadn't attended, comments she had missed from dinner, or things that generally did not concern a woman of her position, Meredith sipped her tea and nursed feelings of acute loneliness.

It made her heart ache.

It made her desperate.

Finally, Mr. Collins took his leave and the family members drifted off to their bed-chambers. Meredith was too restless to sleep, especially when she noticed a light in the duke's study.

She should not go to him.

Under no circumstances should she seek him out. Not when the sky was dark, the hour late, and her heart in turmoil.

But . . . They had found each other after a series of incredible events, and then he had kissed her with all the heat and longing she felt, too. That something between them hadn't gone away, no matter how they had tried.

She wouldn't let it go away.

Meredith knocked on the door and stepped into the study.

When James looked up and saw her, he said her name. "Meredith."

She couldn't quite read his expression. Was he shocked to see her, or nervous? Whatever it was, she didn't see that slow, seductive smile or the sparkle in his eye that she had come to expect. Her pulse started to race, with panic, not passion. "What brings you here?"

"I saw the light . . ."

He lifted one brow as if to say, *and*?

And then she didn't know what to say.

This was a mistake. She should not have come here, like a lovesick girl. She should never have kissed him or even spoken to him that night in Southampton.

But she had done all those things, and somehow her heart had become involved. Now it was bursting with fears and feelings. So here she was, speechless in his study, after midnight, trying to decide where to begin. She needed to explain herself.

"I don't know anything about horses," Meredith blurted out.

"Do you need to?"

"Lady Jemma does."

"Ah. I see."

Comprehension dawned. The man had three sisters. Of course he understood that she was in the throes of jealousy, and in a comparison between herself and another woman, she came up wanting.

"I don't have the connections, or birthright, and I don't know anything about horses or America. But I know you. I know what it feels like when we kiss. When we are together. I haven't forgotten that night, James. I think about it all the time."

"Meredith . . ." His voice was sad. Or was that pity? She couldn't stand if it were pity.

Or sadness. Neither of those boded well for her. For them.

"I know, I shouldn't speak of this. But I cannot help myself. My self-restraint is failing me."

"Why are you saying this? Why are you saying this *now*?"

Because I am losing you.

Because I am losing my surest chance at love and happiness.

"I read the newspapers about you and Lady Jemma," she said. He frowned. "I noticed that you've changed since your trip to Durham Park. This — all this — is changing you. I see it happening. I see you slipping away. And tonight . . . tonight you wouldn't look at me. You're the only one who has ever really seen me, James, and tonight you wouldn't even look at me."

"Meredith, don't." He looked away.

"I'm sorry," she whispered.

"You told me to try to fulfill the duties of my position. To do my duty."

"I know."

He stood abruptly, and in one stride he stood before her, making her feel petite and vulnerable, which made her want to throw herself into his arms even more.

"You told me we could never be together," he growled, gripping her shoulders. "Not in any real way. Not in the honorable, dignified way that I want to be with you every day and every night."

"I know," she cried, anguished. But she had more to say, driven by the panic that she was losing him. "That's still true. But, James, don't we feel so right together? Don't answer, I know you know it, too. What I feel for you, James, it consumes me. It makes me break the rules, throw caution to the wind, risk everything. Because the reward — your love — is worth it. I guess what I am trying to say is pick me, James. Be true to you, and to us, and to hell with what anyone says. We can run away together. We can be happy. If you just pick me."

There was a long, aching silence in which she had laid herself bare, and he released his grip on her and said nothing.

Nothing.

And she knew.

He didn't have to say a word for her heart to break. Because she knew duty, or the duchess, or the dukedom had gotten to him. One or all of them had wormed their way into his head and his heart and there was no more space for her.

If he would only just *look* at her, she might see the sadness and desire for her still in his eyes. Maybe. But he couldn't or wouldn't look at her.

And so, she knew.

This was ending now and it was not going to end well.

James took another small step close to her, close enough to kiss her. But instead of his mouth claiming hers, he spoke in a low voice right into her ear. These were words for her alone to hear.

"I don't want to hurt you, Meredith. Believe me when I say it is the last thing I want to do. If I were being selfish and thinking only of myself I would be kissing you now instead of saying these words. These impossible, sad words that hurt me as much as they hurt you. But I can't be selfish anymore. I cannot think only of myself. Please, believe me when I say my heart is breaking. Because Meredith, we can't be together."

He was close enough to kiss.

He was so close that she could feel the warmth from his body.

He was so close and he murmured these devastating things.

And then he took one step back, then another. The cold rushed in, and the distance between them grew.

James looked at her then. His blue eyes

bright with tears that she knew would never fall.

"I'm so sorry, Meredith."

And he did sound so very sorry. Somehow this failed to console her.

"I was wrong," she said, her voice small and broken. "So wrong. One kiss can hurt."

He just nodded — in agreement. At another time this might have outraged her. In this moment, it was the last little tap of the hammer that sent her heart shattering.

James took another step back and then, with one last look over his shoulder at her, quit the room.

Meredith stood there, shaking, as she listened to his footsteps cross the foyer and up the stairs to the master bedroom.

It was over. Whatever it was, it was over.

She blew out the lone candle on the desk, and darkness enveloped her, a girl who had finally been seen and noticed but still left behind.

CHAPTER 13

Just as a duke must remember his place, so should everyone else in His Grace's household.

— THE RULES FOR DUKES

The house was quiet that evening as Meredith stayed home while the family went to Almack's.

She'd never been so aware of her place before — not quite a servant and not quite a lady. The gratitude she'd previously felt for the advantages of her position had recently given way to a feeling of being nothing more than an ornamental knick-knack on the mantelpiece. These days, she felt like one that continually needed to be put back in its place after the maid moved it for dusting.

Meredith wasn't sure she wanted to be put back, just so. Perhaps she wanted to jump off the mantel, off the shelf, and venture out into the world. Perhaps she wanted more than occupying this middle space, to serve her own ambitions rather than the duchess's.

All this pressure to wed put on the Cavendish siblings was starting to get under her skin. It made her aware that a wedding of her own was unlikely to be in her future — not to James, not to anyone. Her duty was to the duchess.

Now. Forever. Always.

In spite of recent attempts otherwise. Meredith couldn't explain *why*, but there was no denying that at certain moments it became too much to bear, and James was . . . there. Ready to catch her as she flung herself off the shelf and into the world.

But then she would recover her composure and purpose and endeavor to carry on. It had been mortifying to have to face James after she had thrown herself at him, like a lovesick and desperate girl. It was the pity in his eyes that really burned.

Devastation, heartbreak, and embarrassment set in, leaving her hot and irritable from morning through the night. She could not bear to face him, but avoiding him was a challenge.

He was there at the breakfast table.

She was aware of him, busy in his study

as he tackled the business of being a duke — there were account books to manage, correspondence to tend to, meetings with estate managers and other peers of the realm about matters of parliament. This so-called simple horse farmer tackled it all.

She overheard things — like that he was paying yet another call to Lady Jemma. The newspapers reported that they were seen riding together in Hyde Park, attending a horse race, or waltzing more than once at a ball.

I taught him that.

Meredith was *glad* she hadn't joined the family at Almack's. It would have been *torture* to stand on the sidelines with the duchess and all the other old matrons, while watching James dance with Lady Jemma and all the other proper young ladies.

No, she did not need to witness that.

She was *happy* to have spent the evening quietly at home in the drawing room, reading silly novels — the ones that gave her ideas and dared her to dream and ultimately led to this wretched state of heartache.

When Meredith heard the family arrive home, she rose and stood near the slightly open doors of the drawing room, and peeked through to the scene unfolding in the foyer.

The family was in a mood unlike she'd ever seen. Usually they were all in good spirits, if fatigued, upon returning from a ball. But tonight the air was thick with tension and their faces wore grim expressions. Something momentous and terrible must have occurred.

She waited, listened, and did her best to gauge the mood and see how to be of service.

"Well Amelia, I hope you enjoyed yourself this evening," the duchess said crisply while she handed her satin cape and gloves to Pendleton. Meredith recognized the voice; Her Grace was most displeased.

"Immensely." Amelia's voice was thick with sarcasm.

What had she done? What had happened?

"You needn't take such a tone," the duchess said sharply.

"Of course," Amelia said wearily. "Sarcasm and taking such a tone are unbecoming of a lady. I'm so bloody bored of being a lady. And don't tell me ladies don't say words like *bloody* because I am well aware."

Bored of being a lady . . . Meredith knew the feeling.

"Then why must you persist in using such indelicate phrases?"

"Because I must have something to amuse

me. When I am so bloody bored. All the bloody time. Sorry, Duchess, but husband hunting is not my preferred sport."

"Amelia . . ." Lady Claire started.

"Oh, don't *Amelia* me," she said, stomping up the stairs. "Not tonight. I am in no mood for more lectures on how exactly to smile, or the precise tone of my voice or whatever other stupid rules I happen to break because I am some ignorant and uncivilized girl. I won't bend over backward trying to please people who are determined to laugh at me anyway."

"They aren't . . ." Lady Bridget's voice trailed off in her halfhearted defense of the ton. "You don't have to make it so easy for them to laugh. Or hard for me to succeed. And you don't have to be so childish, either, Amelia."

"Expecting that you not divest your foot-wear at a formal ball is not an outlandish request," the duchess said dryly. Meredith wondered: *What the devil had that girl done now?!* And then, echoing the sentiments of the ton, she added, "At least, not in England."

"You are lucky it was just my shoes, when I'd really like to remove this blasted corset, douse it in brandy, and set it afire," Amelia muttered.

"Just don't use the good brandy," James said dryly.

"You're not helping," Claire, Bridget, and the duchess snapped at him in unison, as Meredith also whispered the words under her breath.

Meredith could see, through the crack in the door, that Amelia was halfway up the stairs, on her way to at least removing the offending garment.

"Between her language and the shoes, everyone will think you were raised in the stables," the duchess lamented.

"To be fair, we practically were," James remarked from where he leaned idly against the wall.

"And everyone already thinks so," Lady Bridget muttered.

"Please, do not remind me of that fact," the duchess said, closing her eyes. "I am trying very hard to forget it and very, *very* hard to ensure that the rest of the ton forgets it as well."

"You could always send me back if I'm such an embarrassment to you all," Amelia challenged.

"Amelia, we agreed . . ." Lady Claire started. "And you did say you wanted to see more of the world. Think of this as an adventure. A chance to explore."

"I do want to see *the world*," Lady Amelia said. "Not every drawing room and ball-room in London. I mean, honestly, how much damask wallpaper, gold-framed por-traits of dead aristocrats, and fancy tea sets does one girl need to see?" Her voice was rising now, trembling a little. "I want *more*," she said.

I want more.

Amelia's words echoed in the vast marble foyer. The force of them went straight to Meredith's heart. *Me. Too.*

I want more.

That was the feeling she'd been feeling. That was the hot, irritable sensation — it was that of always wanting, and feeling trapped; always denying or being denied.

She'd felt it that night in Southampton.

She had wanted more than a steady pulse and a perfect reputation. She wanted pas-sion. That night she had wanted it so much that she couldn't deny it. With a man like James to indulge with, why would she?

She felt it every day that she woke up under the same roof as James — but not in his bed. Always, always wanting more than they could give.

And she suspected that not even Just James could satisfy this relentless, driving need for more. Because it was a desire for more than just a man; she wanted more for her life than to be in the duchess's shadow.

Meredith wanted to step into the light and be seen. For herself.

Lady Amelia was ranting now, clearly having reached the end of her tether, and the family stood by.

She ranted about the injustice of a woman being deemed hysterical for wanting more from her life than to marry some inbred Englishman.

Yes! I want more, too.

Lady Amelia carried on about damask-papered prison walls and the interchangeability of corsets and straitjackets.

Yes! Her life so far had been spent pouring and sipping tea in drawing rooms all across town. She spent her hours stitching samplers, writing letters, and arranging flowers. But surely there was more?

Lady Amelia next started pulling the hairpins from the elaborate coiffure. She flung the hairpins one by one around the foyer. They skittered across the marble floor. They ricocheted off crystal sconces. They plunked against portraits and fell to the floor.

"Well," the duchess said. "There is only one thing to do, I suppose. I shall send up Miss Green with some laudanum."

That was her cue to enter and get to work,

quieting the girl who shouted out the words that named the feelings in Meredith's heart.

The next morning, Amelia did not come down to breakfast. Since the girl never did miss a meal, James, Bridget, and Claire thought this odd. It was then discovered that Amelia was missing.

It should not have been a surprise that she'd run away, given the disastrous events of the previous evening. She had caused one hell of a scandal at Almack's. Even James knew it was bad.

James had badly wanted to commiserate with her — he knew how bored and stifled she felt, and how life in London society didn't leave enough room for their big American spirits. But as the Duke of Durham and Head Of The Family he felt he couldn't indulge her behavior.

And now she was missing.

Amelia, whom he'd had to rescue from any number of scrapes — stuck in a tree after trying to rescue a climbing kitten, rescued from a field after falling from an untrained horse and spraining her ankle, rescued from Bridget's wrath after reading her diary aloud at village school — had now embarked on a scrape of previously unforeseen and epic proportions.

Or so he hoped.

The alternative — that she was *taken* — was too horrid to consider.

Sisters. Usually James said the word with a sigh and an eye roll toward the heavens.

But today his lament of *sisters* was half-hearted. He was too sick with worry to be actually vexed.

After arguing with the duchess over the best way to find Amelia — she favored discretion, while he wanted the city blanketed in Bow Street Runners searching for her — he stormed out.

It was impossible and inconceivable that he sit idly at home, sipping tea and waiting for Amelia to return. James knew his baby sister; it would be a while yet before she became too hungry, tired, or scared and overcame whatever need it was that sent her running in the first place.

But London was no city for a young woman alone — especially one like Amelia, a magnet for trouble.

He had to find her.

Not as duke, but as her brother.

As James strode briskly through the streets of Mayfair, hat low over his eyes that skimmed the streets for signs of her, he thought how this was entirely his fault.

If he hadn't brought them to England in

the first place . . .

They would all be happy, at home in America.

If he had fought back more against the duchess as she tried to mold them into Perfect English Ladies when anyone could see they were never cut out for that . . .

They would all be happy, just as they were.

If only he hadn't been so consumed and distracted by Meredith . . .

James would have been able to see sooner that Amelia wasn't happy here and done something about it.

If only he hadn't been busy with this duke business . . .

He would have been able to be a better brother.

James walked the streets for hours, almost getting lost, and then getting caught in a sudden torrential downpour. There was no sign of Amelia, and eventually he returned to the house, hoping to find that she'd returned in his absence. Instead he found a different kind of torment.

If a duke struggles to resist temptation, he should avoid it at all costs. Nothing or no one must interfere with his duty to the estate.

— THE RULES FOR DUKES

For Meredith, and presumably the rest of the Cavendishes, it was one of those days where every second was torture and every minute felt like ten. The family fought — the duchess urged discretion in their search to protect Amelia's reputation, whilst James wanted to call in the Bow Street Runners and probably the cavalry, army, and navy, to boot.

He stormed out, and she knew he would be a one-man rescue mission, stalking the streets of London in search of his beloved sister, for as long as it took, or at least for hours.

Meanwhile, Meredith was confined to the drawing room.

Again. As always.

She sat with the duchess, embroidering only to keep her hands busy, and ensuring the pot of tea was always hot. One could handle anything if fortified with a pot of hot tea. Or four.

They were up to four pots now, and it wasn't even time for luncheon.

After the fifth, Lady Claire decided she needed a walk, and Meredith was more than happy to accompany her. The walk was eventful — the rainstorm they were caught in was the least of it — but they hadn't seen Lady Amelia.

Upon their return, they learned that Lady Bridget had returned from a carriage ride with Lord Darcy — neither of them had spotted Amelia, either.

While everyone was drying off from the sudden storm, Meredith noticed that the door to James's study was slightly ajar, and candles were lit within.

He had returned. Alone.

She shouldn't bother him. More to the point: she should not be alone with him. She was on thin ice with the duchess as it was. She was in a fragile state herself.

But he was hurting, and it had been plain to see all day long. She'd been able to help him before, so why not now?

In the end, she couldn't stay away.

The room was dimly lit. Rain slashed against the windowpanes.

James sat behind the desk. She noted a decanter of whiskey, more empty than full, and a glass.

He looked up when she entered, and then stood, because a woman was present. He looked drawn and tired. He looked sick with worry.

"I wanted to see how you were doing," she said softly.

"Fine. I'm fine. Why would I be anything other than fine?"

His voice was rough, but that might have been the whiskey.

"You're not fine."

"Of course I am not fine," he said sharply, and she flinched. "My sister, my baby sister, is missing. Not only that, but she is missing in a large, foreign city, full of all kinds of danger. Rapists, murderers, thieves, do I need to go on?"

Meredith shook her head *no,* not trusting herself to speak. She suddenly regretted the intrusion because this was not the James she knew.

"Her life could be at stake, if it isn't lost already. So, no, Meredith, I'm not fine."

"She's a smart, resourceful girl. She'll be fine."

Meredith reached out for him, just to touch his sleeve. It was only meant to be a little gesture to show affection and a tangible demonstration that he was not alone. But James jerked back as if burned.

She dropped her hand, mortified.

"You heard the duchess," he said. "Even if she returns, she won't be fine. She'll be ruined. Do you know what that means for the rest of us?"

"Yes," she whispered. She knew. It would not be good.

"It means strategic marriages, quickly, to

powerful members of the haute ton whom we might not love."

She knew that for the Cavendishes it would be an unwilling surrender to wed at all — let alone to do so for such mercenary means. And the thing was: each one of them would do whatever it took to protect the other. Even submit to a loveless marriage for a lifetime.

"I can try to do that myself. And God Above, I am trying," James said. And her heart leapt at the words and the strain in his voice because it seemed to her to mean that he didn't love Lady Jemma. "But I cannot do that to my sisters. I cannot take their choices away from them."

If that didn't make her heart skip a beat with something like love and admiration . . . and then fall and crash and burn when she remembered what it meant for her. Their happiness, for hers.

"It means we could never be together," he said.

"I know that. We both know that."

James shrugged and turned away — but not before a flash of his blue eyes told her something new. Something she had only hoped for in the darkest, most secret corners of her heart.

"You had hoped," she whispered. "A small

part of you still hoped and wanted."

She couldn't tell if this realization made her feel better or worse. Because she, too, had hoped.

"And now with Amelia gone, there is no more hope," he said grimly. "So I hope you understand, Meredith, that I need you to go. I can't stand the temptation. Not now. Not tonight."

The way he looked at her . . . oh, the way he looked at her!

When those blue eyes of his fixed upon her, her knees felt weak. Her heart started to drum in a slow, steady rhythm of wanting. Her skin tingled in anticipation of his touch — one she would never feel again, she was sure. Meredith couldn't move, not when she could barely stand, for melting under the intensity of his gaze.

This is what she wanted. What she dreamt of. And she was just supposed to turn and leave?

"Don't tempt me, Meredith. Please, don't tempt me."

His voice was rough. Desperate.

If she left, he would empty that bottle of whiskey. He would stay up all night brooding. He would be miserable in the morning.

But if she stayed, he would have one more regret to burn over, and she didn't want to be a regret, she wanted to be his joy.

She loved him. The man he was deep down. The man he was trying to be. She realized now that if she stayed, he was going to surrender to the temptation. She would melt against him, kiss him until she was breathless, make love to him on the floor. And they would both be disappointed in him. It was an impossible situation.

"Don't tempt me," he warned once more.

"I want to, but I won't," she whispered. And then she turned and fled, for her own self-preservation as much as his.

James watched Meredith go, carrying his heart and his hopes with her. It had taken every last inch of his self-control not to crush her against his chest, claim her mouth with his, tumble to the floor and lose himself inside her.

Her warmth. Her softness. Her passion. He wanted all of it. Especially tonight.

The way she moved with him, the way she touched him, the way she sighed with pleasure. He needed all of it. Now.

He wanted to lose himself. Lose his mind. Forget everything.

Destroying his family's happiness. Denying his love and lust. And for what? Houses. Duties. Drainage ditches.

James picked up his empty whiskey glass and hurled it at the mantelpiece. It crashed and shattered, and it didn't make him feel better.

The only thing that did improve his mood was the sound of Amelia returning home, which she finally did late, much later that evening.

She was home. She was safe. And he was determined that something had to change.

CHAPTER 14

A duke makes an effort to ensure that his guests enjoy themselves. But not too much of an effort.

— THE RULES FOR DUKES

It was absurd to think that the Duchess of Durham was nervous about hosting a ball, given that she was one of London's most accomplished hostesses. Why, people still spoke about her Egyptian-themed event in 1818 — Prinny himself had attended and declared it a success.

But tonight was different: she was still trying to get the Cavendish siblings to "take" in society. And there was good reason to be nervous: the girls were hardly enthusiastic about the party they had helped to plan for the purposes of showing them off. None of them aspired to ton adulation for their skills as hostesses.

"Tonight *must* go well," the duchess said

as her lady's maid adjusted the tiara in her nearly white blonde hair. The piece was a little too big, but it was part of a breathtaking set of tiara, earrings, and necklace, all made of blindingly sparkling diamonds and deep blue sapphires. It was a family heirloom.

Her Grace took a small sip of sherry, which she usually drank *after* a ball, not before.

"I'm certain that it will," Meredith replied. "There is no reason to think it will not."

"Hmmph. I can think of four of them. Four stubborn reasons that speak in American accents and still don't know how to address the second son of a marquess."

"They are making progress, Your Grace. Lady Amelia tells me that Lady Bridget has taken to writing about Lord Darcy in her diary."

The duchess nodded approvingly. "He would be an excellent match for anyone, but especially Lady Bridget. Such a pairing would take the ton by storm."

"It would be the talk of the town," Meredith agreed. "I daresay Lord Fox might still pursue Lady Claire."

There was also a good reason to suspect he would not, but Meredith decided now was not the time to trouble the duchess with that. The couple had quite the row the other day.

"And Lady Amelia?" the duchess inquired.

"As long as we can keep up the ruse that she's been ill, everything shall be fine."

In order to hide her disappearance, which forced the family to cancel their attendance at another ball, they had spread the word that she had been on her deathbed and then miraculously recovered — all within the span of four and twenty hours. It was a story scarcely believed, but gossip about it diverted people's attention from the scandalous truth: Amelia had spent four and twenty hours gallivanting around London *unchaperoned.*

They would all be ruined if word of that got out.

"That's a tall order," the duchess said. "All it will take is one or two sightings of her around town on her little adventure for people to begin questioning our story and speculating about the truth. The only saving grace is that the duke has been courting Lady Jemma."

The duchess said this breezily, as if Meredith naturally shared her pleasure at the news. As if Meredith hadn't been achingly aware of every afternoon he paid her a visit or every evening that he saw her at balls while she stayed home alone. *Aching* being the key word, of course. That she knew he was following his sense of duty and not his heart, which lay with her, did nothing to ease the pain.

"She's a bit horsey for my taste," the duchess continued, "but I suppose he likes that about her. He could do worse."

"Mmm." It was all Meredith could manage. Breathing was not working for her at the moment, and speaking was a struggle.

"I suspect he might propose soon."

Meredith reminded herself to take a deep breath.

"What makes you say that?"

"He took an interest in the Cavendish family jewels, which I had brought out so the girls might have something to wear tonight."

Meredith smiled tightly. It had nothing to do with jewelry and everything to do with family. She'd always been the one — the only one — the duchess had. And now the Cavendishes all had each other, all dressed in the family jewels. They would welcome Lady Jemma into their ranks, and Meredith would retreat farther and farther from the only life and family she'd known.

But then the duchess surprised her.

"I thought you should have something to

wear as well, Meredith."

"Your Grace, I couldn't possibly . . ."

"Meredith . . . I've never told you . . ." The duchess took a long moment before saying anything else. Meredith watched, and waited, breath bated, as Her Grace seemed to take great care in selecting the words she was about to say. "You're like a daughter to me. I had given up dreaming of one of my own, and then you came along. You have been my true companion for so many years now. Tonight I want everyone in my family to shine and sparkle."

"Your Grace . . ."

"I know. If we were less British we might cry and hug. But then we'd be so . . . American." The duchess shuddered dramatically, and they both burst out laughing. If one looked closely one might have detected a certain slick sheen in their eyes that someone less British might call tears. Because they were Durham and they did not cry. "Let us instead select a brooch for you to wear with that beautiful gown."

After some consideration Meredith selected one shaped like a butterfly, studded with diamonds and emeralds, and affixed it to her cream silk gown.

"That was a gift to me from . . . my brother," the duchess said with a faraway look in her eyes. "On the occasion of my betrothal to the duke. He could scarcely afford it, but restraint and prudence had never been his forte."

Meredith nodded. She had met the earl once or twice as a young girl. He'd died young, in the sort of drunken accident known to befall dissipated lords.

But that was all in the past.

Meredith glanced at her reflection in the mirror: tonight she looked every inch the lady. To look at her, one would never know she was just a commoner, just a girl.

The Cavendish Ball

James was glad, selfishly so, that all the bother of arranging the ball fell upon his sisters and that, as a man, he was excused. This was not fair, but it was the way of the world, and he was not inclined to change it.

James half wondered if Amelia's Great Escape — about which she said nothing, keeping a secret to herself for the first time in her life — was even a desperate ploy to avoid her role in this great soiree. But no, the party must go on, *especially* when the family had rumors to squash. Rumors and speculation that ran rampant throughout the ballroom . . .

■ ■ ■ ■

"Lady Amelia looks quite well for someone who supposedly spent the day abed, and ill."

James gritted his jaw. Amelia had been gallivanting all over London — he knew that much from Bow Street Runner reports and the pinkness on her cheeks from the sun. It was only a matter of time until someone had proof.

And gossiped about said proof.

And then the whole haute ton would know the truth and the Cavendish family would be ruined.

Which meant that any hopes for him and Meredith that he may have harbored in the deepest, darkest, farthest corner of his heart were certainly smothered. He thought they had all been firmly extinguished.

He was wrong.

Every time he thought he had conquered his feelings for her, something would happen to make him fall deeper in love with her.

She was here tonight. She put so many of the young ladies to shame with her beauty, poise, and the way she would captivate him from the far side of a crowded room. When he saw her across the ballroom, saw the glow of candlelight on her skin, saw the sparkle in her eyes, she knocked the breath right out of him.

That last ember of hope or desire flickered back to life and started to smolder.

"Is that Lady Bridget dancing with . . . Darcy? I'm not sure which is more shocking, the sight of Darcy dancing at all, or his choice of partner."

Meredith pretended she hadn't heard Lady Carrington say that to Lady Tunbridge. She also pretended she hadn't heard the disdain and disbelief in her voice. The Cavendish sisters certainly weren't having an easy time of it; even guests at their own party were skeptical about their prospects.

But Meredith did sip her champagne and discreetly glance in that direction to confirm that, yes, Lady Bridget and Lord Darcy were waltzing. It may have been an unexpected sight to those who knew Lord Darcy as He Who Did Not Dance, which was most of the ton.

But it was not unexpected to those who read Lady Bridget's Diary, or had its contents recounted to them by Lady Amelia over afternoon tea.

Nevertheless, it was remarkable to see those two waltzing. Because Lord Darcy was everyone's definition of a catch — tall, handsome, wealthy, powerful, respected.

If Bridget were to land him, then the family would have a powerful ally in the haute ton.

It meant that a little scandal might be bad, but not utterly devastating.

It meant that the rest of the siblings might be able to follow their hearts.

Which is not to say Bridget and Darcy weren't following theirs. The man positively smoldered when he looked at her.

It wasn't unlike the way James had been looking at her tonight.

Meredith glanced around the ballroom, and it was merely a moment before her gaze landed on him and his eyes locked with hers.

It didn't matter that the ballroom was packed with hundreds of people, just like it hadn't mattered that the Queen's Head Tavern in Southampton had been crowded. When he looked at her like that, she felt like they were the only two people alone in the world.

It didn't matter that they had every reason to stay apart. When he looked at her like that, she felt connected to him in a way that society would disapprove of and in a way that felt impossible to break.

Much as they might try.

And she tried. Because it hurt too much to look at him, hurt too much to see the life she could never have, the love she could never really have.

Meredith forced herself to turn away.

"Have you seen Lady Claire this evening? I daresay she is nearly unrecognizable. That girl has transformed from future spinster to utter sensation."

James didn't know why in hell Claire had done what she had done to herself — ditching her spectacles and wearing the sort of frothy, sparkly girl dress she always disdained on others. It may or may not have had something to do with a certain gentleman suitor. She wasn't the sort to lose her head over a man, but then again, there was a first time for everything.

But one thing was plain: she was trying to conform to the ton's standards of delicate, simpering femininity. And by God, she was succeeding. If guests weren't whispering about Amelia, they were gossiping about Claire's transformation.

He wondered if she, too, felt the pressure to fit in so that their younger siblings could follow their hearts and carry on with their irrepressible spirits.

Then James turned around and he saw

Bridget waltzing with the Greatly Esteemed And Dignified Lord Darcy. He turned again, and this time saw that even Amelia seemed to be involved in an engaging conversation with a gentleman that James didn't recognize.

Everywhere he looked, the Cavendish sisters were *trying*.

And then there was Meredith, standing alone along the perimeter of the ballroom, looking lovely and lonely. She was surrounded by members of the haute ton, none of whom took much notice of her because she wasn't A Person Of Consequence . . . and so they missed the loveliness in their midst. It did something to his heart, that.

Perhaps, with his sisters all looking and acting like proper young ladies, it was safe for him to ask her to dance.

Just this once.

To be polite. To be a good host. To be kind. Such were the excuses he made to himself when really, he could not stay away.

James slowly threaded through the crowds on his way toward her, never once averting his gaze. She waited for him, poised and elegant, calm and collected.

But he, and only he, knew what passion burned beneath that cool exterior. Only he knew what she was like when that elegance and restraint gave way to unbridled passion and pleasure. Only he had seen her honey-hued hair spread across the pillow or heard her soft sighs of satisfaction.

James bowed before her. And then, he flashed a grin.

"What is a beautiful woman like you doing alone in a place like this?"

"Really, Your Grace. That line is ridiculous." She fanned herself and glanced away — and then right back at him.

"You must have a story," he murmured. "Tell me your story."

"I do have a story," she replied. "But I'm afraid it doesn't end well. The scene here tonight is too lovely for a tragic tale."

"Shall we see if we can change that?" Before she could reply, he asked, "May I have the pleasure of this dance?"

He held out his hand. Waiting. Hoping.

Meredith hesitated, and he knew her battle was between duty to the duchess and her heart, better judgment versus the rules of etiquette that demanded a woman accept every invitation to dance.

"I would be honored, Your Grace," she replied, finally, accepting his offered hand.

The orchestra began to play the opening notes of a waltz. He swept her into his arms. They started to move.

This time James didn't need her to tell him to hold her more tightly, or to move with more purpose, or to take control of their movements. He did those things. And when she slipped her hands in his, he held on like he never wanted to let go.

It wasn't because he'd had practice with what had felt like nearly every "suitable" lady of the haute ton. With Meredith, he could do this. Whether it was a waltz or running an estate or whatever he was called on to do, with her in his arms or by his side, he could do anything.

She made him strong.

But she was also his weakness.

When James held her, he imagined a future with her — one of love, passion, laughter. He did not think much about his family, the estate, and his duty to both. But he did think of his father; finally, now, he was beginning to understand a love so powerful it would make a man forgo title, family, king, and country.

James knew that soon, *soon*, like his father before him, he would have to decide: duty or love.

"I wouldn't be too sure about a match with Lady Jemma and the duke. Look — he's dancing with the duchess's companion for a

second time this evening. Once is polite. But twice is verging on scandalous."

Meredith should not have consented to the first waltz with James, or the second one a short while later. She had many excellent reasons for saying no: it would cause people to talk, the duchess would disapprove of it, it made her heart ache, it would be more temptation than either of them needed.

But there was also the simple fact that it was Not Done for a woman to refuse a man's invitation to waltz. Meredith suspected this particular gem of etiquette was merely to preserve the delicate egos and emotions of men for whom fear of rejection would keep them from inviting a woman to dance.

Meredith knew The Rules. She would have to say yes to James's invitation because otherwise the people standing nearby witnessing her refusal would talk, and the duchess would disapprove of violating such a basic tenet of good ballroom behavior. Besides, it would make her heart ache to refuse him, and she could not resist temptation.

She could not win either way, and so Meredith chose pleasure. She danced with James a second time.

This did not go unnoticed, or unremarked upon.

And it did make her heart ache to dance with him, to feel his arms holding her, to have him gaze into her eyes like she was the only woman in the world. It all made her imagine what life could be like if they lived in a world where their love could flourish, nurtured by family and friends rather than stifled by widespread condemnation.

Meredith couldn't quite disregard the snide little looks and comments floating around the ballroom. It was impossible to forget that what she and James shared could never be more than this.

"The rumors about Lady Jemma and the duke must be true. He has sought her out and now they are deep in conversation."

James had already learned that very little escaped the attentions of Her Grace, the Duchess of Durham, especially when it concerned the dukedom. The duke dancing twice with her companion was notable. And, in the eyes of the duchess, regrettable.

"You may not have noticed, being so distracted with my companion, but Lady Jemma and her family have arrived," Her Grace said pointedly; her disapproval of his action was abundantly clear.

James took her point. The duchess disapproved of his waltzing with Meredith — once could be passed off as being polite, but twice was nearly tantamount to announcing a betrothal, which was, of course, unthinkable. He wondered if she also happened to notice that *something* between them — the heat and passion, love and heartache — that wouldn't cease.

This, he knew, was not ballroom conversation.

Or a conversation he wished to have with the duchess in any room.

"I shall seek Lady Jemma," James replied. Because of duty. Because of that ten-year-old boy at Durham Park. Because of his sisters.

"See that you do, preferably before the toast at midnight." The duchess snapped her fan open. "And James —" She never called him James. "Do try to remember what matters most."

"It is never far from my mind," he said dryly.

"I am glad to hear it," the duchess said, leveling him with a pointed stare. "Sometimes it does seem like you've forgotten."

Sometimes being every glance, every word, every moment he shared with Meredith. But even then, he didn't forget so much as completely ignore it.

"I should go greet Lady Jemma and her family."

James didn't need to look over his shoulder to know that the duchess wore an expression of satisfaction. He set off into the throngs, intent on finding his intended.

His intended, Lady Jemma.

James tested out the words in his head. And felt . . . nothing in the region of his heart. Not a pang or a skip of a beat or even a clench of agony.

When he stood before Lady Jemma herself, his heart was still unperturbed. This was not a surprise; he liked her, they shared common interests, on paper they were a good match, what with their titles and nearby estates and mutual interest in horses. Love and lust had never entered into the equation.

Nevertheless, he wondered about the state of her heart when she smiled broadly upon seeing him. Did she fancy herself in love with him, or did she also find him an agreeable prospect simply because they were both "horse-mad people"?

"Good evening, Your Grace. This is a splendid affair."

"Thank you. I shall pass your compliments on to the duchess and my sisters.

They are the ones who have done the hard work of planning this ball."

"And somehow you escaped the endless discussions on décor and whatnot," she teased. "How lucky for you."

"I had important ducal matters to attend to," he said gravely. He strove to keep his attentions focused on Lady Jemma.

"Of course you did," she teased. "I don't suppose they were taken care of at the club and involved drinking, card playing, and wagering."

"I wish. A duke can dream."

She laughed, and he forced a laugh, and everything was right and proper, and then what she said next forced the air right from his lungs.

"So tell me, Your Grace, who was that charming woman you were just now waltzing with?" Lady Jemma batted her eyelashes like a coquette, but there was nothing coquettish about her question. There was something steely underneath the words. "I did not recognize her."

In other words, Lady Jemma had just declared Meredith a nobody.

"I was waltzing with Miss Green. She is the duchess's longtime companion."

"Ah, how democratic of you." Here she gave a little laugh as if to say, *oh, you silly*

Americans! James felt himself bristle. "If she weren't a mere companion, one might think she's a rival for your hand."

Now James's heart started to pound in a nervous way. He did not care for the direction of this conversation. He didn't want to discuss Meredith with her. One was love, one was duty.

"I'm sure I don't know what you mean," he replied, warning her off the subject with his voice.

"A man of your station will marry a woman of a similar station. Dukes don't marry companions or governesses or scullery maids, no matter what the novels say. 'Tis the way of the world, I'm afraid. At least, it is the way of the haute ton."

James opened his mouth to offer some sort of protest or lightly dismissive comment. But all he could think was: *How do you know? Why do you say this? Is it that obvious?* But before he could find his voice, Lady Jemma was off on another subject altogether.

"But never mind all that. You'll marry a proper woman, as you are expected to do. Are you familiar with the horses of Arabia? I have this mad scheme to travel there and get one. I'd like to breed them with some of the stock in my stables now."

James blinked, trying to catch up. Horses. Yes. A vastly preferable subject to discuss than what may or may not exist between him and Miss Green.

"I should like to hear more about that," he said, knowing that he could relax and collect himself while she chattered away.

She told him more. He had to agree — it was a mad scheme to travel all the way to Arabia for a horse, no matter what qualities the animal might possess. He wondered if she intended to do this before or after marriage. It would make for one hell of a honeymoon . . .

And then, because it was the done thing, he asked her to dance.

And then, because it was the done thing, she accepted.

As he whirled her around the ballroom, he caught a glimpse of the duchess smiling approvingly. He saw Lady Winston smiling in the way that struck fear in the hearts of unmarried men. He saw so many of the guests watching and discussing the mere fact that he was waltzing with Lady Jemma — again, after dancing with her at so many other soirees.

He noticed all this because he was not exactly riveted by the woman in his arms.

■ ■ ■ ■

"Of course he'll marry Lady Jemma. He hasn't shown an interest in any other woman — except the companion and he would never wed her. The duchess wouldn't allow it!"

After heaven in his arms, Meredith fell back to earth. It wasn't a long, slow tumble, either, but a hard crash. One moment they had been waltzing, and she felt it again — that connection so strong and potent that she considered throwing caution to the wind. *Pick me! Kiss me! Love me!*

But then she'd barely returned to the side of the ballroom when she turned around to see him conversing with Lady Jemma, her eminently suitable horse-mad rival. Meredith stood in the shadows, off to the side and out of the way, and watched.

James didn't hold her as close, nor did he look deeply into her eyes. It was plain to Meredith that James didn't care for her very much, but that only made her feel worse. She couldn't imagine giving up their passion for the sake of a polite waltz, or a mutual interest in horses. If it were love, she would understand.

From her place on the sidelines, Meredith was able to hear as conversations all around her hummed and buzzed along the same theme: what a good match they were, what the odds were in the betting book at White's that he'd propose within a fortnight, what their stables would be like, how he could do worse. No one thought to censor their tongues near her, for what did the thoughts and feelings of the duchess's companion matter? Why, they probably didn't even notice her at all. Not even with her beautiful gown and a diamond brooch that belonged to the duchess. Meredith was still invisible.

When she could wrench her gaze away, Meredith noted more than a few smug, approving smiles. The duchess and Lady Winston, especially, were particularly pleased by the sight of James and Lady Jemma whirling around the ballroom.

Meredith was quite certain that when she had danced with the duke tonight, the sentiments were vastly different. She'd seen the skeptical expressions and overheard the questions. She *knew* what they would say — did say — *Why is he dancing with* her *twice? Just who does she think she is?*

The duchess was not pleased. No one shared in Meredith's joy. And that was only for the grave sin of a second waltz. Imagine what would happen if, *if,* IF they were to marry!?

The stares. The whispers. The questions. The skepticism. The condemnation.

Could this intangible something between them withstand all that? Could their love — or whatever it was — withstand the guilt of wrecking his sisters' prospects and crushing the duchess's dearest wish for the dukedom? Could James live with himself after choosing love over duty?

Could she?

She feared not.

The hour was approaching midnight. Meredith had enjoyed her fairy-tale moment with the handsome, charming duke. Now it was time to return to her bedchamber and turn back into a pumpkin. It was best to get out while she still could.

She started making her way out of the ballroom when she heard someone — James — calling after her. He shouldn't. He really shouldn't. Hadn't they given everyone enough to discuss this evening? Hadn't they already caused enough gossip? She rather thought yes. Best to get out before permanent damage was done to either of their prospects.

"Meredith, wait," he called out after her. "Where are you going?"

She paused.

Don't look. Don't look. Don't look.

But then she gave in and turned around.

"I'm tired, James. I think I'll retire for the evening."

He smiled. "You can't be tired. It is not yet midnight. The night is young."

"But I am tired, James. I am tired of standing on the sidelines of the ballroom . . . of life. I am tired of watching life happen to other people while I stay in the shadows. I am tired of feeling like I don't quite belong — not here in the ballroom with the ton, nor downstairs with the servants. When I am tired like this I just need to be alone."

"Dance with me." He held out his hand. She wanted, badly, to take it. While dancing with someone twice in one evening was scandalous enough, a third dance would be ruinous.

"We should not."

"Dance with me." He waited, his hand still extended. All she had to do was place her hand in his. *A woman must always accept a man's invitation to dance.*

"If we dance for a third time in one evening, people will talk and they will not be kind."

"I don't care. Dance with me."

She was aware of people watching them.

They were watching her, mere companion, have the nerve to put up a fuss about dancing with a duke. The whispers were already starting.

She knew that she had more to lose than he did, if she were to accept. That was the way of the world — the women always paid the consequences. If she were going to ruin her prospects, it would have to be for more than just a dance.

"Your Grace, I must refuse."

Meredith turned and quit the ballroom.

James followed. He should *not* have followed.

"You should not be following me," Meredith said in a low voice. "We should not be alone together."

"But I can't help myself, can you?"

"I'm trying to, thank you very much. I am trying so hard, but you aren't making it easy. So I just have to keep trying harder."

"Why, Meredith, why?"

"You woo me. And then you tell me we can never be together. Then you say that I tempt you. When I'm not trying to. And now you insist on a third waltz, at midnight, like a bloody fairy tale."

James reached out for her, grasping her hand. Meredith tugged it away and he relinquished his grasp. But he kept his hold on her with words.

"I don't want to woo you," he said in a low voice, right in her ear. "I don't want to be tempted by you. I don't want to think about marrying you, and I don't want to agonize over what it would cost us both to be wed. I don't want to want you, Meredith."

There was no need for him to say the rest for her to hear what he left unspoken: *But I do.*

This should have made her heart sing. This should have made her feel like a fairy princess with the prince. Just. Within. Reach. But she had felt that before, and each time the inevitable crash took a little more out of her. Soon there might be nothing left.

"You say that tonight, Your Grace. But I'm not sure you'll say it for the rest of your life."

The way he looked at her was too much: with love and desire and sadness, all at once, all in those blue eyes of his. At that point, Meredith no longer cared about causing a scene. She only cared about self-preservation.

Abruptly, she turned and fled down the corridor.

"Meredith."

He caught up with her in just a few steps. She kept walking as he fell in step beside her. With every step, they retreated farther and farther from the ballroom and all the guests.

"You should not follow me," Meredith said in a low voice as she tried to get away from all of it. "You should be in the ball-room with your guests, and your family, and your Lady Jemma. You should be talking about horse things, and counting how many acres you both possess and how the ton will fawn over your match."

"Strangely, I don't find those things as compelling as you."

"I am touched, truly."

"Mer . . ." He tugged her into the nearest room. One candle provided the only light. Her eyes adjusted; it was his study.

The soft click of the door shutting behind them.

It was dark. They were alone. Her heart started to pound. Not with fear, but with wanting. It was dangerous in the dark, behind closed doors, with no one watching. Cut off from the world like this, there was no one and nothing to keep them in check.

Her heart beat hard with wanting. James was so close.

"We shouldn't," she whispered.

"I know."

"We can't," she said in a low voice.

"I know," he growled. "Oh, Meredith, I know."

And then his mouth crashed down on hers.

CHAPTER 15

If a duke is going to break the rules, he should have a damn good time doing it . . . and ensure his partner does, too.

— THE RULES FOR DUKES

The soft click of the door shutting behind them . . .

It was the sound of shutting out the rest of the world until there was only her and him and this something between them. It was invisible, but oh, so real. Meredith could feel it in the pounding of her heart. She felt the way it made her breath catch in her throat. Her skin was hot with anticipation.

James's mouth came crashing down on hers and she gave up the fight.

I shouldn't. I shouldn't. I shouldn't.

But how could she say no to the gentle pressure of his lips on hers, when it was everything she'd ever wanted? How could she help but yield and welcome him in when it was the only thing she wanted to do?

How could she do anything but kiss him back?

Meredith wrapped her arms around him and kissed him with all the pent-up heartache and desire inside of her. When she closed her eyes and concentrated on the kiss, everything melted away — Durham and duty, the haute ton crowded in the ballroom — and she was back in that room, that night when it all began.

A spark.

Burning brighter and brighter with each moment.

Just her and Just James.

When they were like this, mouths caught in a kiss, bodies melting into each other, desire flowing freely, it was enough. It was everything.

The soft glow of a lone candle . . .

There was just enough light for James to see her — the outline of her jaw, the plump curve of her lips, the delicate curve of her neck. James paused in the kiss to look at her, really look at her, seeing all her hopes and dreams and desires in her eyes. He saw love there, too. Real love for the man he was and the man he was becoming.

Just a girl, she had said that night.

She would *never* be just a girl to him.

He caressed her cheek gently, finding the skin soft and warm. Then he sank his fingers into her hair, cradling her as he lowered his mouth to hers for another kiss, this one gentle and deep and sure and promising forever.

Somehow, someway, forever.

He felt her sink against him, giving up resistance and giving herself up to him, and he swore he would find a way for them to be together.

Forever.

But first, tonight.

One kiss led to another led to another. He couldn't get enough of her, her touch, her taste, the sound of her breath catching.

"Meredith . . ."

There was so much he wanted to say, but he couldn't find the words. He could only tell her with his touch and the way he crooned her name.

His hands — rough, scarred, and strong hands that had worked — caressed her, savoring her every curve: the way her full breasts fit perfectly in his hand, the way her hips flared. She felt better than he remembered. Oh, how he had wanted her. Oh, how it'd been torture to know she was under the same roof and yet off-limits.

James pulled her flush against him, his hardness cradled in the soft vee of her thighs. He wanted to lay her down on a bed and lose himself in her. Or find himself. Whatever it was, he wanted that connection.

Still holding her close, James took one step, then another, guiding them toward the light of that one candle until she was up against the desk, the big ducal desk.

The sound of fabric rustling . . .

Meredith didn't protest as James pushed the fabric of her skirts aside. His fingertips skimmed the inside of her thighs, and she shuddered at the delicate pleasure of it.

She did not protest as he pressed a kiss to her lips and dropped to his knees before her, reverentially. Feeling beautiful and adored, she parted her knees and leaned back.

A kiss.

James kissed her there, at the sensitive spot between her legs. She gasped at the initial touch of his mouth to her, and she sighed as he teased her with his tongue, tasting her and taking her to heights of pleasure she'd only imagined.

What had started with a kiss, a spark, was

now a smolder. She burned, oh, she burned, as the heat within her grew hotter and the pressure in her core grew stronger.

I want. I want. I want.

More, she wanted more.

"James . . ." She whispered his name, and she wasn't sure if it was a question or a plea.

His hands gripped her thighs and she moaned. She was close, so close to losing herself completely.

The sound of soft sighs and frantic breaths . . .

James stood before her, and Meredith reached for the buttons on his breeches. He didn't stop her, no, she knew he wanted this as much as she.

Want being too small a word for the driving need to be melded as one and lost in each other.

In the quiet of the dim room, there was only the sound of fabric rustling aside — her skirts, his breeches — and the sound of her breaths or his, she didn't know. They were one, or about to be, and she couldn't wait much longer.

A kiss. His mouth found hers for a kiss that was frantic and desperate.

James kissed her deeply as he eased into her, and she moaned softly as the hot, hard length of him filled her up. Her head fell back and he kissed her exposed throat.

She wrapped her legs around his back, urging him deeper.

"Oh, God, Mer . . ."

He thrust into her, slow and steady.

"I want . . . I need . . ." she panted.

"I know."

He thrust again, slow and steady and sure, finding exactly the rhythm that somehow matched the pounding of her heart. She lost herself in that rhythm, letting go of everything except for the wild pleasure building within her.

This. Here. Her. James didn't know who he was or where he belonged in the world, but here in Meredith's arms and buried deep inside her, he knew *this* was where he wanted to be.

Now.

Forever.

He moved into her, losing himself in her warmth and taking pleasure in the sound of her sighs. He was driven by the pounding of his own heart, thudding hard and strong in his chest.

This. Her. Kiss.

There was nothing else in the world in that moment except for him and her and the pleasure between them. He was so attuned to her that he felt the moment she began to peak.

Sighs, more frantic. She tightened around him. Her fingers gripped his jacket and shirt like she was falling and holding on for dear life. He thrust hard and harder as he lost himself to his own climax. When she cried out he captured the sound with a kiss.

She wrapped her arms around him and sagged against him. James held her tight and breathed her in.

And then the room fell silent except for the sound of their breathing.

The soft glow of a lone candle . . .

It took a moment, but Meredith finally opened her eyes and drifted back to the present reality, slowly and achingly. They were in the study at Durham House. A ball for hundreds of guests raged just down the hall.

He was The Duke.

And she was still just a girl, the companion.

They had just made love, frantically, passionately, and without a care to the consequences. There would certainly be consequences. Her mind was still too hazy in the aftermath of their lovemaking to fully consider the implications.

She could only ask the question that begged to be asked.

"What does this mean?"

"I don't know," James admitted as he stepped back from her and buttoned his breeches. His shirt was rumpled, his hair tousled, and his cravat in a state of disrepair.

"You don't know," she repeated.

"I don't know. I lose my mind around you," he whispered, pressing a kiss to her lips. But he was distracted now, and she felt it. Because this meant something, but neither of them knew what. "But everything will be fine. I swear to it."

"We shouldn't have let this happen."

"But it happened."

It certainly had happened. Her heart was still pounding. Her breath hadn't quite returned to normal. She was sitting on the ducal desk with her legs wantonly spread apart. Hastily, she adjusted her skirts and slid to her feet.

"It happened," James confirmed. Then he pushed his fingers through his hair, mussing it up even more. "I'll figure something out."

She started trying to smooth her skirts, as if wrinkles in silk were the worst of her problems right now. Lifting a hand to her head, she realized her coiffure was beyond repair. And her brooch . . .

Her heart sank. She suddenly felt ill. The brooch was gone.

"I will take care of this, Meredith. I will take care of you."

She glanced at him, now more panicked about the loss of a piece of jewelry than what had just transpired. How could she lose such a precious heirloom? And what if it were found here, in the duke's study? How would she explain it?

"My brooch. I lost my brooch."

"I'll help you look," James said, fumbling for another candle.

The sound of a door clicking open . . .

They were in a state of semi-disarray and panic, searching for the missing brooch, when a maid pushed open the door to the study.

"Your Grace?" She bobbed into a curtsy. But Meredith saw her eyes widen as she took in the duke with his hair and cravat askew, as well as her own disheveled appearance. The maid was young, but she was no fool.

Oh, God. Oh, damn.

"Your Grace, the duchess is inquiring as to your whereabouts. She would like to do a toast at the ball."

Oh, God. Oh, bloody hell. The duchess

had noticed he was missing. And presumably Meredith, too. What, oh, what, had she been thinking?

She hadn't been thinking. And now . . . she did not know what now.

James glanced at her, looking for guidance as to what to do — stay with her or return to his guests.

"You should go," she said. It was the right thing to do. People were waiting upon His Grace, the Duke of Durham. And far be it for her, a mere Miss, to keep him from them.

"This is not over," he vowed. And then he followed the maid and the door clicked shut behind him. She was alone.

This is not over, James had said. But what did that mean?

Later that night, Meredith fell asleep with the question dancing circles in her head, his taste still on her lips, the feeling of his touch still warm on her skin. She spent the night in a hazy, fevered sleep, reliving those glorious moments when nothing mattered but her skin against his. And yet it was always, always followed by the question, *what did it mean? What would happen now?*

Would they wed?

Would she have to leave?

Would she be content as his mistress if he

took a proper wife?

Meredith woke up with the question still stuck in her head and still unanswered. James had some choices to make, but so did she.

CHAPTER 16

A duke mustn't make promises that he cannot keep.

— THE RULES FOR DUKES

The next morning, Meredith encountered James in the corridor as they made their way down to breakfast. The timing was so perfect she wondered if he had been listening and waiting for her. Perhaps his night had been as sleepless as hers.

They had to talk.

They approached the grand staircase in the foyer, where footmen and the butler stood at attention and maids bustled about. This was not the place for a private conversation.

"Meredith, wait." He fell in step beside her.

"We'll be late for breakfast."

"This will only take a moment."

"If we are late, people may notice something is amiss. There will be questions. And I don't know how to answer them. I have spent a sleepless night thinking of how to answer them, and I still am not prepared to do so."

"Leave that to me," he said confidently. Ducally.

Leave it to me.

She couldn't just leave her entire future to him to figure out over breakfast, especially when she suspected that he didn't know what to say, what to do, how to manage it all so that no one was hurt. He could hardly have given the matter more thought than she.

Then again, maybe he knew.

"All right." She paused on a step halfway down and turned to face him. In a hushed whisper, she asked, "What does it all mean? Has last night changed anything?"

"Yes. No." He glanced at the servants in the foyer and, in a low voice, murmured, "You know that I still have to be mindful of my sisters, and their reputations. Their prospects."

"But not of mine."

"I'll find a way for us to be together, Mer, I promise you." He reached for her hand, giving it a quick squeeze that was hidden by the volume of her skirts. She found it only mildly reassuring because her future with the duke — or without him — was not the only trouble weighing heavily on her mind.

"I have more pressing concerns at the moment. The brooch the duchess lent me is missing."

The diamond and emerald brooch that she could never afford to replace, which did not even matter, given that its sentimental value made it irreplaceable to the duchess. Meredith was heartsick just thinking about telling her.

"I will find it," James said confidently, easily, like some fairy-tale prince who would handily fix every little thing. "If not, I'll buy another."

"That's not the point."

"I'm a simple man. You'll have to explain this to me."

"We have both betrayed her trust," she said. "She trusted me with a family heirloom. And then she trusted me to help polish you into a duke. And now I have lost the brooch, and while you look the part, you are still entertaining very un-ducal ideas of running off with the penniless companion and threatening to expose the family to scandal? Or you are not entertaining such thoughts and I shall be heartbroken when you marry Lady Jemma. There is no way out of this without someone getting hurt."

That is what had kept her up all night. It wasn't new, but it felt more raw after she lost her head last night . . . lost her wits, her sanity, and a little more of her heart. She had wondered if perhaps they could not even be together under the same roof, whether or not they were *together,* for it was too much temptation for one pair to fight and she was so, so tired.

"I lose my head around you," he murmured.

"And I, you."

It was a simple truth, and Meredith was beginning to see what she needed to do.

A duke's duty is to the dukedom — *not* his heart.
— THE RULES FOR DUKES

A short while later
The drawing room

There was no way around it: James lost his head around her. He lost his wits, his reason, and his sense of duty. Meredith turned him into nothing more than a single-minded man, consumed with lust, driven only to please her and to love her at the expense of everything else in his life, even the things that truly mattered.

Oh, he put up a good fight.

Every minute he didn't glance her way, every day he didn't steal a kiss and every night that he didn't make love to her could be considered a triumph.

But after last night, James was forced to consider whether fighting his feelings for Meredith might, just might, be a losing battle.

Surrendering could feel like winning, because he would then be with her. He felt deep in his bones that he could survive anything, as long as he had Meredith by his side to give him strength and to show him what needed to be done in this mad new role of his.

Maybe he didn't see how he would survive it and thrive in it without her.

James drummed his fingers on the arm of the chair. Today. He would say something to the duchess today. Something like, *Josie, I've fallen in love with Meredith and need to make her my duchess and I know it will be a scandal but we'll just have to make things work.*

Probably.

It was the terms of surrender that gave him pause and stopped him from waving the white flag.

And those terms of surrender were made

clear to him as the duchess continued her reading of the gossip columns to the family, as they all lounged about the drawing room, moods muted from the party the night before.

Frankly, he didn't think those news rags were good for anything, not even lining horses' stalls. James's opinion was not revised when he heard what those hack reporters wrote about his family now.

"*The London Weekly* is reporting that Amelia was seen quaffing an excess of champagne," Josephine said with a frown. "When she wasn't quaffing champagne," the duchess read, "she was seen shooting daggers with her eyes at Mr. Alistair Finlay-Jones, the vaguely disreputable heir to Baron Wrotham."

His littlest sister certainly did look like she was suffering from the aftereffects of too much champagne.

When, he idly wondered, had she become a woman who drank champagne and shot daggers with her eyes at a man at a London ball? In his mind, she was still ten and stealing a sip of his ale before spitting it out all over the floor and declaring it revolting.

And for that matter, who was this Mr. Alistair Finlay-Jones, presumably wounded by Amelia's eye-daggers? Was he a prospect, or a rogue? Were they newly introduced or was he a previous acquaintance? Was she lovesick, too, or was this bloke a good-for-nothing scoundrel?

James had no idea, either because he'd been too consumed with his own affairs, or because it had something to do with Amelia's Great Escape, which she still did not speak of. But the bottom line was plain: she was changing and growing up and might need him. He had been too distracted of late to know any of these things. This was not the sort of older brother he imagined himself being.

This truth felt like a door slamming shut on his future dreams with Meredith.

"I don't know what you are talking about," Amelia muttered.

"It's not *I* that am talking about it, but rather *The London Weekly* and thus the entire town. My only consolation is that they are not speaking about your mysterious illness."

"The *Morning Post* is," Claire said. "The Man About Town says that Lady Amelia appears to have made a remarkable recovery from her grave and sudden illness." Then she read from the column. *"In fact, the lady looked as if she had spent a day out of doors rather than a day on her deathbed."*

Oh, damn. James pushed his fingers through his hair. This is what they had been afraid of. Rumors. Discovery. Being caught in a lie.

Another door slammed shut.

He felt the walls closing in.

James glanced at Meredith, who concentrated very carefully on her embroidery.

"If only they could see you now," Bridget teased. "You look incredibly ill."

Amelia halfheartedly swatted at her.

"Sisters," James lamented dryly, but lovingly. "What did I ever do to deserve three sisters?"

More to the point, why did he have to care so much about their happiness, especially at the expense of his own? His intentions to declare his love for Meredith and insist on marrying her were fading away in the face of his sisters' happiness being compromised by too much champagne and eye-daggered scoundrels. To say nothing of whatever was going on with Claire and her Lord Fox or Bridget and that Darcy fellow. James was afraid to ask.

"Oh, you are not off the hook. Your Grace," Claire said, smiling devilishly. James scowled as she read aloud from one of the papers. *"His Grace crushed the hopes of many a young maiden by waltzing twice with*

Miss Meredith Green, companion to the duchess, while eligible young ladies languished on the sidelines."

A long, heavy silence descended upon the drawing room.

Should he say something? Was this his moment to declare his love for her?

James glanced at Meredith, who concentrated very hard on her sewing, keeping her head down and attention focused on every perfectly tight little stitch.

"I wanted Miss Green to have a pleasant evening," James said blandly.

His sisters didn't bother to reply, as if they all knew his words were simply a pathetic attempt to hide the truth of his feelings. He even caught his sisters exchanging glances to the effect of *are you going to say something? Shall I?*

"That is very admirable and I share your sentiment. But might I remind you that you have one job, Duke," Josephine said sharply. "In fact, all of you have one task. To marry and marry well."

More than one Cavendish sibling rolled their eyes heavenward, because Lord knew they'd heard that a hundred thousand times before.

He knew this, they all knew it, and yet the duchess kept saying it . . . as if she were still waiting for it to sink in, waiting for him to follow the command. That she was still saying it suggested that she would not be amenable to the declaration he had half planned.

I intend to marry your lowborn companion.

No, that was not marrying well. It was not what the duchess would approve of. James felt another door slamming shut, the walls closing in.

"Well, perhaps Lady Bridget might do us proud," Claire said. Then she continued reading from the paper. "*Lady Bridget was seen waltzing with Lord Darcy. It would be an excellent match for her, and . . .* oh."

"What does it say?"

Claire closed the sheet. "Nothing."

"Liar."

"It says it would be an excellent match for you and a surprising choice for him."

"She is the sister to a duke. It wouldn't be surprising at all," Josephine said flatly.

"Does it say why?" Bridget asked suspiciously.

"It just says that it would be surprising if one of England's most refined gentlemen wed the girl who fell," Claire said with an apologetic smile.

And then there was that. Bridget was trying so hard — more than anyone in the fam-

338

ily — and yet she was constantly dogged by her one misstep. Literally. It seemed that nothing she could do — not dozens of perfectly well-mannered appearances at balls, or snagging a suitor like this Darcy fellow — could make the ton forget about the one time she slipped and fell on her backside at their debut ball.

What happened when there was a greater scandal?

Like, say, the duke eloping with the companion? The family might never live it down. It would be whispered about for years. Their children would have to grow up in the shadow of such gossip. Could he do that to all those unborn Cavendish brats?

Ah, yes, the doors were slamming, the walls were closing in, the windows were shutting on his hopes and dreams.

"Your Grace," the butler intoned from the doorway. "A caller."

It was Mr. Collins, their "cousin" and James's heir. At first James was relieved when the odious man requested an audience alone with Bridget — the less he had to suffer through the man's insufferable company, the better — but it was only a hot second before James realized why and what for.

"No, wait —"

"Come along, Duke." The duchess ushered him out. "Lady Amelia and Lady Claire, I insist you come, too."

Meredith didn't need to be told twice; she had already set aside her sewing and made her way to the foyer. The duchess shut the drawing room doors all the way.

"Josephine . . ." James warned.

"Shhh. We cannot hear when you are talking."

They could hardly hear through the thick oak doors anyway. They being the duchess, Amelia, Claire, Meredith, a downstairs maid, and one footman. But it was unnecessary, for they all had a good idea what transpired on the other side. Mr. Collins was proposing, and, James prayed to God, Bridget was refusing him without a second of hesitation.

If she threw her life away on that odious and small-minded worm because of some notion of duty to the family, he'd never forgive himself.

Pendleton returned with a bottle of champagne. James was about to order it away when suddenly, the doors burst open, and Mr. Collins burst out, clearly in an agitated state. Bridget followed behind. It was clear what had happened: Mr. Collins had proposed, Bridget refused him, and the duchess expected to celebrate a betrothal.

"Mr. Collins was just taking leave of us," Bridget said firmly.

The butler had to hand over a bottle of champagne to the footman in order to hand Mr. Collins his hat and cane. Everyone watched in awkward silence as the man, red in the face, took his leave.

The door shut behind him.

"Don't bother to open the champagne, Pendleton," the duchess said with a disapproving frown. "It is clear we have nothing to celebrate."

"Did you honestly think that we would?" Bridget asked incredulously.

"You must marry. You must all marry!" For once, the duchess actually raised her voice.

"I do not think we are opposed to marriage," James said evenly.

"We are just opposed to pledging our troths to morons," Bridget said.

"Well if you continue to flout society, you may only have the likes of Mr. Collins to choose from!" the duchess cried. "And he is not the worst possible person. At least the dukedom would stay in the family. You would be provided for. What if your brother dies and you are all unwed? How will you support yourselves? Who will marry you then, when you have no dowries because everything has gone to Mr. Collins?"

"James won't die," Amelia protested.

"People die, Amelia. Look at our parents," Claire said softly.

"Yes, but people love, too. Look at our parents," Bridget said. "Don't we all want that?"

Everyone, from the duchess to the butler, fell silent. Thoughtful. Amelia bit her lip. Claire exhaled deeply. James felt his heart clench.

"We want what our mother and father had, Josephine. Love," James said quietly, looking at Meredith. "The kind of love you throw a dukedom away for."

One might already say they were throwing the dukedom away with every rule broken, every convention flouted, all the daggers shot from eyes, excessive quantities of champagne quaffed, unchaperoned London adventures, accidental slips and falls in ballrooms, Claire's scandalous attendances at mathematical lectures . . .

They should at least get love out of it.

There was little Meredith could do about that, other than get out of the way of it happening.

As she stood there in the foyer while the

metaphorical smoke cleared between the duchess and the Cavendishes, Meredith knew two things as sure as she knew her own name.

James could never put his own happiness ahead of his sisters. This was one reason she loved him. And if he prioritized their love over his sisters' happiness, they would never be truly happy together knowing the price his sisters paid.

Meredith knew the duchess would be devastated if she failed at her life's goal of assuring the succession of Durham. She had watched for years as the duchess tried and failed, tried and failed. So desperate was she to assure success that she had tracked down a long-lost *American* relative in the desperate hope that he might be a decent duke.

Everyone said she was mad to go searching the colonies for a long-lost heir. But James was her last hope. Here he was, *so close* to being the man Durham needed him to be, save for Meredith tempting him to throw it all away.

One by one, the Cavendishes drifted away from the foyer to be alone with their thoughts. She'd never seen them so quiet and pensive before.

"Meredith, if I might have a word with you."

"Of course, Your Grace."

Meredith followed the duchess upstairs to Her Grace's private sitting room. James started after her, and Mer shook her head *no.* This was between her and the duchess. She had to do this alone.

Once in familiar environs of her private sitting room the duchess settled into her favorite chair, and Meredith took her usual place on the settee opposite.

They'd sat together like this a hundred times, a thousand times. They had discussed light topics, like the latest ton gossip: who wore what to the theater, how best to attire the Cavendish girls, or which parties to attend.

Meredith had also been privy to more private concerns: the duchess's ongoing distress about a lack of heir, or even a girl child; the late duke's declining health, the duchess's worries about the dukedom.

Something in the air, or maybe it was something in Meredith's heart, told her this would not be a lighthearted gossip session about the fashion choices at last night's soiree.

"Well, did you enjoy the ball?" The duchess's voice was heavy.

Meredith answered truthfully. "Very much. It was an honor to attend."

"I suppose we should see to it that you attend more engagements. You might find a suitor," the duchess said and Meredith stilled. This was unexpected. "I suppose it's been selfish of me to keep you with me on the sidelines, and thus on the shelf, so that I might have your company for longer."

"I understand why you do." Until a few Americans tumbled into their lives, Meredith was the only person the duchess could rely on. She was like the daughter she'd never had. She was her companion for now and for her old age.

Remember that. Remember that. Remember that.

"But never mind such sentimental thoughts." She reached into the drawer at the side table and withdrew something shiny and sparkly. Something that made Meredith suck in a breath. "I found this last night."

There it was, in the duchess's palm, the butterfly brooch with nary a diamond or emerald out of place. The one Meredith had borrowed and lost.

"Oh! I had been looking for that last night and this morning. I was wretched with worry. I thought it might have fallen off on the stairs . . ."

"Actually, one of the housemaids found it in the duke's study, near the desk. Which is, oddly, where she found the duke when I sent her to find him for the toast late last night."

Meredith stilled. She *knew* this wasn't a pleasant afternoon chat. She just hadn't realized how much the duchess knew, and she was achingly sorry that Her Grace had found out from someone other than herself.

"I can't imagine why the brooch might have fallen off your gown there. Or what His Grace was doing in his study during a ball. It *sounds* like you might have been with him. But I shouldn't like to make assumptions, especially about such a grave matter. Especially not about *you,* Meredith."

There were just enough holes in the story for Meredith to fill them in with lies and half-truths that would be to her benefit. She could dispel any suspicions. She could buy time, and wait for James to come to her rescue with his excuses and noble declarations of *blame me, not her* and *I am the duke.*

And then what?

Meredith would be left standing in the shadows again. Besides, she wasn't some fairy-tale miss who counted on Prince Charming to swoop in and save her. No, she had been raised by none other than the Duchess of Durham, and as such, she was no shrinking violet.

This was it then, the moment of reckoning.

This was not even about her and the duke.

It was about her and the duchess. If nothing else, Meredith owed her the truth.

"I think I might love him."

Meredith hadn't said the words aloud before. She had barely even allowed herself to think them. But she had felt them with each beat of her heart, with every breath, with each and every heated gaze between her and the duke. But saying them aloud . . . that made it all seem real.

Perhaps she should have said those words to James first.

I think I might love you.

While she was mostly certain of his reply, she was on tenterhooks as to how the duchess would answer. And Dear Lord in Heaven, was she taking her time crafting a response.

First, her gaze sharpened.

Next, her lips flattened into a thinly pressed line.

Meredith stopped bothering trying to control her inhales and exhalations; she gave up and let the air get stuck in her throat and her lungs grow tight and fiery. She had not expected acceptance. But this waiting for her sentence was excruciating.

"Well," Her Grace said after an endless silence. "That is inconvenient."

And that is what broke Meredith's heart. She and her feelings were nothing more than an *inconvenience* to the woman who raised her. Who, presumably, loved her. Who, unlike her own *mother,* recognized and remembered her.

"Meredith, you know that he needs a bride. A . . . suitable bride." The duchess spoke delicately, with a small sigh of lament.

It was one thing for Meredith to have said it herself, always with a little hope that she might be wrong. But if the Duchess of Durham said it, it was not wrong.

"My question is *why* I am not suitable."

"Meredith, you know how the ton works . . ."

"I do know," Meredith said, voice tight. "But I want to hear *you* say it. All of it. Because we both know that the only person who knows Durham better than you is myself. We both know that I possess all the accomplishments of a lady. I am well mannered, well spoken, well educated. I am experienced in society. I have been taught by the best."

"And we both know that is not enough."

"You mean my family is not enough. My father, the duke's valet, was not enough. My mother, who served you faithfully for years, is not enough. We're too common. But that's just it, isn't it? She served. Just as I serve you . . ." She bit back the word *faithfully*. She was in no position to say that this morning.

"It is not what I think, it is what the ton thinks. And we both know ancestry is everything. Connections are everything. Wealth is everything. Class is everything."

"And there is no hiding the truth with me."

"Never mind the truth about you. I have had one purpose in life, one purpose in a world that allows women to be little more than decoration. My life's work is to secure Durham for another generation. I love you like a daughter, Meredith. I only want what is best for you. And I don't think this is it. The ton will be cruel. Your children will struggle for acceptance . . . especially if your mother's condition proves to be heritable."

"I think he might love me, too."

"Passion fades, Meredith. And then how will you and the duke get on when the ton has turned against you both? When they refuse to accept your children?"

As much as it pained her, she knew what the duchess said was true, and spoken with only the best of intentions. She knew the right thing to do. Meredith swallowed hard. She loved James. But she loved the duchess, too.

"I think I should go away for a spell. I'll go visit my mother. Perhaps when it comes to the duke, out of sight is out of mind. Perhaps while I'm gone, he and the girls will make *suitable* matches."

"Meredith — you should keep this brooch. One day I'll explain why." The duchess held out the brooch. A peace offering, perhaps. A mere token of affection. A little treasure from the Cavendish family vaults. But she didn't ask her to stay.

A duke must always respect a woman's wishes. Even if they break his heart.
— THE RULES FOR DUKES

It took Meredith a few days to make the arrangements for her departure, and all the while she pretended as if nothing were amiss. She sat in during the family's afternoons at home, and was present when Amelia's suitor came calling. She consoled Bridget over Darcy and served as a confidante and rather lax chaperone for Claire

350

when Lord Fox came to call.

She did her very best to avoid James.

She almost succeeded in avoiding him entirely, but he caught her in the foyer — the great, vast, marble and gold foyer that made a person feel oh, so small — as she was trying to sneak out without saying good-bye.

She watched as James took note of the footman walking ahead toward the open door with her luggage. Next he took note of her traveling dress, and the gloves and reticule in her hands.

There was a stormy look in his blue eyes. He didn't like what he saw.

"You're leaving," he said.

"I am leaving."

"Why?"

James stood at the bottom of the stairs. She noticed his grip on the balustrade tightening.

"Because it is the right thing to do. We both know that, James."

"We need you. I need you. Amelia now has this suitor and I'm not certain of him. Bridget is heartsick over this Darcy fellow. And I have no idea what is happening with Claire and Lord Fox. I need you to advise them. And me."

"Exactly," Meredith said, her resolve to

leave strengthened, even as she looked into James's blue eyes, which always made her melt a little.

"Exactly?"

"Your sisters have real chances at true happiness. I shall not stand in the way of it."

"Why would you stand in the way of it?"

Meredith gave him a sharp look, because he very well knew the answer to that.

"Besides," she continued. "I need to visit with my mother. She is not well."

"I'll go with you." He started toward her. "You will want company."

"Your sisters need you here and I need to visit her alone." She took a few steps back, careful to maintain a sensible distance between them. If he got too close, she would lose her resolve. But then he took another step or two in her direction.

"I see what you are doing," he said, standing close, oh, so close. "You are being my better judgment. You are demonstrating the strength and restraint that I should show but cannot. And here I am some lovesick fool, begging you not to go."

"I'm not going away forever."

"But who knows what will have happened by the time you have returned. I might fall in love with someone else." He said this softly. The words hung in the air between them.

Or rather, one word.

Love.

He paused.

She paused.

"If your heart is that fickle, then I suppose I should be rid of you now."

"It isn't. That's not what I meant. Mer . . . I feel like . . ." She watched his hand gripping the railing. The knuckles were white as he held on for what seemed like dear life. "I don't want to be parted from you. This house will feel incomplete without you. I will feel incomplete without you. Meredith, I don't know how to do this without you."

The anguish in his voice almost made her lose her resolve. Almost.

"I don't know who I am outside of the shadow of the duchess, and of Durham," Meredith explained, because this wasn't entirely about him, and he needed to know that. "I don't know what world or life awaits me outside of this role. This might be the best I could hope for. Or there might be more for me. There is so much I don't know, James, and I won't know as long as I stay here. And you and your sisters won't know as long as I am here, distracting you from becoming someone great, someone you were born to be."

"You are certain. I can see in your eyes, and the stubborn tilt of your jaw that there is no persuading you otherwise."

"And I can see in your eyes that you know I am right, and that you know better than to try to change my mind."

"This is goodbye then."

"Goodbye, James. Just James."

She reached out and caressed his cheek, one last time. He gripped her hand and held it to him.

"Goodbye, Meredith," he said, finally letting go. "You'll never be just a girl to me."

CHAPTER 17

A few days later
Hampshire

"How good of you to visit us," Mrs. Bates said, with no small amount of sarcasm as she opened the door to the small cottage. Meredith stood on the step, holding her few belongings. "It's so very good of you to spare some time for your mother between all your fancy parties and shopping sprees."

In London, Meredith was a nobody who barely clung to the fringes of fashionable society. But here she was considered fancy and above herself. In spite of her best efforts to be modest and obliging, they all thought she put on airs.

Especially Mrs. Bates, a large and bullish woman, who was left with the thankless task of caring for Meredith's mother, Mrs. Clara Green, former and beloved lady's maid to the Duchess of Durham.

"How is she?" Meredith asked, stepping

into the small foyer.

"She was fine an hour ago, actually. You'll have to see for yourself how she is now. You know how she changes and how quickly."

Meredith followed Mrs. Bates into the parlor, where her mother was in her usual seat of the rocking chair near the window, with a view of the garden. Her hair had long ago gone gray, and the wrinkles that lined her face had deepened as the years went by.

"Who is it? Who is there?"

Meredith looked into her mother's eyes — ones that were an awful lot like Meredith's — and saw the confusion there. Long ago, those dark eyes had looked at her with love, worry, joy, delight, and all the feelings a mother had for her daughter. These days, they barely registered her existence.

"It's me, Mother. Meredith."

"I am not at home to callers," her mother said archly.

"She's not at home to callers," Mrs. Bates repeated with a snort.

"I heard her," Meredith murmured. Then, playing along with whatever scene was unfolding in her mother's head, she said, "Perhaps I shall call another time."

"Leave your card, if you will." Her mother gave her a dismissive wave.

"She thinks she is the duchess," Mrs.

Bates confided. "High and mighty, like mother, like daughter."

Meredith bit her tongue. Mrs. Bates had no idea of high and mighty — perhaps one day she would, if she actually met the duchess. Her Grace could freeze that sneer right off Mrs. Bates's face. And yet, the duchess provided the funds for Clara's care, but left Meredith to manage Mrs. Bates.

It couldn't have been easy, putting up with her mother in this state. All those hours shut up alone in this cottage with a madwoman who, more often than not, was confused about the day or the year or her own past or even her own daughter. *She forgot she had a daughter.*

Meredith knew this was merely a symptom of whatever afflicted her mother's mind. But today, after leaving the duchess and parting with James, she worried, *am I so forgettable then?*

The next morning
In London, there was always plenty to do, and with the arrival of the Cavendish family, there had been plenty of conversation at meals and laughter ringing through the corridors. Never a dull moment with that lot.

So it was strange now to be in this small, quiet house.

In London, Meredith just felt small and in the shadows, but here she felt large and ungainly and intrusive. There was little to do and few people with whom to associate.

In fact, the only thing to do was sit in the parlor with her mother and attempt conversation whilst Mrs. Bates sat nearby, hemming bedsheets.

"Good morning, Mother."

"Who are you speaking to? Who is it?" she asked, alarmed.

"It is I, Meredith. Your daughter."

Her mother laughed. "I'm only one and twenty and unwed. I can't have a daughter."

Ah, so her mother's mind was lodged in the past again. Meredith did some calculations in her head (though admittedly not as quickly as Claire would have performed them). Her mother must think it was 1783. She and the duchess would have both been one and twenty, and the duchess married for three years already.

Her mother then fixed her attentions on Meredith. For a second, she thought her mother's mind had cleared, so sharp was her gaze.

"Your Grace, it is time to get ready for the ball tonight."

"She thinks you're the duchess," Mrs. Bates said with a smirk. "She must be off

358

on another one of her flights of fancy again. Happens more and more these days."

This just made Meredith sigh. And oh, what a sigh. Her mother thought her the Duchess of Durham, a role Meredith was at once trained to play and yet could never truly embody. So much for her efforts to escape.

"Best just play along then," Mrs. Bates advised. Grumbling under her breath, she added, "She never mistakes *me* for the duchess."

"I've pressed the blue dress for you," her mother continued, reenacting some scene from her day as a lady's maid. "And we must decide whether to wear it with the diamond parure or the set of emeralds."

"The problems some people have," Mrs. Bates muttered. Privately, Meredith agreed.

Meredith didn't know the blue dress of which she spoke, but she was familiar with the diamond parure — a set including a tiara, necklace, and earrings all made with diamonds and deep blue sapphires.

"The tiara doesn't quite fit," Meredith said. They'd confirmed this just the other night at the Cavendish ball.

"That's right. It was made for the dowager duchess's fat head."

Her mother cackled.

"Clara," Meredith said reprovingly, as she imagined the duchess might do.

Then to no one in particular, her mother said, "Her Grace usually tucks into the sherry after the ball, not before."

"Better than before breakfast," Mrs. Bates muttered.

Meredith gave a small huff of laughter.

But she also felt a pang of homesickness for life with the duchess and a newfound kinship with her mother as she thought of all the evenings she'd handled that diamond parure with the too-big tiara and poured Her Grace a glass (or two) of sherry and listened to her recount the evening. Like mother, like daughter.

"We talk about the dowager's fat head all the time," her mother said.

Well this was a side of the duchess Meredith had never seen. A younger, less restrained side. She could scarcely imagine it.

"Perhaps it's not so much fat as stubborn," her mother continued. "With all her rules and nagging for an heir and all that. Lord knows you're trying. I've never seen anybody try so hard at anything."

Meredith glanced over at Mrs. Bates, who was presently concerned with a knot in her thread. Perhaps she'd heard this scene a thousand times before or maybe she simply didn't care.

But Meredith blushed slightly, considering the intimacy that must have existed between the duchess and her lady's maid — how much her mother must have known of Her Grace's efforts and failures to conceive, all her hopes and heartaches, and all the pressure the duchess must have been under to not only produce an heir, but to rule society and manage multiple households.

"You are so determined to be the perfect duchess in every other way," Clara said sagely.

Knowing the duchess as she did, Meredith couldn't imagine the duchess confiding such stresses in anyone else. But as her lady's maid, Clara must have observed so much, and what she said now rang true today. No wonder Her Grace supported her mother in her mad old age; it was only fair as her mother had supported her.

"I don't suppose you know if the earl will be attending the house party?" Clara asked. Was she still reliving her memories? Was this a continuation of the same scene or a new one? And which earl?

"Why do you ask?" Meredith inquired.

"You know why, Duchess." Her mother gave her a sassy wink. Meredith raised an eyebrow at the audacity, the familiarity.

"Remind me," Meredith said.

Her mother shrugged and said, "He seems to have taken a liking to me."

Mer's breath caught in her throat. As a lady's maid, did she really speak of earls and romance to the duchess like that? Or was this a fantasy scene? Meredith was confused, but intrigued, by this window into the past or at least her mother's inner life. Too much rang true for her to immediately discount it as merely fantasy.

"What kind of liking?"

"The kind that makes a girl dream of better things," her mother said. And Lud, if that didn't start a crack in Meredith's heart because she knew all about that kind of liking and loving. "But don't worry, Your Grace, I know my place. And his place. He's just quite handsome."

"He won't marry you," Meredith said. Surely that is what the duchess said then, just as she said it recently. And, because she knew how this story played out, Meredith added, "You'll marry someone else."

"That's probably true. Doesn't mean I can't have a bit of fun first." Her mother burst into a girlish laughter, which was something else coming from her mouth, lined with wrinkles.

Meredith was momentarily mortified to

be faced with the prospect of her mother being young and wild and potentially having flings with handsome lords. There were some things a child did not want to consider about her parents.

"The lax morals of the upper classes . . ." Mrs. Bates clucked.

"What do you mean, upper classes? My mother was a lady's maid. Not quite the same."

"But the earl is upper class," Mrs. Bates said. "And Lud, do my ears burn when she gets started on reliving those encounters between her and the Earl of Cambria."

"The Earl of Cambria?"

Her heart stopped beating. Truly, for a moment, it stopped. The air stopped rushing in and out of her lungs. It couldn't be . . .

Before Meredith could even think through the implications, Mrs. Bates was chattering away.

"How can a London girl like yourself be shocked by some lord dallying with a lady's maid at a house party?"

Meredith wasn't shocked by that; it happened all the time, then and now. She knew that well enough, not that she'd share that with the judgmental Mrs. Bates.

But she was shocked by what it might

mean for her parentage. Because if she wasn't the daughter of the duke's valet, as she'd always assumed . . . if there was blue blood in her veins after all . . . *if her father was the Earl of Cambria . . .*

She still wouldn't have a name, or connections, or a dowry or any adjoining acres. But she would have one more thing to make her a little more of a suitable bride for James: blue blood pulsing through her veins.

Because she still thought of James even after all these days and nights away. She thought of him struggling to make sense of being a duke and wanted to be there to help him through. She thought of all their stolen moments on the stairs, or kisses in the corridors. At the breakfast table or in the parlor, she wanted to look up and catch his eye. She had questions for him, about the horses she saw in the fields or how this little cottage compared to his home in Maryland. She craved his touch.

He might have been out of sight but he was hardly out of mind.

And now her mother — her mad, out-of-her-mind mother — was saying things that led Meredith to hope that her case might not be so hopeless after all.

Meredith took a deep breath. She shouldn't get ahead of herself.

"Clara, do remind me what month and year it is," Meredith said in her best imitation of the duchess. It was pretty good, if she said so herself. She'd had years of observation and practice. In a way, no one was more perfectly prepared than her to be the next Duchess of Durham.

But her mother was now off in a different reverie and any questions remained vexingly unanswered.

A few days later

Days passed while Meredith helped Mrs. Bates with the housekeeping and kept her mother company. This usually entailed listening and playing along as her mother relived scenes from her past. It was illuminating — what better way to get to know her mother than to dramatically reenact scenes from her whole life?

But it was also exhausting to be constantly performing various roles, leaping from the duchess, to her father (or so she thought), to shopkeepers and Lord only knew who else.

There were dull scenes in which she discussed what the duchess should wear and when she'd like her breakfast and recounting of gossip from over twenty years earlier.

There were more troubling scenes in

which her mother reenacted fights with her father — or the man she'd known as her father. Mr. Green had been Durham's valet; he and her mother had met in service to the duke and duchess, had wed, and had Meredith — or so she'd been told. They had all lived in a small cottage on the estate, and from a very young age, Meredith was left to help run the household while her parents worked. She'd been close to her mother, but had scarcely any memories of her father. The ones she did have weren't ones to warm the heart.

At least, this is what she had known and the story she had been told.

There was no mention of this earl, in spite of Meredith's efforts.

"Tell me about you and the Earl of Cambria," she said again in her best impression of the duchess.

"I'll press the blue dress for this evening. Would you like to wear it with the diamond parure or the sapphires?"

Sometimes Meredith answered the diamond parure, or the sapphires, or suggested the green dress instead.

Sometimes, Meredith tried to prompt her mother to start on a particular scene or topic she wished to know more about. How had Mr. Green proposed? How had the duchess persuaded her to give up her daughter? Why had the duchess brought Meredith to live with her anyway?

It was such an effort, a game, to set up these scenes in the hopes her mother would say something revelatory. If only she could *just ask.* Sometimes all Meredith wanted was to have a simple, basic conversation where her mother recognized her. Knew her. Saw her.

"Do you know who I am, Mother?"

"You're the Duchess of Durham," her mother said, having no idea how that rent a fresh tear in her daughter's warm, beating heart. "Honestly, Josephine, what kind of question is that?"

And so the days passed, full of maddening conversations that prompted questions that only Her Grace, the Duchess of Durham, could answer.

And Meredith wanted answers.

CHAPTER 18

Very often dukes will excuse themselves with the pretense of important estate business. But sometimes there actually is important estate business.

— THE RULES FOR DUKES

Durham Park

When one's heart was broken and one's future seemed to be some vague disappointment, there was only one thing to do: take solace in drainage ditches.

At least, that was James's plan.

Meredith had left, and it was not clear when she would return, if ever. The duchess was tightlipped about it — not wanting to encourage him, presumably. There was gossip about him and Lady Jemma; it seemed that she and the rest of the haute ton were expecting a proposal, oh, any second now. But he just. Couldn't. Do. It.

But James did learn that important ducal

estate business provided a very convenient excuse to avoid problems in London that he'd rather not deal with. He invented an emergency at Durham Park, had Edwards pack up his belongings, and left.

Now here he was, digging drainage ditches with Mr. Simons and Mr. Sprock in what seemed to be a very fine pair of breeches and a linen shirt. Edwards would have an apoplexy when he saw the bottle green wool jacket lying in a heap under a tree, to say nothing of the long-lost cravat and the state of his boots.

"It's very good of you to come to assist us, Your Grace," said Simons, eyeing him warily.

"No need to call me Your Grace. Just James will do." Then James winced as *Just James* brought back a storm of memories that he was trying to forget.

The sight of her across a crowded room. Her shy smile. The soft click of the door closing. The soft sigh from her kissable lips.

James pushed his shovel into the dirt and heaved a pile of it off to the side. Drainage ditches. He needed to focus on drainage ditches.

"Begging your pardon, Your Grace," Sprock added. "But it seems improper to address you any other way."

"But we're digging a drainage ditch," James said, pausing to take a breath. Bloody hell, London was making him soft. Back home in Maryland, this labor wouldn't even have him breaking a sweat. "I think we can do away with all that formality."

"But you're still the duke."

A duke who was digging a drainage ditch as an escape from romantic troubles.

"It is a bit odd to have the duke himself personally assist us with this manual labor," said Simons. "This hot, dirty, sweaty, messy manual labor."

"Surely dukes have more important things to attend to," Sprock added.

"Just a lot of paperwork, mainly," James grunted. Gasped, really.

"Don't blame you for being out here then."

James shrugged and got back to work digging. It was a known fact that drainage ditches didn't dig themselves and if they were to be an effective distraction from romantic troubles, then he would have to focus.

And so, he dug while Sprock and Simons chatted away while they worked.

"The previous duke, may he rest in peace, would never concern himself with something like this."

"I dunno, Sprock, I reckon he would have done, but the duchess would never allow it. She kept him busy with all that important duke business."

"I shudder at what this place would be without her firm hand behind it."

"I thought the late duke was well regarded for his management of the estates and his work in parliament," James cut in.

At least, that was the impression he got from his review of the account books (very well, Claire's review) and conversations with the late duke's colleagues in government. By all accounts, he was an upstanding man who knew his duty and performed it well. No sins, no scandals. It was a tough act to follow.

"Oh, he was a good man. Knew his duty. But he still understood that the life of an aristocrat wasn't all it's cracked up to be."

It's not just me, James thought. He kept digging.

"Not that we know."

"So we've heard."

"That's why he let your father run off with that horse."

James paused in his digging. *Let?*

"Whatever happened to that horse?" Sprock asked. "Mess something it was called. Can't quite remember."

"Messenger," James answered, picturing the tall black stallion. "My father took the horse and used him to establish his breeding and training program."

"Never saw a horse like that one before or since."

For once, James didn't want to talk about Messenger. Or horses. Or home. He was stuck on a casually spoken string of words that weren't compatible with the story he'd grown up hearing.

"What do you mean the duke *let* my father run off with the horse?"

What about the secret plans, galloping through the darkness at midnight? The risks if he were caught?

"Oh, I thought you knew."

"Sprock, look at him: he obviously didn't know."

"Your father was never very happy after he came back from the war. Everyone thought it was the aftereffects of battle, but the duke knew your brother was lovesick for a woman he met in the colonies."

For once James didn't correct the saying of *the colonies.*

"The duke was just married himself. Or about to be? I can't recall, it was so long ago. I think he and the duchess figured they'd have an heir and a spare soon enough, so the duke let him go. Helped with the arrangements, but didn't let the missus in on it."

"There was a scandal," said Simons. "My wife read about it in the London papers. Months after the fact, of course, before we got the city papers out here. But then she told me and everyone. We all talked about it."

"Aye, the duchess didn't like that. She had an aversion to scandal," Sprock said, smiling at the memory. "Not one bit. Her lady's maid told her husband, the valet. Or was it the other way around? Either way, he learned about it and he told us."

"Were they married then? I can't seem to recall."

"It did happen awfully quick. One of *those* weddings."

James kept digging. And thinking. He was learning a lot from these two old tenants, not the least of which was that old men seemed to gossip as much, if not more, than young women.

Later that day
James spent the last hours of daylight in the portrait gallery. He didn't know what he was looking for, exactly, but after listening to Simons and Sprock all day, he supposed

he wanted something like understanding.

He paused in front of a portrait of the duke, painted in the man's later years. With his distinguished gray hair, strong pose, His Grace, the fifth Duke of Durham, looked so . . . ducal.

Was he really the sort of man who would encourage his younger brother to leave *everything* behind for love in another country, on another continent, knowing they might never see each other again? If he was anything like the duchess it was hard to imagine it.

Nearby was a portrait of his father as a young man, and James stood in front of it for a long time, marveling at how it was like looking in a mirror. He was the spitting image of his father in this picture — the same blue eyes, the same light brown hair (though worn in a different style these days), the straight nose and strong jaw. His attentions were fixed to something — someone? — off the canvas.

Messenger was in the background. James recognized the shiny black coat and spot of white on his nose and the lively look in the animal's eye. James grew up with that horse; he'd recognize him anywhere.

That the animal should be in a portrait with his father suggested that horse belonged to him. One didn't often commission a portrait with oneself and stolen goods. James began to wonder if perhaps there wasn't some truth to what Sprock and Simons had said. On that note, it was remarkable that this portrait still had pride of place in the family gallery in the preferred family estate.

But one thing was clear to James: his father hadn't run off or escaped. He'd left with the blessing of his family. Otherwise, the portrait would be burned or in the attics.

So why couldn't James have that love, too?

Farther down the gallery was a painting of the duchess as a young woman; it was one of those portraits done to commemorate a betrothal or a marriage and the triumph of snaring a duke.

It was strange seeing the duchess as a young woman. James had only ever thought of her as he knew her now: older, wiser, all knowing, and vaguely terrifying at times. In this painting, her hair was blonde instead of white, and her skin was dewy with youth. Her gaze was as shrewd as ever and there was no mistaking that it was her.

There was something about her smile, though . . . something that made James stop in his tracks and take a second look. It was a sweet smile, but a knowing one at the same time.

Something about the upturn of her lips and the slight tilt of her head seemed familiar, but James was having a hard time placing it. It was a smile he knew, but one he'd never seen on the duchess in real life.

James stared at it for a long time before it finally dawned on him.

No . . .

It couldn't be . . .

That didn't make sense . . .

And yet . . .

James turned and strode briskly from the portrait gallery. He would depart for London at first light because he had questions that couldn't wait and questions that only the duchess could answer.

Upon occasion, a duke may find it beneficial to seek advice from trusted and respected persons.
— THE RULES FOR DUKES

Durham House, London
James arrived back at Durham House in London late in the evening. The duchess had already retired, so James sought out his sisters for company. He knew exactly where they would be: in Claire's bedroom for

some quality family time, in which they could chatter away without being reminded of duty and etiquette and in which it would feel like *home* before everything changed.

Claire, Bridget, and Amelia were all lounging on Claire's bed and, as was his habit, James was sprawled in a chair pulled up beside them. His sisters were nattering on about some girlish stuff he wasn't quite listening to, though he found their familiar voices and accents comforting and a welcome distraction.

But then, the conversation took a turn.

"Remind me again why Meredith left us?" Bridget wondered aloud.

So much for the thoughts he was trying to avoid.

"I miss her," Claire said. "My maid Pippa is not nearly as good a chaperone. She actually pays attention unless I find some way to distract her. Meredith and I had an understanding."

"A good chaperone is so hard to find," Bridget mused.

"She didn't *leave*," James replied. Insisted, really. This was just a temporary absence, not a permanent one — or so he told himself. The alternative was too much to even contemplate. Although it had felt awfully permanent when they'd said goodbye. "She's visiting her mother, who is ill. She'll return."

"That's the *only* reason she left?" Amelia asked. "The one and only reason?"

"What other reason would there be?" James replied evenly, evasively. Discussing things of a romantic nature with one's sisters was no man's idea of a good time.

He was treated to the sight of three Cavendish sisters rolling their eyes at once. Synchronized eye rolling. Only his sisters would excel at that.

"Brothers." Amelia sighed mightily.

"So does anyone know when Meredith will come back?" Claire asked.

"That question was addressed to the group at large," James pointed out. "So why are you all looking at me?"

"You can give a man a dukedom, but you can't give him basic, common sense," Bridget said.

"Even Lord Fox isn't this obtuse," Claire said, referring to her suitor who was well liked but widely regarded to *not* be the sharpest knife in the drawer.

"Even Darcy isn't this stubborn," Bridget said.

"Even Alistair isn't this evasive," Amelia added.

James never imagined the day that all his

sisters would compare him to their suitors and that he'd come up wanting. But he'd had plenty of experience with their prying and needling. There was only one way to deal with it.

"Why don't you just tell me what you'd like me to say and I'll say it?" James asked. He didn't know what to say otherwise. He suspected that she wasn't just visiting her mother but fleeing from him and his cowardice.

Try as he might to rationalize it as duty or whatnot, James was starting to suspect he might just be scared — scared of the enormity of his feelings, scared of the duchess, scared of failing in this new role.

"We want you to speak from the heart," Bridget said.

"Yes, confide in us all your deepest feelings," Amelia added.

"I must be becoming more English than I realized because I feel nauseated at the thought of discussing my feelings. With my sisters. Without copious amounts of whiskey."

"Shall I fetch us some?" Amelia offered mischievously.

The other siblings simultaneously offered a swift and sure "NO."

"Why did she really leave, James?" Claire asked.

That was the thing about sisters: they were relentless and unmoved by his diversionary tactics. They didn't care if it was scary or painful for him to examine his feelings or to *speak from the heart.* And they were the only ones in the world who could make no bones about any of that, and insist that he toughen up and speak the truth. It was probably for his own good.

He would go to his grave before he said a word of any of that aloud, though. Naturally.

With three pairs of eyes staring at him expectantly, James knew he had to tell them something.

"As you know, the duchess is keen for me to wed," he began.

"No!" Amelia said, feigning surprise.

"You don't say," Bridget drawled.

"I am shocked," Claire said flatly. "Simply shocked."

He made a face at them and carried on.

"I might have half a mind to marry Meredith, but the duchess favors someone more suitable. Or rather, anyone more suitable."

There was a long moment of silence. And frowning sister faces.

"I see why she left," Claire said, sticking her nose in the air.

"*Half a mind* to marry her indeed," Bridget added. "If that isn't a nail in the coffin of romance I don't know what is."

"Best she got out while she could," Amelia, his baby sister, said sagely, nodding.

"That's not what I meant," James protested.

"Isn't it?" Claire asked. "If you were wholeheartedly and whole-mindedly determined to wed her, would she really be gone right now?"

That was a good question.

A fair question.

A question that it pained him to consider.

"Her mother. She's ill. She went to be with her." He said this weakly, knowing it was a weak excuse, and he clung to it desperately.

"Hasn't her mother been ill for quite some time now?" Claire asked. "Before we even arrived, I think."

"You could have gone with her," Bridget pointed out. "To provide comfort and company."

"Romance isn't just flowers and waltzes, you know," Amelia said. "It's showing up for someone and standing up with someone in their hour of need. In all of the hours, in fact."

"That is awfully wise of you, Amelia,"

Bridget said, sounding impressed.

"Our little sister is growing up," Claire said with a loving sigh.

"Now if only our older brother would, too," Amelia said. "Emphasis on *old.*"

"This is some way to treat your beloved brother."

"Unless we've only *half a mind* to love you," Bridget said pointedly. The others nodded and shrugged their agreement.

After all he had done for them! After all he had sacrificed for them! After all the life choices he had made on their behalf or with their happiness in mind! After all that and they made cracks about halfhearted loving!

No. Just no.

"It's because of all of you, all right?" James said. "Because of my three *beloved* sisters, whose happiness I prize more than my own."

"Me?"

"Moi?"

"Us?"

"I cannot risk a scandal while you are all unwed," he explained, voice tight with frustration. "I cannot ruin your prospects with my own selfish desires."

There was a moment of silence in which it was apparent that this was only occurring to them now. Which was fine — as it should be. But any moment at least one of them should say, *Thank you, dear beloved brother, for your noble sacrifice and for putting our happiness before your own.*

That was not what they said.

"That is awfully sweet of you," Bridget began *politely.* "But . . ."

"Really thoughtful of you," Amelia added. "But . . ."

"But what makes you think we'd want to marry men who wouldn't stand by us for better or worse, for scandal or not?" Claire asked, with a pointed arch of her brow.

"Honestly, James, if we were content with such lily-livered, spineless beaux we would have married some of the fortune hunters and scoundrels the duchess has kept throwing in our way," Bridget said.

"But . . ." James didn't know what to say.

But the truth was so blindingly bright now. He didn't want to make things harder for them. He wanted them to have choices.

But most of all, he wanted them to find men who would proudly stand by them for better or for worse, and who valued true love over whatever the ton might say. They wouldn't be truly happy with anything less anyway.

"So don't mind us," Amelia said with a wave of her hand.

"Don't ruin happily ever after on our account," Bridget added. "I could never live with myself."

"So back to the original question," Claire cut in. "When is Meredith coming back?"

This time, when three Cavendish sisters stared at him expectantly, he knew why. And he knew exactly what to say.

"As soon as I can bring her back."

CHAPTER 19

A duke has his priorities in order.
— THE RULES FOR DUKES

The Queen's Head tavern
Southampton, England
The sun was setting when James dismounted and threw the reins to a groom idling in the courtyard and strode up the wooden steps and into the tavern with much more certainty than he had the first time he'd been here. He pushed open the door, and a little of the late evening light spilled in behind him.

A quick glance of the room — nearly full with travelers — told him that she wasn't there.

Even though he hoped she would be here, James knew it was unlikely. If he were to see Meredith here, now, it would mean that she was returning to London or leaving England entirely.

Then again, her goodbye had felt so final.

Hopefully, he'd find her soon, as early as tomorrow, even, at her mother's cottage, which was another full day's journey away. He'd learned her whereabouts from Claire, who had wheedled the information from the housekeeper.

His sisters, bless them, conspired to help make his departure possible.

Then again, James suspected that if he didn't go himself, they would have fanned out en masse over the countryside until they found Meredith, pleaded his case, and persuaded her to return to London.

It was better this way. There were some things a man had to do on his own.

He had told the duchess there was urgent estate business requiring his attentions at Durham Park. Again. She seemed pleased that he was taking such an active role in the management of the estate, which made him feel a twinge of guilt for deceiving her.

Amelia and Bridget, who had just a day ago each become betrothed to excellent gentlemen, promised to involve (and distract) the duchess with wedding planning.

"Go," Claire said. "Go running off for true love. Meredith deserves happiness and so do you."

He rode hard for a few days and stopped

at the Queen's Head Tavern for the night and for the memories. And so he was here, in the room where it all began.

Meredith had not anticipated returning to London, and certainly not so soon. But she had questions for the duchess and now the carriage wheels couldn't turn fast enough.

Meredith tapped her toes on the floor of the mail coach and drummed her fingertips on the reticule in her lap. She'd spent what felt like an inordinate amount of time in the carriage already. If what she suspected about her past was true, it would certainly change her future.

But first, a stop in Southampton.

Particularly, the Queen's Head Tavern. She had debated spending the night at a different inn — there were more than a few — but she wanted to return to the place where her life had changed.

Meredith climbed the few steps to the entrance, pushed open the door, and stepped inside. It took a second for her eyes to adjust to the dim light, but when they did, there was no mistaking the sight that greeted her.

There he was: leaning against the wall, a mug of ale dangling from his fingertips. Even though the room was full with other travelers, she found him straightaway.

Meredith's breath caught and her heart lurched.

He was here. He was *here*!

What did this mean?

What did this mean?!

Heart pounding, Meredith deliberately ignored him and took a seat in the far end of the bar and gave her order to the barmaid — a tea, please. She was a proper lady and as such, proper ladies did not make advances upon men in tavern common rooms.

She glanced over, just to be sure that it was him and her eyes were not deceiving her. Then another fleeting look before looking away. All these quick glimpses when she wanted to gaze at him forever.

He caught her eye every time.

Her slight smile was the invitation he needed to come over.

Meredith's heart started to pound with every step he took across the room toward her, just as it had done that night. It was as if her heart knew that she wasn't just a girl and he wasn't Just James.

Finally he stopped beside her and took to leaning against the bar. And then, he smiled. A wicked, beautiful smile that made her start to melt.

"What is a beautiful woman like you doing alone in a place like this?"

"That is *such* a ridiculous line. I've been meaning to tell you that since the first time you said it to me."

"But it works."

"Does it?"

"It's the third or fourth time I've said it to you, and you're still talking to me, aren't you?"

James grinned at her, and his blue eyes were doing that thing where they sparkled with love and a hint of wickedness and a whole lot of wanting. The rogue had a point. Given the way he looked at her, he could say almost anything, and it would make her heart giddily overrule her brain.

"I don't suppose you're here waiting for the first ship back to America," she said, trying not to get her hopes up that he was here for her. Those were the only plausible reasons that would bring him to this place.

"It so happens that I'm here for a girl."

His words hit her heart hard. *Ba-bump.*

"Oh? What girl?"

"Just a girl."

Ba-bump. Ba-bump.

"I do hope you find her."

Ba-bump. Ba-bump. Ba-bump.

"I already have."

She knew, just knew, that he was here for

her. Once again fate or something like it had brought them together. It took all of her elegance and self-restraint to keep from throwing herself into his arms and pressing her mouth to his. But proper ladies did not do such things, and she was a proper lady. She knew this now.

But under her skirts, her toes were tap, tap, tapping out a quick rhythm, something like the rapid pace of her heartbeats.

"So tell me," he asked, leaning in. "What brings you to the finest inn and tavern in all of Southampton?"

"I'm on my way to London," Meredith answered. "I have some important business there."

"Words I'd hoped you'd say," he murmured. Her lips turned up in a little smile. Her heart was beating hard, and she felt it in her chest and the blood rushing through her veins. She was alive. This was real. Fairy tale or not, this moment was happening. To her.

"You know, I never did tell you my story," he said. "I started to the night we first met but then I got . . . distracted."

"I suppose you're going to tell me now," she murmured.

"Well, you wouldn't want to live your whole life not knowing it, now would you?"

"I suppose the answer to that is no," she said softly. Teasing. "Tell me your story, Just James."

"I know I'm a strong, impressive, handsome, wealthy duke now," he admitted, eyes sparkling. "But once upon a time, I was just a nobody, a horse trainer from America. And I was happy with my life there, and reluctant to start over here. But opportunities to be a duke don't come along every day, so I traveled across an ocean for a role I wasn't sure I could fulfill and a fate I wasn't sure I wanted. The night I arrived in England, I met a girl at a tavern."

Meredith was silent, waiting for him to go on with this story. She knew the broad strokes and outlines of it, but there was something mesmerizing about hearing him tell it to her now, and putting herself into the context of his life.

"I think I might have fallen in love with her that night," he said. "She certainly cast a spell on me. Even though she broke my heart by running away without so much as a goodbye. Isn't that the cruelest thing you've ever heard?"

"Maybe she had her reasons."

"She didn't even leave her name. I thought she was lost to me forever."

"But you found her."

"I had made a promise to myself, you see. I wasn't going to be a duke until I set foot in London, until I placed my boot on the ground. I was just about to leave when I saw her. So if it weren't for this girl, I would be back in America now, out in the country with my horses, the worst sort of coward who abandons family and duty."

"You were going to run away?"

"I was. But this girl made me a man. She was the only reason I stepped out of that carriage in London. My love for her is the only thing that has made it possible for me to do my duty. And she does it all just by being herself."

There was a hint of tears in Meredith's eyes when she asked, "What happened to the girl?"

"She got away. Almost. Maybe." He reached out and took her hand in his. "You see, Meredith, I've been sent to fetch you and bring you back."

"*Fetch* me?"

"I have three sisters. They all possess, shall we say, strong opinions and forceful personalities. They have insisted that I cannot live without the woman I love. And so I have been told, in no uncertain terms, that I am to find her and declare my intentions and hopefully persuade her to marry me so that we can be happy. Once you meet my sisters, you'll see that they are quite forceful and impossible to disregard."

"You're here on orders from your sisters?"

"In truth, Mer, it's more like their blessing. I'm given to understand that I might cause a scandal by wedding a woman who doesn't appear in *Debrett's* or other rubbish like that. My sisters have wholeheartedly encouraged me to risk scandal for love. They told me they have found their happiness, and it's time for me. And, I hope, you. I love you, Meredith. I want to be with you as man and wife, duke and duchess, and I don't care what anyone else has to say about it."

"James . . . Just James." She sighed his name, and it felt like she forgot how to breathe. This man had seen her — and that was enough for her to lose her head for him. Now this man loved her — and she was ready to give him her heart. But where to begin when one's heart was beating like mad and breath was stolen? "I don't know what to say."

"Say you love me, too. Say you'll marry me. Say you'll be my duchess."

A short while later . . .

The soft click of a door closing in the latch,

shutting out the rest of the world, because the rest of the world didn't matter in a moment like this.

The scratch and spark of a match coming to light, and the soft glow from a candle illuminating just enough: him and her, together, alone. Eyes dark with desire, an expression full of love.

The quiet sounds of whispers, promising things like tonight and forever, love and happy ever after. Promises they both knew they would keep.

The quiet rustle of fabric as dresses and coats and jackets and all such things were removed and cast aside so that there was nothing between his bare skin and hers. There was nothing to hide and nothing more would keep them apart.

The soft and silky sound of sighs and sharp intakes of breaths and slow exhales as they kissed. Mouths colliding, touching, tasting, knowing.

The feeling of bare fingertips along heated skin, of nerves tingling with wanting, doing nothing, *nothing* to diminish desire but only stoking it further.

The feeling of becoming one, so connected and tangled up in each other there was no knowing where one ended and one began.

The sound of crying out in pleasure, his a low possessive groan, hers breathless. And then, underneath the silence, the sound of beating hearts and promises whispered.

But this, *this* was not the end.

Chapter 20

A duke is not above love.
— The Rules for Dukes

The following day
The next morning, James and Meredith woke up in each other's arms. The moment was all the sweeter for having longed for it and worked for it.

But not everything was sunshine, roses, and happily ever after. They would marry, and they would be happy. But it would be all the more joyful if they had the blessing of the duchess.

By unspoken agreement, they set off for London as soon as possible.

The carriage rolled away from the Queen's Head, pulled by a matching set of white horses — as if in a fairy tale, Meredith noted wryly. For a while she watched the scenery pass by, but then she took James's hand in hers.

"I never told you my story," she said, turning to face him.

"Tell me. Start with *once upon a time* and then let's ensure that it concludes with *and they lived happily ever after.*" He pressed a kiss upon her cheek, and she gave a quick smile.

"There are a lot of blank pages in my story, though. There are things I will have to ask the duchess."

"Such as . . ."

"Who my father really is," Meredith said, saying the words aloud for the first time.

"My mother and her caretaker, Mrs. Bates, said some things that raised questions in my mind as to whether or not the man she had married was also the man who had fathered me," Meredith explained. "Mr. Green, may he rest in peace, never showed much interest in me as a child, and as I matured he wasn't very interested in protecting me from the boys in the village. He said the sooner I was married off the better — didn't matter to whom."

"Oh, Mer . . ."

"That was when the duchess swept in and took me under her wing. She *saved* me, James. Just think of where I would be without her attentions."

One did not want to think of such things.

James gave a squeeze of her hand, which was more than words could say.

"Sprock and Simons said something about the duchess's lady's maid having a quick wedding. Maybe it signifies. Maybe it doesn't." James shrugged.

"Who are Sprock and Simons?"

"Tenants at Durham Park. We were digging a drainage ditch in the north field. Did you know that digging drainage ditches is a better remedy for a broken heart than sitting in the dark with decanters of brandy?"

Meredith laughed. "I did not. I shall keep that in mind."

"But hopefully you'll never have a broken heart," James murmured, pressing another kiss on her lips. "Apologies. You were saying something and I distracted you with a kiss."

"That's all right," she said, smiling.

"Tell me what other questions you have for the duchess."

"I want to know why she took me in, the daughter of her lady's maid, and raised me as her companion. I thought all these years it was because she was lonely, and because she felt obligated after my mother fell ill. But now I wonder if it's more than that. I wonder, James, if I might have noble blood after all."

"It doesn't matter to me one way or

another," he said, and she knew it. To be honest, it didn't matter much to her, either, though she did want to know the truth and she did want to understand if perhaps she and the duchess shared a deeper connection than she had realized.

"I know." She gave his hand a squeeze. "I want to be with you, James, with or without her blessing, but I would rather have it. She has made me into the woman I am."

"And the woman I love," he murmured.

> If he does nothing else, a duke must fight for those he loves.
> — THE RULES FOR DUKES

Durham House

This time when the carriage pulled up in front of Durham House, James leapt out first and extended his hand to help Meredith alight.

It seemed like only yesterday that she had stood with the rest of the household staff to greet him. She clearly remembered the feeling of her heart leaping and sinking when she set eyes on the New Duke and saw that it was none other than the man she'd made love to at the inn. Conflicting emotions crashed through her — joy to see him again, fear that he would reveal her indiscretion, lust and longing and confusion.

Now he was proudly standing before her, holding out his hand to welcome her. This time when she entered Durham House, things would be different.

Despite James's assurances that he would love her forever and wed her immediately, she still felt no small measure of trepidation. She cared greatly for the good opinion and affection of the duchess — especially if Meredith's suspicions about their connection were true — and she worried about the looming conversation.

She found the duchess in the south drawing room.

"Meredith! It is good to have you back. You won't believe what you have missed." The duchess smiled, and Meredith couldn't help but smile back, though hers was a nervous one.

And then James stepped in after her.

"I suppose the duke has told you that two of his sisters are betrothed!" The duchess beamed. "Bridget has even landed *Lord Darcy.* The ton speaks of little else." And then upon seeing their serious expressions, the duchess said, "What is on your mind? What brings you back to London?"

James and Meredith took seats on the settee beside each other. If the duchess noticed anything intimate or equal between them, she didn't say it. But her eyes did narrow, so she must have seen.

"Your Grace, while I was visiting with my mother she said some things that have raised questions in my mind. While in one of her states, she spoke of your brother, the Earl of Cambria. I am wondering if you might tell me what transpired between them."

The duchess visibly stiffened. Meredith plunged ahead. Her heart was racing but if this was true . . .

"I know it may be nothing more than the rantings of a madwoman, but it did make me wonder. Because, Your Grace, if it wasn't the rantings of a madwoman but her real memories . . ." Meredith paused. "You look as if you've seen a ghost."

"Best ring for tea. This is a story that requires some fortification."

"Who is the Earl of Cambria?" James asked.

There was a long pause before Her Grace answered.

"My brother, may he rest in peace. My reckless, devil-may-care, rakehell brother who never met a scandal he didn't want to tangle with. My brother, who knew no limits, knew only privilege and entitlement and no sense of duty."

James seemed confused. But Meredith wasn't.

Was it true? Her heart raced, her mind raced with the implications.

"An earl's dalliance with a lady's maid is hardly a scandal," Meredith said softly. "It is, alas, so often the way of things."

"But she was *my* lady's maid," the duchess said in a tight voice. "My trusted confidante, my one source of constancy as I left a tumultuous home to become the wife of a man I hardly knew. I was expected to find my way in the ton with little guidance and to manage all the duke's households. She was good and loyal to me. But my brother . . . distracted her."

The duchess paused and so much started to make sense now. Why she worried so much about scandal, why she relied so much on Meredith's constancy by her side, why she fretted about James assuming his duty.

The duchess had more to say: "And the result of his dalliance with her, *my niece,* was destined to be born a bastard or a commoner. I made arrangements for your mother to quickly wed the late duke's valet, so at least you weren't born a bastard. Marrying Cambria was out of the question, of course."

"I am your niece," Meredith whispered. "I am your niece."

"You are my niece," she confirmed.

And like that, so many pieces clicked together and fell into place. This explained why the duchess plucked her from her surroundings and brought her to live in the grand ducal residence, why she instructed her in all the proper ladylike arts, from pouring tea to addressing the third son of an earl and his wife in both speech and writing, to managing a household. But these things were not just items on a Perfect Lady checklist, they were the hard-earned knowledge of how to survive that the duchess had learned and passed along to her flesh and blood, and the closest she'd had to a daughter of her own.

Meredith understood her now, in a way she never had before.

But one question remained unanswered. If she had noble blood . . . if she was as polished as any gently bred young lady . . . if she was the one who made James want to stand up and *be* Durham . . . and if they were in love . . .

"Why am I not suitable for James then?"

"As far as anyone knows, you are merely a commoner," the duchess explained, sounding very sorry about it. But still. "We all know that dukes do not marry commoners. Durham has weathered enough scandals, we cannot have more. And the ton will talk — oh, will they talk. They will be vicious and cruel. And I don't wish to see you hurt."

"You're trying to protect me." The duchess nodded *yes*. "But I don't want to be protected. I want to marry the man I love, who loves *me*."

"If it weren't for the dukedom needing James . . ." the duchess mused. "If you could just get away . . ."

"Like my father. And mother," James added. "He ran away to be with her, and the horse-thieving story was just to serve as a distraction from the real potential scandal: that love mattered more than duty to the dukedom."

"You have seen how much people depend upon you, James, or the person in your position. You have seen how there is too much at stake to entrust it to someone like Mr. Collins. I do not wish to stand in the way of love and happiness, but we cannot lose you now, Duke. It would be far more devastating if you ran away now than when your father did."

"I won't run away," James said firmly. "As long as I have Meredith as my duchess."

"I know that the ton will talk and people will turn their noses up at us. Between the commoner and the American duke, we shall certainly struggle for acceptance that would have come easily otherwise," Meredith said. "But I have your blood in my veins, and you have taught me well. Josie."

"Hmmph," the duchess said at being addressed as *Josie* by Meredith for the first time. "That's right. You have my blood in your veins. When I have said that you are like a daughter to me, I have meant it in ways that you didn't know. I couldn't let my own niece grow up impoverished with few opportunities to advance and none to succeed. But the world is cruel and quick to judge. I don't want to see you hurt — not from society, and certainly not from a marriage that cannot withstand the pressures of society."

"The love I have for Meredith won't be swayed by what people think or say or whether we are invited to parties or not. The love we share is the kind of love you throw a dukedom away for," James said evenly. "But I would like to stay. Duchess, you and Meredith have shown me that duty and love needn't be at odds. It is my love for Meredith that has made me want to stay and become the Duke of Durham and the man I am destined to be."

Was that, perhaps, a glimmer of a tear in the corner of the duchess's eye? For that matter, was that a glimmer of a tear in Meredith's eye? At least one tear wouldn't be amiss. She had found love, family, and home, more than she had ever imagined. She had, luckily enough, found her place and purpose in the world. This was a gift she would treasure always.

"Besides," James continued. "What's a little scandal when it comes to true love?"

A moment later
When Meredith, James, and the duchess opened the doors from the drawing room to the foyer, a not altogether unexpected sight greeted them: three Cavendish sisters leaning close to the door, making a valiant attempt to eavesdrop.

Claire, Bridget, and Amelia all jumped back, wearing vaguely guilty expressions. A smile tugged at Meredith's mouth. *Sisters.*

"Did you know that these doors are remarkably thick?" Bridget mused.

"They are not very good at transmitting sound," Claire said.

"I do believe that is the point of them," James said. "Ensuring privacy, whether visual or auditory."

"They are the bane of eavesdroppers everywhere," Bridget said.

"Or just us," Amelia added with a grin. "Your *beloved* sisters."

"Please, tell me that long private discussion was about you two getting married," Bridget said, getting right to the point. "And that I have not sent Pendleton for a bottle of champagne for no good reason."

James and Meredith glanced quickly at each other, and then at Pendleton, who stood nearby with a bottle of champagne, and then at the duchess. They would have a wedding soon — their love would not be denied. The only question was whether they would have the approval from the one person whose good opinion mattered most.

"There will be a wedding," the duchess said, then a pause, and a smile. "With my blessing."

EPILOGUE

A duke is often the most important and highest-ranking person in a room — unless the duchess is present. Any man of sense defers to her.

— THE RULES FOR DUKES

Twelve years later
Durham Park

Her Grace, Josephine Marie Elizabeth Cavendish, the dowager Duchess of Durham, had *one* job in life: to assure the succession of the dukedom for the next generation.

In this, she succeeded.

Spectacularly.

The evidence was all around her.

Oh, there was the house and grounds at Durham Park — as grand as ever, and just one of the well-run estates in the family. But the best evidence of success was all the happy couples and children frolicking all

408

about her. There was no special occasion for this picnic, other than that it was a beautiful summer day, there was not even a hint of rain in the blue, sunshine-filled sky, and they were all together.

Each of the Cavendish siblings had wed and multiplied. For this, she breathed a prayer of thanks because, for a few moments there, it seemed *highly* unlikely that they should make any match. But love had prevailed.

There had been a scandal when the duke wed his common-born duchess, Meredith. But the family had weathered the social storm admirably, due to the unbreakable love between them. And it didn't hurt that the sisters had landed some very well-connected and powerful husbands. Their acceptance of the new duchess helped smooth her way in society.

Lady Bridget had captivated Lord Darcy, a pillar of the ton.

Lady Amelia had wed the heir to Baron Wrotham.

Lady Claire had snared the charming Lord Fox.

And James, the duke, had married the duchess's own niece, Meredith.

Now there were children *everywhere*.

The duchess, seated elegantly on a blanket

spread out on the grass, sipped her lemonade and counted them. There were at least two in the trees, another two pulling a rowboat to the water's edge without a care at all for wet shoes and clothes, and at least four were running around shrieking in a game that she did not understand, nor care to. Though even the duchess had to admit it looked like fun.

Bridget, Amelia, Claire, and Meredith came and sat down with her.

"Remember the time that Bridget and I —" Amelia began, eyeing the two girls tugging the rowboat out into the pond. Beside her, Bridget groaned.

"Yes," the duchess said crisply, "though I have made an effort to banish it from my memory."

But how, oh how, could she forget the day the two sisters fell into the lake at Lady Winterbourne's garden party?

"Remember the time you and Aunt Bridget did what?" This question came from Caroline, Amelia's daughter. Her cousins Miranda and Katharine were equally intrigued in the answer.

Oh, the duchess did so enjoy watching the elder hoyden having to answer the younger hoyden, painfully aware that she ought to set an example for her daughter, and especially for her nieces.

"Are you going to tell her what scandalous antics her mother engaged in?" Josie couldn't resist asking.

"I have to set an example," Amelia grumbled. Turning to her daughter: "We fell into the lake because we were standing on the boat while dramatically reciting poetry. One mustn't *stand* in a rowboat and recite poetry. It's best done in a seated position."

"Unless there are handsome men around, ready to save you from thrashing about in the water," said Darcy, joining the group.

"Don't listen to him. This is why you must learn to swim. So you aren't reliant on stuffy lords," Bridget said. Then she kissed her husband, a notoriously stuffy lord.

"Where is James?" Meredith asked. "Is he engaged in vitally important estate business?"

She asked this with a twinkle in her eye. *Vitally important estate business* often meant mucking about in the stables with his horses, as opposed to *actual* estate business.

"He is with Fox," Claire said. "They are teaching little Josie and Henry how to ride on one of those horses bred from the Arabian that Lady Jemma brought back from her travels. Soon they'll be jumping."

"When they're older I'll show them how

to ride standing atop the saddle," Amelia said with a wicked grin.

"Please. Do not." Meredith put her hand over her heart. "I beg of you. I shall be too nervous."

"I'll make sure she doesn't," Alistair said. "I'm sure we can find some *other* trouble for her to get into."

"Or perhaps I still need lessons from Meredith at her new school," Amelia said. With so much expert knowledge of how to be a Proper Lady In Society, Meredith and the dowager duchess were considering starting a school for young women of all social classes.

"Perhaps?" Bridget asked pointedly, taking a bite of a biscuit. Amelia scowled.

"Sisters," Claire sighed. She and Meredith shared a smile and laughed. Even the duchess joined in.

As the afternoon drew to a close, nannies came to herd the children back to the house, and one by one the couples wandered off, hand in hand. They were all so happy.

Especially Meredith and James. The duchess had been so worried about how their marriage would endure the gossips of the ton and the strain of the dukedom, but now she couldn't imagine two people more in love and devoted to each other. Aye, the dukedom was secure in a changing world, and her children — she thought of *all* of them as her children — were happy. Truly happy.

Josie thought she'd done quite well with her life: she'd dedicated her life in service to Durham, something greater than herself, and she grew old surrounded by the love and laughter of family as they all lived happily ever after.

ABOUT THE AUTHOR

Maya Rodale began reading romance novels in college at her mother's insistence. She is now the bestselling and award winning author of numerous smart and sassy romance novels. A champion of the genre and its readers, she is also the author of the non-fiction book *Dangerous Books For Girls: The Bad Reputation Of Romance Novels, Explained* and a frequent contributor to *The Huffington Post, Bustle* and more. Maya lives in New York City with her darling dog and a rogue of her own.